continued . . .

"Full of excitement, humor, suspense, and loads of hot, hot sex. Anyone who enjoys a good paranormal should *not* miss this one!"
—*Fresh Fiction*

"[Marked by] the subtlety of the writing. The characterizations, the backstories, the world-building are deftly intertwined with the story."
—*Dear Author* (July Recommended Read)

"An absolutely fantastic paranormal/fantasy read . . . Gorgeous, complex, and fascinating."
—*Errant Dreams* (5 out of 5)

"What a refreshing and unique world Virginia Kantra has created for Children of the Sea! Full of sensual magic, intrigue, and compelling characters, *Sea Witch* is a book to be savored."
—*CK²S Kwips & Kritiques* (4½ clovers)

"A bestseller arises from the depths of the sea and floats to the top of the romance/paranormal list! *Sea Witch* is enthralling!"
—*A Romance Review* (5 roses out of 5)

Home Before Midnight

"Sexy and suspenseful . . . A really good read."
—*New York Times* bestselling author Karen Robards

"Virginia Kantra is a sensitive writer with a warm sense of humor, a fine sense of sexual tension, and an unerring sense of place."
—*BookPage*

Close Up

"Holy moly, action/adventure/romance fans! You are going to *love* this book! I highly, highly recommend it."
—*New York Times* bestselling author Suzanne Brockmann

"A story fraught with intense emotions and danger . . . Kantra clearly demonstrates that she's a talent to be reckoned with." —*Romantic Times*

"Kantra's first foray into single-title fiction is fast-paced, engrossing, and full of nail-biting suspense."
—*New York Times* bestselling author Sabrina Jeffries

"Honest, intelligent romance." —*Romance: B(u)y the Book*

MORE PRAISE FOR
VIRGINIA KANTRA AND HER
BESTSELLING NOVELS

"Smart, sexy, and sophisticated—another winner."
—*New York Times* bestselling author Lori Foster

"An involving, three-dimensional story that is scary, intriguing, and sexy." —*All About Romance*

"Kantra creates powerfully memorable characters."
—*Midwest Book Review*

"Virginia Kantra is an autobuy . . . Her books are keepers and her heroes are to die for!"
—*New York Times* bestselling author Suzanne Brockmann

"Spectacularly suspenseful and sexy. Don't miss it!"
—*Romantic Times*

Sea Lord

VIRGINIA KANTRA

BERKLEY SENSATION, NEW YORK

THE BERKLEY PUBLISHING GROUP
Published by the Penguin Group
Penguin Group (USA) Inc.
375 Hudson Street, New York, New York 10014, USA

Penguin Group (Canada), 90 Eglinton Avenue East, Suite 700, Toronto, Ontario M4P 2Y3, Canada
(a division of Pearson Penguin Canada Inc.)
Penguin Books Ltd., 80 Strand, London WC2R 0RL, England
Penguin Group Ireland, 25 St. Stephen's Green, Dublin 2, Ireland (a division of Penguin Books Ltd.)
Penguin Group (Australia), 250 Camberwell Road, Camberwell, Victoria 3124, Australia
(a division of Pearson Australia Group Pty. Ltd.)
Penguin Books India Pvt. Ltd., 11 Community Centre, Panchsheel Park, New Delhi—110 017, India
Penguin Group (NZ), 67 Apollo Drive, Rosedale, North Shore 0632, New Zealand
(a division of Pearson New Zealand Ltd.)
Penguin Books (South Africa) (Pty.) Ltd., 24 Sturdee Avenue, Rosebank, Johannesburg 2196,
South Africa

Penguin Books Ltd., Registered Offices: 80 Strand, London WC2R 0RL, England

This is a work of fiction. Names, characters, places, and incidents either are the product of the author's imagination or are used fictitiously, and any resemblance to actual persons, living or dead, business establishments, events, or locales is entirely coincidental. The publisher does not have any control over and does not assume any responsibility for author or third-party websites or their content.

SEA LORD

A Berkley Sensation Book / published by arrangement with the author

PRINTING HISTORY
Berkley Sensation mass-market edition / May 2009

Copyright © 2009 by Virginia Kantra.
Excerpt from *Kissing Midnight* by Emma Holly copyright © 2009 by Emma Holly.
Cover art by Tony Mauro.
Cover design by Rita Frangie.
Logo by axb group.
Interior text design by Laura K. Corless.

ISBN: 978-0-425-22636-0

BERKLEY® SENSATION
Berkley Sensation Books are published by The Berkley Publishing Group,
a division of Penguin Group (USA) Inc.,
375 Hudson Street, New York, New York 10014.
BERKLEY® SENSATION and the "B" design are trademarks of Penguin Group (USA) Inc.

PRINTED IN THE UNITED STATES OF AMERICA

10 9 8 7 6 5 4 3 2 1

To Michael.
I couldn't do this without you.

ACKNOWLEDGMENTS

First of all, thank you to Cindy Hwang and the wonderful team at Berkley.

Thanks to my fabulously supportive agent, Damaris Rowland.

Thank you to my wonderful first-draft readers, Kristen Dill and Melissa McClone.

Huge thanks to my family, who deal patiently with blank stares, interrupted phone calls, humming, and deadlines.

And finally, thanks to twelve-year-old African AIDS victim and activist Nkosi Johnson for these words: "Do all you can with what you have, in the time you have, in the place you are."

So, in one moment,
Or almost one, she was seen, and loved, and taken
In Pluto's rush of love. She called her mother,
Her comrades, but more often for her mother.

—OVID, *METAMORPHOSES*

I tell you naught for your comfort,
Yea, naught for your desire,
Save that the sky grows darker yet
And the sea rises higher.

—G. K. CHESTERTON,
"THE BALLAD OF THE WHITE HORSE"

In the time before time, when the domains of earth, sea, and sky were formed and fire was called into being, the elementals took shape, each with their element: the children of earth, the children of the sea, the children of air, and the children of fire.

After earth had flowered and life crawled from the sea, humankind was born.

Not all of the elementals were pleased with this new creation. The children of fire rebelled, declaring war on the children of the air and humankind. The others, forced to cohabit with the mortals, withdrew—the fair folk to the hills and wild places of earth and the merfolk to the depths of the sea.

Yet there are still encounters between the elementals and humankind. Of such meetings, souls are redeemed and lost, wars are waged, great art is created, empires are raised. Of such meetings legends—and children—are born.

The whaleyn sing of a prophecy, that a daughter of the

sea witch Atargatis will one day alter the balance of power between the elements. Over the centuries, the children of fire have grown strong, while the children of the sea have declined in numbers and in magic. The daughter of the prophecy could prove their salvation. Or the weapon of their destruction . . .

Prologue

~≈~

CONN AP LLYR WALKED THE BROKEN SHORE OF
the crescent island, just out of reach of the seductive curl
of the water, ignoring the siren call of the waves and the
lap of the surge like the tempo of his blood. He needed the
sea like he needed a woman.

But he could control his needs. He must. Let his
father, Llyr, wallow in the ocean's seductive embrace.
Conn had held himself above such things for a very long
time.

Yet sometimes in the evening, he left his tower to walk
with his hound among the rocks and tide pools at the water's
edge.

The sun slipped in the bronze sky, staining the pewter
water to gold and veining the clouds with fire. Conn lifted
his face to the raw western wind. He could have sought or
summoned a partner. There were females on Sanctuary
eager to satisfy the moods and needs of its prince.

But that was indulgence, too, another slide into sensation, another plunge into loss of control. Unlike his father

the king, Conn could not afford to expend himself and his energy on passing pleasure.

The dog ranged up and down, head low. The water shrugged. A line of foam rustled to shore, whispering for Conn's attention. In the time before Conn's father's time, when the flood of magic ran full and hot, the sea kings had grasped and wielded power like a sword. But the gifts of the merfolk had declined with their numbers. Conn's own magic was a subtler thing, pale and shapeless as water, that trickled through his clenched hands.

Which was why the vision burning in the tide pool at his feet almost tripped him up.

Light struck the surface of the water and blazed. The pool caught the colors of the sky, orange and gold. Power shimmered in the air. The hound whined.

Conn narrowed his gaze as the glare resolved itself into a female shape. A girl, with long bones and strong shoulders and hair as thick and pale as straw around a lean and quiet face.

Well.

Conn frowned. Not selkie. He would have known one of his own. There were only a few thousand of his people left, enough to recognize, barely enough to rule.

Not even particularly beautiful.

Human, he thought. And therefore unimportant.

But then why had his gift shown her to him?

Her image shimmered, trapped in the safe, shallow little pool like a fish caught by the retreating tide, oblivious to the rich dark depths of the ocean teeming yards away.

She meant nothing, Conn told himself.

She was nothing.

But her vision refused to go away.

1

CONN AP LLYR HAD NOT HAD SEX WITH A MORtal woman in three hundred years.

And the girl grubbing in the dirt, surrounded by pumpkins and broken stalks of corn, was hardly a reward for his years of discipline and sacrifice.

Even kneeling, she was as tall as many men, long boned and rangy. Although maybe that was an illusion created by her clothes, jeans and a lumpy gray jacket. Conn thought there might be curves under the jacket. Big breasts, little breasts . . . He hardly cared. She was the one. Her hair fell thick and pale around her downturned face. Her long, pale fingers patted and pressed the earth. She had a streak of dirt beside her thumb.

Not a beauty, he thought again.

He knew her name now. Lucy Hunter. He had known her mother, the sea witch, Atargatis. This human girl had clearly inherited none of her mother's allure or her gifts. Living proof—if Conn had required any—that the children of the sea should not breed with humankind.

But a starving dog could not sneer at a bone.

His hands curled into fists at his sides. In recent weeks, the girl's vision had haunted him from half a world away, reflected in the water, impressed upon his brain, burning like a candle against his retinas at night.

He might not want her, but his magic insisted he needed her. His gift was as fickle as a beautiful woman. And like a woman, his power would abandon him entirely if he ignored its favors. He could not risk that.

He watched the girl drag her hand along the swollen side of a pumpkin. Brushing off dirt? Testing it for ripeness? He had only the vaguest idea what she might be doing here among the tiny plots of staked vines and fading flowers. The children of the sea did not work the earth for their sustenance.

Frustration welled in him.

What has she to do with me? he demanded silently. *What am I to do with her?*

The magic did not reply.

Which led him, again, to the obvious answer. But he had ruled too long to trust the obvious.

He did not expect resistance. He could make her willing, make her want him. It was, he thought bitterly, the remaining power of his kind, when other gifts had been abandoned or forgotten.

No, she would not resist. She had family, however, who might interfere. Brothers. Conn had no doubt the human, Caleb, would do what he could to shield his sister from either sex or magic.

Dylan, on the other hand, was selkie, like their mother. He had lived among the children of the sea since he was thirteen years old. Conn had always counted on Dylan's loyalty. He did not think Dylan would have much interest in or control over his sister's life. But Dylan was involved with a human woman now. Who knew where his loyalties lay?

Conn frowned. He could not afford a misstep. The survival of his kind depended on him.

And if, as his visions insisted, their fate involved this human girl as well . . .

He regarded her head, bent like one of her heavy gold sunflowers over the dirt of the garden, and felt a twinge of pity. Of regret.

That was unfortunate for both of them.

* * *

Lucy patted the pumpkin affectionately like a dog. Her second graders' garden plots would be ready for harvest soon. Plants and students were rewarding like that. Put in a little time, a little effort, and you could actually see results.

Too bad the rest of her life didn't work that way.

Not that she was complaining, she told herself firmly. She had a job she enjoyed and people who needed her. If at times she felt so frustrated and restless she could scream, well, that was her own fault for moving back home after college. Back to the cold, cramped house she grew up in, to the empty rooms haunted by her father's shell and her mother's ghost. Back to the island, where everyone assumed they knew everything about her.

Back to the sea she dreaded and could not live without.

She wiped her hands on her jeans. She had tried to leave once, when she was fourteen and finally figured out her adored brother Cal wasn't ever coming back to rescue her. She'd run away as fast and as far as she could go.

Which, it turned out, wasn't very far at all.

Lucy looked over the dried stalks and hillocks of the garden, remembering. She had hitchhiked to Richmond, twenty miles from the coast, before collapsing on the stinking tile floor of a gas station restroom. Her stomach lurched at the memory. Caleb had found her, shivering and puking her guts into the toilet, and brought her back to the echo-ing house and the sound of the sea whispering under her window.

She had recovered before the ferry left the dock.

Flu, concluded the island doctor.

Stress, said the physician's assistant at Dartmouth when Lucy was taken ill on her tour of the college.

Panic attack, insisted her ex-boyfriend, when their planned weekend getaway left her wheezing and heaving by the side of the road.

Whatever the reasons, Lucy had learned her limits. She got her teaching certificate at Machias, within walking distance of the bay. And she never again traveled more than twenty miles from the sea.

She climbed to her feet. Anyway, she was . . . maybe not happy, but content with her life on World's End. Both her brothers lived on the island now, and she had a new sister-in-law. Soon, when Dylan married Regina, she'd have two. Then there would be nieces and nephews com-ing along.

And if her brothers' happiness sometimes made her chafe and fidget . . .

Lucy took a deep breath, still staring at the garden, and forced herself to think about plants until the feeling went away.

Garlic, she told herself. Next week her class could plant garlic. The bulbs could winter in the soil, and next season her seven-year-old students could sell their crop to Regi-na's restaurant. Her future sister-in-law was always com-plaining she wanted fresh herbs.

Steadied by the thought, Lucy turned from the untidy rows.

Someone was watching from the edge of the field. Her heart thumped. A man, improbably dressed in a dark, tight-fitting suit. A stranger, here on World's End, where she knew everybody outside of tourist season. And the last of those had left on Labor Day.

She rubbed sweaty palms on the thighs of her jeans. He must have come on the ferry, she reasoned. Or by boat. She was uncomfortably aware how quiet the school was now that all the children had gone home.

When he saw her notice him, he stepped from the shadow of the trees. She had to press her knees together so she wouldn't run away.

Yeah, because freezing like a frightened rabbit was a much better option.

He was big, taller than Dylan, broader than Caleb, and a little younger. Or older. She squinted. It was hard to tell. Despite his impressive stillness and well-cut black hair, there was a wildness to him that charged the air like a storm. Strong, wide forehead, long, bold nose, firm, un-smiling mouth, oh, my. His eyes were the color of rain.

Something stirred in Lucy, something that had been closed off and quiet for years. Something that should *stay* quiet. Her throat tightened. The blood drummed in her ears like the sea.

Maybe she should have run after all.

Too late.

He strode across the field, crunching through the dry furrows, somehow avoiding the stakes and strings that tripped up most adults. Her heart beat in her throat.

She cleared it. "Can I help you?"

Her voice sounded husky, sexy, almost unrecognizable to her own ears.

The man's cool, light gaze washed over her. She felt it ripple along her nerves and stir something deep in her belly.

"That remains to be seen," he said.

Lucy bit her tongue. She would not take offense. She wasn't going to take anything he offered.

"The inn's along there. First road to the right." She pointed. "The harbor's back that way."

Go away, she thought at him. *Leave me alone.*

The man's strong black brows climbed. "And why should I care where this inn is, or the harbor?"

His voice was deep and oddly inflected, too deliberate for a local, too precise to be called an accent.

"Because you're obviously not from around here. I thought you might be lost. Or looking for somebody. Something." She felt heat crawl in her cheeks again. Why didn't he go?

"I am," he said, still regarding her down his long, aquiline nose.

Like he was used to women who blushed and babbled in his presence. Probably they did. He was definitely a hunk. A well-dressed hunk with chilly eyes.

Lucy hunched her shoulders, doing her best turtle impression to avoid notice. Not easy when you were six feet tall and the daughter of the town drunk, but she had practice.

"You are what?" she asked reluctantly.

He took a step closer. "Looking for someone."

Oh. Oh, boy.

Another slow step brought him within arm's reach. Her gaze jerked up to meet his eyes. Amazing eyes, like molten silver. Not cold at all. His heated gaze poured over her, filling her, warming her, melting her . . .

Oh, God.

Air clogged her lungs. She broke eye contact, focusing instead on the hard line of his mouth, the stubble lurking beneath his close shave, the column of his throat rising from his tight white collar.

Even with her gaze averted, she could feel his eyes on her, disturbing her shallow composure like a stick poked into a tide pool, stirring up sand. Her head was clouded. Her senses swam.

He was too near. Too big. Even his clothes seemed made for a smaller man. Fabric clung to the rounded muscle of his upper arms and smoothed over his wide shoulders like a lover's hand. She imagined sliding her palms through his open jacket, slipping her fingers between the straining buttons of his shirt to touch rough hair and hot skin.

Wrong, insisted a small, clear corner of her brain. *Wrong clothes, wrong man, wrong reaction.* This was the island, where the working man's uniform was flannel plaid over a white T-shirt. He was a stranger. He didn't belong here.

And she could never belong anywhere else.

She dragged in air, holding her breath the way she had taught herself when she was a child, forcing everything inside her back into its proper place. She could *smell* him, hot male, cool cotton, and something deeper, wilder, like the briny notes of the sea. When had he come so close? She never let anyone so close.

His gaze probed her like the rays of the sun, heavy and warm, seeking out all the shadowed places, all the secret corners of her soul. She felt naked. Exposed. If she met those eyes, she was lost.

She gulped and fixed her gaze on his shirt front. Her blood thrummed. *Do not look up, do not . . .*

She focused on his tie, silver gray with a thin blue stripe and the luster of silk.

Lucy frowned. *Just like . . .*

She peered more closely. *Exactly like . . .*

Her head cleared. She took a step back. "That's Dylan's tie."

Dylan's suit. She recognized it from Caleb's wedding.

"Presumably," the stranger admitted coolly. "Since I took it from his closet."

Lucy blinked. Dylan had left the island with their mother when she was just a baby. Four months ago, he'd returned for their brother Caleb's wedding and stayed when he fell in love with single mom Regina Barone. But of course in his years away Dylan must have made connections, friends, a life beyond World's End.

Lucky bastard.

"Dylan's my brother," she said.

"I know."

His assurance got under her skin. "You know him well enough to help yourself to his clothes?"

A corner of that wide, firm mouth quirked. "Why not ask him?"

"Um . . ." She got lost again in his eyes. What? Crap. No. No way was she dragging this stranger home to meet her family. She pictured their faces in her mind, steady, patient Caleb, edgy, elegant Dylan, Maggie's knowing smile, Regina's scowl. She blinked, building the images brick by brick like a wall to hide behind. "That's okay. You have a nice . . ."

Life?

"Visit," she concluded and backed away.

*   *   *

Conn was affronted. Astonished.

She was leaving him.

She was leaving. Him. Sidling away like a crab spooked by the rush of the water. As if his magic had no power over her. As if he would pounce if she turned her back.

His lips pulled back from his teeth. Perhaps he would.

He had not exerted the full force of his allure, the potent sexual magic of his kind. Why should he? He had felt her yield, smelled her arousal. Her eyes, the soft gray-green of the sea under a cloudy sky, had grown wide and dark. For a moment, as he held her gaze, Conn had felt a twist in his belly, a click of connection like a barely audible snap in his skull.

And then she blinked. When she met his eyes again, her own were shallow and bright.

Frustration tightened his gut.

He concentrated until his head pounded, bending his gaze and his will upon her, seeking . . . what? Surrender? Or a vision, a sign, something to guide him.

Nothing, he acknowledged wearily.

Nothing but her face, pale between the curtains of her straw-colored hair, and his own reflection, trapped within her eyes. The magic that had goaded him here had drained like a wave from the rocks, leaving him high and dry.

Conn set his jaw. He wished, not for the first time, that he had the old kings' power—or shared his father's disregard for anything beyond his own pleasure. But he was not his father. He had not left Sanctuary for the first time in centuries to satisfy a need as simple as lust.

"Come with me," he urged.

She jerked. "What?"

He would deal with her resistance later. What he would not do, now that he had found her, was let her get away. Both his magic and his glands were clear on that score.

"To see your brother," Conn improvised smoothly.

The girl shook her head, making her pale hair fall forward like a veil. "Dylan and I see enough of each other, thanks."

Conn's face must have revealed his surprise, because she added, "He moved back home a couple of months ago. Didn't he tell you?"

"No. We lost touch," Conn said grimly. Another reason Conn had been forced to leave Sanctuary and seek out the woman of his visions. Dylan was on World's End at Conn's command. But Conn had expected him to report back to Sanctuary weeks ago.

She tucked her hair behind her ears, regarding him with

confusion and a hint of challenge. "Then what are you doing here in his suit?"

Conn stiffened. He was not accustomed to having his
actions questioned. To avoid explanations, he had donned
clothes. Uncomfortable, modern clothes, the best in Dylan's
wardrobe, befitting Conn's rank. And now this girl was
challenging his selection.

"Perhaps you would prefer I take it off," he suggested
silkily.

She had very fair skin. Every blush showed. But she did
not back down. "I just think you should have asked before
you raided his closet."

"Very well. Take me to him."

She bit her lip. "I don't know if . . . He's probably at the
restaurant at this time of day."

What restaurant?

"Then we will go there," Conn said.

He watched politeness war with reluctance on her face.
He admired both her manners and her caution. But of
course, he could not allow her to refuse.

"Or we could wait at your home," Conn added.

Her eyes widened. Something flashed in those soft green
depths, like a fish darting below the surface of the water,
before she dropped her gaze.

He stared, frustrated, at the top of her head.

"This way," she said.

*   *   *

The road zigzagged to the harbor, bumping around hills
between snug, square houses and trees burning red and
gold. Lucy followed the pavement like a spool of black ribbon unrolling to the sea, uncomfortably conscious of every
step, every breath of the man beside her.

She wasn't afraid of him, exactly. Growing up on the

island, you learned to take care of yourself and your neighbors. Her brother Caleb, the island police chief, was rarely called for anything more serious than teenagers lifting beers from Wiley's Market or fishermen settling a dispute with their fists.

Until this past summer, when some madness had infected World's End beyond the usual "germs"—vacationers, in island-speak. A woman from Away had been murdered on the beach by a lawyer living on the point. A homeless vet had attacked Regina Barone in her own restaurant. And just two months ago, an unknown intruder had broken into the clinic, nearly killing Regina and the island doctor.

Lucy swallowed the flat taste of fear in her mouth. Not that the guy striding next to her looked like a killer. But you never knew, did you? Bruce Whittaker, the lawyer convicted of the beach murder, hadn't looked like the kind of man who tortured women in his living room either.

She was relieved when the road unfurled into town. The afternoon sun danced on the waters of the harbor, painting the peaked roofs with yellow light. Shadows stretched under cars and between buildings, gathering under the eaves like cobwebs. The storefront windows were papered with flyers advertising a shellfish commission meeting, a bake sale in support of the community center, free kittens.

The faded red awning of Antonia's Ristorante extended over the sidewalk, casting a warm glow over the tables inside. Empty tables. Empty chairs. A typical Wednesday in the off-season, between the lunch and dinner rush.

"This is it," Lucy announced.

Her companion glanced from the hand-lettered chalkboard in the doorway to the cat napping in the restaurant window. "Dylan is here?"

Lucy pushed the door—he didn't try to open it for her, she noticed—making the bell jangle. "Usually. He—"

"Hi, Lu." Regina straightened from the refrigerated case behind the counter, her dark hair tied under a jaunty red bandana and a wide, white apron wrapped over her baby bump. Her Italian heritage showed in the tiny gold cross at her neck and her big, dark, expressive eyes. Her gaze wandered over Lucy's shoulder; brightened with interest. "Friend of yours?"

"I just met him."

"Oh?" The interest sharpened. "Nice. As long as you're here, you can take his order. Maggie's off the clock."

Lucy cleared her throat. "I don't think—"

"Maggie?" repeated that deep, cool voice.

"Maggie Hunter." Regina shot him a smile. "I'm Regina Barone."

He inclined his head, acknowledging the introduction. "Conn ap Llyr."

Regina stilled. Her eyes narrowed. "Nice suit."

He regarded her the way he'd looked at the cat, as if she were a species of creature barely worthy of notice. "Nice place."

Regina crossed her arms over her middle. "We like it."

Lucy's stomach knotted. Something was wrong. She didn't know what. But you didn't grow up in an alcoholic household without learning to pay attention to eyes and hands and tones of voice.

The door behind them opened. Lucy jumped.

But it was only her brother Caleb, still in his police uniform, coming to pick up Maggie after her shift. Relief relaxed Lucy's shoulders. Strong, patient Cal, steady as an oak tree despite the limp he'd acquired in Iraq. His hair was darker than hers, his eyes the same gray-green.

His smile faded as he picked up the tension in the room. "What's going on?" he asked evenly.

"This guy"—Regina jerked her head without taking her eyes off the stranger—"is Conn ap Llyr."

Lucy watched the two men size each other up like ten-year-olds on the playground. Only ten-year-olds never left her feeling shaky and breathless, as if they'd sucked up all the available oxygen.

Few men had the height or the balls to look down on her brother. Conn ap Llyr apparently possessed both. "And you are . . . ?"

"Caleb Hunter. Chief of Police."

Neither man offered to shake hands.

Lucy reminded herself to breathe. She had brought this stranger here. It was her responsibility to smooth things over. "He knows Dylan, he said."

Caleb aimed a look over her shoulder at Regina. "Where is Dylan?"

Regina pressed her lips together. "In back. With—"

"Get him," Caleb ordered before she could say Maggie's name.

Regina disappeared through the kitchen door without a backward glance, leaving Lucy alone with the two men. And no idea what was going on.

It was like a scene out of some old Western, she thought fancifully. The local sheriff facing down the visiting gunslinger in the bar. Her heart bumped. She had never liked confrontation. Still, she could appreciate the picture they made, solid Caleb in his wrinkled uniform, the big stranger in his elegant suit.

Her brother's suit.

Dylan swung through the kitchen door and completed the set: tall, dark, and lean in a black T-shirt tucked into faded khaki shorts.

The air fairly boiled with tension and pheromones, almost too thick to breathe. Lucy shrank into herself, retreating to the line of booths along one wall.

"Is it just me," Regina asked from the doorway behind him, "or is it crowded in here?"

Caleb's wife, Maggie, spoke from the kitchen, amusement smooth in her voice. "Crowded and hot."

She strolled forward, and every man in the room watched her move. Lucy sighed. Caleb's new wife was exotically beautiful, full-lipped, full-bosomed, with masses of wavy dark hair and sleek, female confidence.

She took her place by her husband and smiled around the room. "Very hot."

"Margred," Conn said gravely. "You look . . . recovered."

Caleb jammed his hands in his pockets, his shoulders squared.

Conn knew her, Lucy realized. How did he know her? Maggie was a newcomer to the island, a victim of the violence earlier in the summer. Caleb had found her, bloodied, dazed and naked on the beach, and brought her home. Maggie said that the attack had robbed her of her memory. But she certainly seemed to recognize Conn.

"I am well." Margred touched her husband's arm, a subtle gesture of restraint or support. "As you see."

It really was like watching a movie, Lucy thought. Or taking part in a play. Only she'd wandered into the second act, and nobody had handed her a script.

Red stained Dylan's high cheekbones. "My Lord," he exclaimed. "Conn." Except he ran the phrases together: *My Lord Conn.* "What are you doing here?"

Conn raised his eyebrows. "Have you forgotten your responsibilities, that you must ask?"

Lucy looked at her brother's face. *Ouch,* she thought.

Regina stuck out her chin. "Maybe he has other responsibilities now."

"Then I should have been informed."

Dylan took Regina's hand and pulled her to his side. "Regina is to be my wife."

"Ah." Conn's gaze, light as frost, surveyed her face;

dropped briefly to her belly. "Congratulations. You will want this, then."

He slipped a silver chain from under his shirt and around his neck, and laid it on the glass display case.

Lucy heard the clink of metal and felt a buzzing in her head like a hive of bees. Her fingertips tingled.

Through the swarming in her head, she saw Caleb step closer to the counter. "What is it?" he asked.

"A warden's mark," Margred breathed.

A what?

"A wedding present," Conn said at the same time.

Dylan's face went from red to white. Whatever it was, Lucy thought, her brother wanted it very badly. She blinked, trying to clear the cloud from her eyes, to quiet the hum inside her.

Caleb rocked back on his heels and shot him a challenging glance. "A present? Or a bribe?"

Conn's mouth became a hard, flat line. "You underestimate the gift. And your brother."

"Say, instead, that my husband does not underestimate you," Margred murmured. "The timing—"

"Dylan earned this."

Forgotten in her corner, Lucy wondered, *Earned what? Earned it how?*

She squinted at the object on the counter, a flat silver disk engraved with swirling lines that looked a lot like Regina's tattoo: three flowing, connected spirals bound in a circle. The pattern pulled at her, coiling, dangerous, mesmerizing as a snake. Staring at it, she felt her head fill with bees, her bones turn to sand.

Deep breaths, she told herself, and held everything still inside her until the dizziness passed.

Dylan raised his gaze from the medallion to Conn's face. "I cannot accept it," he said jerkily.

"I have never known you to be stupid before," Conn said. "I can feel your influence all over this island. You are a warden now, whether you wear the mark or not. Take it."

Dylan shook his head. "My loyalty is pledged elsewhere. To them."

"Them," Conn repeated, testing the word in his mouth.

Dylan tightened his hold on Regina's hand. "My family."

His new family, Lucy thought, watching unobtrusively from the shelter of the booths. Which was the way it should be. But his gesture did not make her feel any less alone.

"Yes." Conn's pale gaze sought Lucy in her corner. She trembled, pinned. Dismayed. Disconcerted that he had noticed her, when her brothers and her friends had forgotten she was there. "Let us discuss your family."

"We can't now," Regina objected. "I need to get back to work. Dinner service starts in less than an hour."

"I do not believe your participation is required in this discussion," Conn said coldly.

"That's because you don't know me very well."

Lucy bit down on a smile.

"We're all in this together," Caleb said firmly. "Except for Lucy, of course."

Lucy's smile died. Of course.

"Caleb." Margred touched his arm again, nodding to where Lucy stood, frozen in her corner.

Her family turned to look at her with varying degrees of concern, regret, surprise.

She cringed inside, feeling the veil she had drawn around herself thin to cobweb.

Strangely, it was Conn who rescued her.

"Then we must postpone our discussion until you all are available," he said. "Tonight. At your house."

Dylan and Regina exchanged glances.

"Ma is closing tonight. I can ask her to watch Nick," she said, referring to her eight-year-old son.

Dylan nodded.

"We'll be there," Caleb said. "Eight o'clock?"

"Eight." Conn's cool, opaque gaze rested a moment longer on Lucy.

She felt again that dangerous quiver, that liquid tug deep in her belly, and stared at her feet.

Go away, she thought fiercely. *Please, just . . . go away.*

After a long moment, the bell jangled. The door closed behind him.

Regina's cheeks puffed out. "Well."

Margred's smooth forehead creased.

Caleb rubbed the back of his neck. "Listen, Lu—"

"I'm fine," she assured him quickly.

And she would be. As soon as she could be alone. As soon as she could pull herself together, repair the chinks in the careful wall she'd built around herself and her emotions.

"I'll see you all later. Or, um, not," she said and edged toward the door.

"It's not you," Dylan said. She was sure he meant to be kind. "This doesn't have anything to do with you."

She managed to find a smile from somewhere and fixed it on her mouth. "Right."

She didn't know what was going on. She didn't know why she was excluded, even in her own family. Why she was *different.*

Her hand trembled as she reached for the door. She yanked on the handle, desperate to escape before the emotion seething inside her found its way through the cracks.

She climbed the road toward home, hugging her sweatshirt and her composure against the fog rolling in from the sea. Like Dylan said, Conn's visit didn't have anything to do with her.

And yet . . .

She reached the top of the hill. The last light spilled

through a tear in the sky, daubing the waters of the harbor red and gold. The breeze that plucked her hair carried the scent of salt and the cries of the gulls. For one moment, Lucy lifted her face to the wind and let herself breathe, let herself dream, let herself yearn.

Then she set her steps inland, toward the dark spires of spruce and the white church tower rising from the streaks of fog. Going home. Alone.

A bird mourned in the trees.

Her heart pounded.

Without turning her head, she knew when Conn came out of the mist to fall into step beside her.

2

SHE DID NOT JUMP OR SCREECH.

Conn supposed he should be grateful for that. She either was brave or particularly unexcitable. *A lioness?* he wondered. *Or a sheep?* Either suited his purpose.

They walked together in silence under the lengthening shadow of the trees. The air swirled with moisture and the scent of pine. Mist sheened the black road and collected like a veil of pearls on the girl's fair hair. She walked with long strides like a man's, her arms crossed tightly in front of her. She did not look at him.

Conn had thought that she was shy. He wondered now if she was actually guarded. There was a stillness in her that did not feel completely natural, a watchfulness he recognized, almost like the discipline he had learned to impose on himself when he came to rule.

Which was absurd. She was too young to have learned such control, too human to need it.

He did not know what to say to her.

Her brother Dylan was selkie. Her brother Caleb had

married one. It was clear to Conn, however, that her family had told her nothing. Why should they? The recent trouble between the children of the sea and their fellow elementals, the children of fire, had nothing to do with her.

Yet the vision of her face had dragged him from his tower and drawn him halfway across the world. He eyed her almost resentfully.

"I thought you were talking to everybody later. At the house," she said to her feet. Long, narrow feet, he noticed, in shoes that might once have been white.

"I am." He clasped his hands behind his back. "I am talking to you now."

She turned her head. "Why?"

Such directness was unexpected and somewhat disconcerting.

"I would like to get to know you better," Conn said carefully.

"Why?" she repeated, nettling him.

Conn was not used to accounting for his actions. Even his wardens did not question him. He could hardly tell her he was trying to figure out what possible use or interest she could be to him. "I cannot be the first man to seek your company."

She smiled crookedly. "Yeah, I have to beat them off with a stick."

He stared. He could not have heard her correctly. "I beg your pardon?"

Pink suffused her lean face. "I meant . . . It's been a while."

Could he turn that to his advantage? Did human females want sex, miss sex, as selkies did?

"How long is a while?"

She blinked. "Boy, you take this getting-to-know-you shit seriously, don't you?"

"You do not have a husband?" he pressed. "A suitor?"

"You mean a boyfriend?"

Was that the word?

"Yes."

Her shoulders hunched, almost hiding her ears. "Nope."

Conn was aware of a faint release of tension. The claims or existence of another sexual partner meant nothing to him, but they might matter to her.

He was glad she was not married.

Her shoes scuffed the wet, black road. "What about you?" she asked.

"I live alone," he said truthfully. Selkies did mate, but few pairings lasted through the centuries.

"No one special?"

"Not for some time. My, uh, work does not permit many distractions."

"What kind of work do you do?"

"You ask a great many questions."

A smile lit her narrow face. "I work with five- to seven-year-olds. Taking an interest is part of my job description."

He stared. "You are a teacher."

He had once gone to great lengths to secure a teacher for the half-grown, half-feral whelps of Sanctuary. But there were no children on the selkie island anymore. Not in over twenty years. Dylan had been the last.

Conn's people were dying out. He needed more than a teacher to save them this time.

"You have a problem with teachers?"

"Not at all," he said politely. "I admire those who can teach. I simply have not known many."

"You must have known some."

He raised his eyebrows in question.

"When you were a kid," she explained.

"Ah. No. I received instruction—what there was of it— from my father."

She nodded. "Homeschooler. We don't get a lot of those

on World's End. Most islanders are just grateful we have enough children to keep the school running, you know?"

"Indeed."

"Did you like learning from your father? Or was it lonely without other children?"

Conn frowned. It was not the sort of question anyone had ever asked him. That anyone would dare to ask him. He did not talk about himself or what he missed or what he liked. He especially did not talk about his father.

He looked down grimly at the woman walking beside him with long, free strides. Now that the conversation was fixed on him, she was animated, even attractive, her quiet face bright with encouragement.

It was her job, she had said, to take an interest. He thought it must be her nature as well.

But then why did she shrink into herself earlier? Was she so averse to attention? She had a trick of lowering her lashes and ducking her head that made her almost disappear.

Like magic.

Not magic, Conn reminded himself. She was human. She could have no understanding of him or his needs.

"I am never lonely," he said.

"You and your father must be close, then," she observed.

"Not particularly," Conn said, his tone cool.

Her soft green eyes reflected her confusion. "But if he taught you—"

"I have not seen my father for many years." Centuries, if he kept track of such things. Which he certainly did not. "He abandoned all claim to affection or allegiance"—*or the throne*—"when he abandoned us."

" 'Us'?" she queried softly.

Conn regarded her with annoyance. "My people."

"Your family."

He was silent.

"It's hard," she said. "Dealing with a parent who walks out. I mean, I miss my mother, and I don't even remember her. She left us when I was a baby."

Conn frowned. Was she actually offering him sympathy? He was selkie, one of the First Creation. He did not require her pity. "So I heard."

She turned her head sharply.

"From your brother," he said.

Her brow cleared. "That's right. Have you known each other long?"

Ever since Dylan's Change at thirteen, when Atargatis discovered her older son was selkie. She had returned with him to the sea, leaving her human family behind.

A year later, she was dead, trapped and drowned in a fisherman's net, and Dylan became Conn's ward on Sanctuary.

"Long enough," Conn said.

Fog dripped from the trees like tears. The houses grew smaller and farther apart. Rusting vehicles and stacks of lobster traps littered yards like wrecks on the ocean bottom.

"Did you ever meet her?" Lucy asked abruptly. "My mother?"

"Yes."

"What was she like?"

Discontented, Conn remembered. As unhappy with the life she had returned to as the one she left. Away from the magic of Sanctuary, in human form, selkies aged as humans did. The years on land had dragged at Atargatis, coarsening her hair, wearing on her spirit, etching lines at the corners of her eyes. But she was still selkie, still alluring, still . . .

"Beautiful," he said.

"That's it? Just beautiful?"

What did she want him to say? She was not like the
mother who had abandoned her. Not selkie. And not beautiful either. Appealing, perhaps, with her lean, quiet face
and coltish grace, but . . .

"Beautiful and sad," Conn said. "Perhaps she regretted
leaving you."

"Maybe," the girl said doubtfully.

"You could ask your brother."

"After twenty-three years?" Unexpected humor lit her
eyes. "I don't think so."

"Your father, then."

"We don't talk about her." Her shoulders were rigid.
She stared straight ahead at the darkening road. "We don't
talk about much of anything, really."

She *was* guarded, Conn thought. More comfortable asking questions of him than offering anything of herself.

He remembered the way she stood apart at the restaurant, an observer in her own family.

Isolated.

And vulnerable.

He could use that, he thought.

"You can talk to me," he said.

*　*　*

Lucy unlocked the front door, uncomfortably aware of
Conn on the porch behind her. Her palms sweat. Her stomach jittered. For a moment, she was catapulted back to fifth
grade, afraid to bring a friend home after school.

The door creaked open. "Dad?"

No answer.

Her stomach relaxed.

The reassuring aroma of the beef and vegetables she'd
dumped into the Crock-Pot that morning rushed to greet
her, almost masking the smells of must and old carpet.

Lucy had come home from college with a bucket of cleaning supplies and a guide to keeping house, as if spotless tile would bring sparkle to their lives, as if she could banish bad memories along with the dust.

Maybe her efforts could not make up for the years of disorder and neglect, for the cracked vinyl and the cramped spaces and the mildew that sprouted mysteriously at the bottom of the stairs. At least her floors were clean.

Conn followed her as she marched past the shadowy living room, flipping on light switches as she went. He stood in the middle of her scrubbed kitchen floor, overdressed, out-of-place, dark, and wild. Her heart thundered. She felt breathless, as if he'd done his sucking-all-the-oxygen-out-of-the-room trick again.

And yet he did not move, only stood there with his hands still clasped behind his back.

"Where is your father?" he asked.

She grabbed a spoon and lifted the lid of the Crock-Pot, hoping he wouldn't notice her hot cheeks. "Out," she said, stirring.

Conn glanced at the now-dark windows. "It is late to haul traps."

He knew her dad was a lobsterman. Lucy's hand tightened on the spoon. What else did he know?

"My father's on the water by five every morning. In by four, most days. He off-loads and does his business at the co-op." She set her spoon on the counter, pleased that neither her hand nor her voice trembled. "And then he goes to the bar at the inn and drinks until they won't serve him anymore."

She fit the lid carefully back on the pot and turned to face Conn, her back to the counter, her chin high. "Are you hungry?"

A short, charged silence vibrated between them.

Conn studied her face, his silver eyes inscrutable. "Yes. Thank you. That smells very good."

She almost sagged with relief and disappointment.

What had she expected?

That he would say he was sorry for her, for her alcoholic father, her crappy childhood?

That he would sweep her off her feet and take her away like a prince in a fairy tale?

Stupid, stupid. She wasn't looking for sympathy. Or rescue. Especially not from some cold-eyed stranger who twisted her insides into knots.

What a good thing he hadn't offered either one.

"Sit down," she said. "I'll get you a plate."

His eyebrows raised. "You must join me."

Not, *"Would you join me?"* Not a question or a request. Obviously, he expected her to sit down and put a good face on things and pretend that everything was normal.

Lucy bit her lower lip. And she would, too.

Because she always did.

*   *   *

Conn generally paid scant attention to what he ate or did not eat. But hot food was a change from his usual raw diet. The simple stew had stirred his appetite.

He watched the girl—Lucy—as she cleared the table and washed their few dishes. In her own venue, she was really quite competent. He observed the neat, practiced movements of her hands as she rinsed a plate and set it on the counter to drain. Narrow, brown hands, with long, slender fingers and strong wrists.

She stirred his appetite, too.

Conn frowned. He was revising his opinion of her attractiveness. He still did not understand what he was doing here.

She turned from the sink, a cloth in her hands, and thrust it at him. "Dry."

"I beg your pardon?"

She gestured toward the counter stacked with dishes. "I'm running out of room. I need you to dry." A sudden gleam appeared in her eyes. "You do know how to dry, don't you?"

He regarded her with mingled appreciation and annoyance. Was she laughing at him?

"I believe I can learn," he said and took the cloth.

They worked in silence until all the dishes had been dried and put away.

"What about that one?" he asked.

She glanced over her shoulder at the big pot on the counter. "It's fine."

"There is food inside."

Not much. Conn had filled his plate twice. But . . .

"It will be wasted," he said.

She took the dishcloth from him without meeting his gaze. "My father might want something when he comes in."

Might?

"*He goes to the bar at the inn,*" she had said, "*and drinks until they won't serve him anymore.*"

"And if he is too drunk to eat?" he asked.

Lucy fussed with the cloth, arranging it over the bar of the oven door to dry. "Then in the morning before I go to work, I'll throw it out."

"Will you wash the pot then, too?"

"Yes."

"And prepare something else." Not a question, this time.

She lifted one shoulder in a shrug. "I guess you think that's stupid."

Stupid, yes. And gallant.

He admired her tenacity. He understood what it was to meet one's obligations, day after day, year after year, without hope or expectation.

"Why do you do it?" he asked.

She smiled crookedly. "Who else will?"

He understood that, too.

Their gazes locked. Beneath the surface of her eyes, kelp green shadows swayed. Conn's chest tightened. *Why was the sea reflected in her eyes?*

The doorbell rang.

She dropped her gaze.

For a moment, he could not breathe.

No, he thought. *Stay.*

But she was already moving past him to the door. "That will be Cal and Maggie."

She sounded relieved. Or perhaps she was merely pleased to see her brother.

Conn observed their greeting, the tall, quiet police chief in his rumpled uniform, the tall, quiet schoolteacher with garden dirt on her jeans. They did not embrace. But their silent exchange—his long, assessing look, her quick, reassuring smile—revealed their bond.

"Touching, is it not?" Margred murmured in Conn's ear. "The Hunters are a very loyal family."

He recognized her warning.

"And you, Margred?" He challenged her softly, this woman who had once been selkie. "Where do your loyalties lie?"

She widened her eyes. "Why, with my husband, my lord," she said and moved away.

The door opened again, and Dylan entered with the small, dark, pregnant woman he intended to marry. Around his neck, he wore the silver medallion, the warden's mark: three interconnected spirals representing the domains of earth, sea, and sky. The sign of Dylan's new power . . . and his duty to his prince.

He did not make the mistake, this time, of addressing Conn by title. He bowed stiffly.

Conn nodded in acknowledgment.

"Well." Dylan's woman cocked her head like a bird, her gaze darting around the hall. "I don't know about the rest of you, but I've been on my feet since four this morning, and I'd like to sit down."

Lucy jumped. "Of course. Why don't we use the living room?"

"Actually, Lu . . ." Her brother Caleb's slow voice dragged her back from the doorway. "Maybe you could put up a pot of coffee."

"I don't . . . Tea?" she offered.

"Tea would be great. Thanks."

She changed course toward the kitchen while the others flowed into the darkened living room.

Dylan switched on a lamp, casting a pool of yellow light over a table. "That's better."

Did he refer to the light? Conn wondered. Or his sister's absence?

Caleb took a stand with his back to the wall and his eyes on the door. "What have you told her?" he asked Conn.

Conn raised his eyebrows. "Very little. Though I am curious why you have not told her more."

"She is human," Dylan said.

"So is your brother," Conn said.

On the sofa, Margred crossed her legs. "Caleb faced a demon for me. He deserved to know who I was. And what their mother was."

"Milk or sugar?" Lucy asked breathlessly from the hall.

Silence thickened the air.

They did not want her there. Conn felt their discomfort

as a living, pulsing barrier, drawing them together, leaving Lucy alone on the outside.

She felt it, too. Conn saw the red tide sweep her face.

He had already learned what he could from her. He needed Dylan's report.

Yet looking at her flushed cheeks, her soft, stricken eyes, he felt almost sorry for her.

"Sugar, please," Margred said.

The other woman, the pregnant one, pulled herself to her feet. "I'll help," she said kindly.

But Lucy was already backing away, shaking her head. "I've got it."

"Why don't you set out everything in the kitchen," Caleb suggested. "We'll join you when we're ready."

Lucy flinched and then was still, like a wounded animal that will not call attention to itself. "Actually, I just . . . I have lesson plans to do. Upstairs."

They sat, listening to the sound of her retreating footsteps.

The pregnant woman crossed her arms over her stomach and shot Caleb an accusing look. "Smooth, Cal. Very smooth."

Caleb rubbed the back of his neck.

"She couldn't stay," Margred said.

"Not after that," the woman—*Regina, that was her name*—said.

"Not at all," said Dylan. "She's not involved. She doesn't even know what's going on."

Conn was struck by a sudden vision of Lucy's face burning in the water of the tide pool.

She was involved. Somehow.

He had to find the reason, a pattern, a clue.

He clasped his hands behind him and directed a look at Dylan. "Neither do I. Yet. No doubt you are about to enlighten me."

3

CONN WAS NOT HIS FATHER. HE DID NOT EX-
pend energy in needless emotion. But listening to Dylan's
report, Conn was aware of a hard, cold lump beneath his
breastbone, a warning pulse in his blood, that felt discon-
certingly like anger.

Buggering hell.

He tightened his hands behind his back. "They tried to
kill your child," he said. "A selkie child. A daughter of
Atargatis."

It was the threat he feared.

And the answer he had come looking for.

Regina spread her hands over her stomach. "We don't
know yet if the baby's selkie. Or even if it's a girl. The ul-
trasound won't be accurate for another couple of weeks.
But that woman—the devil woman—was definitely trying
to end the pregnancy. I was just . . . What do you call it?"

"Collateral damage," Caleb said in a grim voice.

Conn ignored them both. "And you did nothing," he
said to Dylan.

Dylan flushed the way he used to when he first came to live at Sanctuary, a thin, sulky adolescent with more attitude than sense. "I warded the island."

"You knew I was waiting to hear from you."

"I sent the *whaleyn*."

The humpbacks' song was rich and nuanced. But it lacked the clarity of human communication.

"You should have come yourself," Conn said.

He had wasted weeks in the expectation that Dylan would return to Sanctuary to make his report—a mere eyeblink in the centuries of a selkie's existence. However, in the current contest with the children of fire, even time was Conn's enemy.

Dylan gave him a level look, reminding Conn he was not a boy any longer. "I couldn't leave them," he said.

Them. His woman. His child. *The daughter of the prophecy?* Conn wondered. The *targair inghean.*

"You could have brought them with you," he said. Though what in all the seven seas he was to do with them . . .

Dylan shook his head. "Regina shouldn't travel."

"I wouldn't leave anyway," she said. "I've got family here. A kid. A life."

Conn raised his eyebrows. "And if you lose your life? What becomes of your child then?"

She pressed her lips together.

The big man with the quiet eyes—Caleb, Dylan's brother—stirred by the door. "She fought. We all fought the battle that came to us. Where the fuck were you?"

In his tower on Sanctuary, trying to hold a castle of sand against the encroaching tide.

"You see a battle," Conn said coldly. "I see the war."

Caleb stuck his thumbs in his pockets. "So we're just more collateral damage?"

"Not if you come to Sanctuary," Conn said.

They all gaped at him.

Not the reaction he was hoping for.

"In attacking you, the children of fire have exposed their weakness. They fear you. Or at least," he added carefully, "they fear the children to come after you. The daughters of Atargatis are a threat to them."

And an advantage to me, Conn thought but did not say. A tool. A weapon to be grasped.

Lucy's face—watchful eyes between curtains of thick, fair hair—flashed briefly in his brain.

But it was her brothers who concerned him now.

"Come to Sanctuary," he repeated. "Where I can protect you."

"Protect?" Margred asked. "Or control?"

"You will be safe there," Conn insisted.

"We're safe here," said Dylan's woman. "Dylan warded the whole island."

"Dylan is but one," Conn said. The youngest and least of his wardens. "There are a dozen guardians on Sanctuary."

Or there could be.

He would call them back, he decided. The ranks of the wardens had thinned as their people dwindled, as their magic declined. There were fewer than a hundred now. Too many of the seaborn had been lost as Conn's father was lost to the bliss of the land beneath the wave. Atargatis had been among the last of the old ones to still take human form. Which made preserving her bloodline even more important.

"Well, I'm the only cop on World's End," Caleb said. "I can't just pack up and leave. I have a responsibility to the people here."

Conn looked pointedly at Margred. "Greater than your responsibility to her? To the children you might have together?"

Margred sucked in her breath.

"There aren't going to be any children," Caleb said flatly.

"There could be," Margred said.

Her husband's face set like stone. "I'm trying to protect you."

"So you keep saying. Or we would have a baby by now."

Conn, sensing weakness, pressed his argument home like a sword. "Have your baby on Sanctuary. Where you both will be safe."

Margred's mouth opened. Closed.

"Want a piece of candy, little girl?" Regina muttered.

Dylan shot her a warning look.

"What? We already talked this over," she said. "I won't leave Ma. And I'm not ripping Nick away from the only life he's ever known to hang with the lost boys in Neverland."

"All right," Dylan said. "If—"

"You need time to consider," Conn said before they could refuse.

The lump under his ribs had coalesced into a hard, cold knot. More was at stake here than their human ties or loyalties, than their practical considerations or their pride. More was at risk than their safety.

The demons were circling World's End, drawn to the promise of power like sharks to the scent of blood. If Conn could preserve Atargatis's bloodline . . .

He regarded them a moment: two humans, a selkie who had lost her pelt, and a warden just coming into his power. The heirs of Atargatis. The key to the prophecy.

The knot in his chest tightened.

"I'll leave you to talk," he said.

Caleb gave a short nod.

But at the entrance to the hall, Conn paused. "You should ask your sister what she wants."

"Lucy?" asked Regina.

"She's not selkie," Dylan said.

"She carries the bloodline," Conn said. "She has a right to choose."

"Lucy would never leave the island," Caleb said. "She almost didn't go away to college. She's happy here."

Conn raised his brows. "Is she?"

"Isn't she?" Margred asked.

"Ask her," Conn said again.

He gripped the door handle when something—a noise, a scent, a sense like a breath at the back of his neck—dragged his gaze upward.

Lucy stood almost hidden in the crook of the narrow stairs, a hand pressed to her mouth. In the shadows, her eyes blazed.

His heart leaped.

Their gazes locked.

She blinked, and it was as if the brightness had never been.

Conn swallowed a snarl of disappointment. "A message at the inn will find me," he said tightly to no one in particular. "When you are ready to talk."

Opening the door, he stalked into the night.

*   *   *

Lucy stabbed her spade into the soil. *Nobody loves me, everybody hates me, think I'll go eat worms . . .*

Which was stupid. She knew her family loved her. She loved them. But the silly jingle played over and over in her head like a bad song on the radio, complete with a slide show of scenes from last night.

The Hunter family had never been big on Sharing Their Feelings. Every child growing up in an alcoholic household learned to protect its secrets. Lucy had spent most of her life avoiding questions from friends, teachers, and well-meaning neighbors. *Where is your mother? How is your father? Why did you move back?*

But now the things her family would not say were threatening to split them apart. And the people with the answers, the people Lucy loved, weren't talking.

At least not to her.

She ripped a potato from the garden. The fat root exploded from the ground in a shower of dirt that did nothing to relieve her hurt or frustration.

Use words, she told her students when they were overwhelmed by the need to scream and kick and bite. Well, she'd tried, hadn't she? After Conn had left, she'd gone into the living room to talk to her family. But all her questions, all her overtures, had died a slow and miserable death in the face of their determined noncommunication, killed by Dylan's stubborn silence and Caleb's dismissive reassurances.

She rubbed the potato against her jeans, leaving a long smear of dirt.

Caleb's reaction hurt the most. Her brother had raised her from the time she was in diapers until he left on a ROTC scholarship the year she turned nine. All through middle and high school, Cal had still been there for her, making trips home for holidays and school assemblies, sending checks on her birthday. She trusted him with . . . almost everything.

He didn't trust her. His lack of faith stung.

Well, if Cal couldn't treat her like a grown-up, she knew someone who would.

She glanced toward the edge of the field. Assuming he came.

She thought—she hoped—he would come. Otherwise, why bother making that cryptic announcement at the door? *"A message at the inn will find me when you are ready to talk."*

She wiped her sweaty palms on her jeans, smearing them

even more. Ready to talk? Maybe. Ready to listen anyway. Anything was better than being cut off from her family by this awful not-knowing.

She watched him emerge from the shadow of the woods like a surfer sliding from beneath a wave. He wasn't a stranger anymore.

That didn't stop the drop in her stomach, the scrambling of her pulse.

"You came," she said foolishly as Conn approached over the sun-streaked furrows.

No jacket today. No tie. The collar of his dress shirt—Dylan's dress shirt—was unbuttoned, the sleeves rolled up. Fine, dark hair dusted his arms. Otherwise, he looked the same, same slightly hooked nose, same unsmiling mouth, same cool eyes.

The color of rain, Lucy thought again and shivered with apprehension and desire.

She wished suddenly, passionately, that she could turn the clock back, roll the world back to the way it had been twenty-four hours ago when he had first walked across the fields and into her life. Before she knew her brothers were lying to her. Before she was forced to a decision.

His brows arched. "You asked me to come."

"*You can talk to me,*" he'd said.

"Yeah." She swallowed. She must have been out of her mind. "You said . . . Last night you said I had the right to choose."

Silence. A long, assessing, how-much-should-I-tell-her kind of silence, while her heart beat faster and her blood drummed in her ears.

"I was mistaken," he said at last.

Disappointment flattened her mouth. She took a step closer. "I want to know what's going on."

His cool, light eyes considered her face. "What did your brothers tell you?"

"Dylan didn't say anything. And Caleb . . ." Lucy bit her lip, a small pain to counter the ache at her heart. "Cal said what I don't know can't hurt me."

But it hurt already.

"They treat you like the girl they left behind," Conn said.

She met his gaze, grateful for his understanding. "Pretty much."

"You are very young," he observed.

"Twenty-three."

"Almost a quarter century," he said, gently mocking.

She narrowed her eyes. She was tired of being shut out, frustrated at being dismissed, sick of being good and quiet and alone. "Old enough," she said.

His gaze met hers. The air charged between them. She felt a tingle like static electricity all along her skin, the shock of wetness between her thighs.

"Are you indeed?" he murmured.

She swallowed. "I didn't mean . . . I don't want . . ."

But her lips wouldn't release the lie. She did. Oh, she did. She felt a contraction deep inside, powerful as a fist. It had been so long since she'd allowed herself the freedom to feel. To take. And in this moment, faced with the temptation of his firm, unsmiling mouth, the challenge of those cool gray eyes, she had trouble remembering why.

His gaze dropped to her mouth. His nostrils flared. Her nipples beaded. She sensed the wildness in him, churning deep below the surface, and an answering hunger uncurled in her belly, whetted by loneliness and lust. She leaned in, drawn beyond caution, beyond reason, pulled irresistibly closer by the promise of his kiss.

He bent his head and paused, his breath on her lips.

She felt a spark, a current arcing between them. His lips touched hers, and her heart gave a startled jump and flew up behind her teeth. He coaxed her mouth open with his mouth, pressing his tongue inside. He tasted wild and salty as the sea. She surged to meet him, meeting his tongue eagerly with her own, sucking it deeper, twining her arms around his neck. She was starving for the taste of him, for the feel of his man's hard body against her body, for the touch of skin on skin.

She wanted . . . She rose on tiptoe, straining to get closer. She needed . . .

He broke the kiss, leaning his forehead against hers. His breath was hot on her lips, his skin warm and damp. She wanted to burrow under his shirt to touch him, his flesh. His erection was long and thick, pressed against her.

His fingertips brushed her cheek, her jaw, her throat. "Come away with me."

Yes.

No.

"Where?" A silly, breathless sound.

"Does it matter?" He sounded impatient. Amused.

No.

Yes.

She wanted to pull him down among the broken corn rows, open his pants and straddle him. She swallowed hard. "It might. I don't know you."

"What better way to learn?"

He had the trick of answering a question with another question. Like a cop. Like Caleb. Like a man with something to hide.

"We could try talking."

"Come with me," he urged. "Away."

The possibility pulled at her like an undertow. She almost staggered. "I can't *leave.*"

"Why not?"

"I have . . ." She searched for solid ground, reasons that would stand against the tug of his temptation, the demand clamoring through her blood. "Obligations. School. My father."

"This is no place for you." His voice beat at her like the sea on the rocks at night, whispering along her nerves, eroding her control. "This is no life for the woman you have become."

She pressed her hands to her temples. Her body throbbed like a bruise. "You don't know anything about what kind of woman I am."

And he couldn't.

No one must ever know.

"Tell me."

Oh, God, she wanted to.

She stared at him, tempted, appalled, dismayed. Her heart pounded in her chest. *This* was what came of asking questions.

His eyes darkened and expanded until they filled her vision. Twin black whirlpools, drawing her in, dragging her under.

She could barely hear over the rushing in her ears. Her head buzzed. Her blood itched and crackled. She worked her tongue, trying to lick her words into shape. "I don't want to talk about it."

He smiled slowly, the first time she had seen him smile. "Then we will not talk."

"I should . . ." *What?* "Go home," she managed.

"I will take you where you need to go."

Take me. Yes.

His mouth possessed hers in a long, deep, drugging kiss that blanketed her brain like fog rolling in from the sea. She was lost in it, in him, in her rising need. His lips followed the trail blazed by his fingertips, the curve of her cheek, the hollow of her jaw, her throat. His hands pushed under her shirt to close on her breasts, and her knees folded like wet string. He shifted her, pulling her sweatshirt over her head, throwing it to the ground. Sliding his hands to her hips, he turned her against his body. His chest was fitted to her back, his erection pressed her buttocks. She panted with excitement, liquid heat running through her veins, surging through her body, melting her insides. She could not see his face. She could only feel, his breath hot at her ear, his arm hard around her waist, his solid body pulsing, rocking against her. His free hand unbuttoned her jeans, tugged on her zipper.

"Uh," she said. Assent? Or warning?

Then it didn't matter because his hand was there, in her panties, between her legs. His long fingers stroked her, pressing firmly and then delicately, making her hot, making her wet, making her shudder and cry out. It wasn't enough. His beard rasped the side of her face. His hand was busy, making her mindless. She arched against him, frantic, pushing her hips into his hand, fighting the constricting denim.

"I need . . ."

More.

"Yes. Trust me," he said.

She struggled to turn, to face him, and he used the break in her balance to sweep her off her feet and onto the ground. The sun dazzled her eyes, silhouetting his head. He came down hard on top of her, still fully clothed. Her hair spilled among the leaves and vines. The smell of rich, ripe, growing things enveloped them.

Hooking his thumb into the neckline of her tank top, he dragged it down, exposing her to the cool air and his heated gaze. The stretchy fabric caught beneath her breasts, pushing them upward like an offering. The sun glinted on her navel ring.

He paused. With one finger, he touched the tiny aquamarine sparkling like a tear against her belly. "Beautiful."

But she was too far gone for compliments. Or delays. Grabbing his head, she guided it to her breasts. He suckled her strongly, his mouth hot and wet. She tangled her fingers in his sleek, warm hair, feeling the pull all the way to her womb. The earth exhaled as the sun poured down like honey, sealing her eyelids. It still was not enough. Never enough. Something had seized her, a hunger, a fever. She rose to meet him, her heels pressing the earth, feeling the clods cool between her shoulders, the soil damp beneath her buttocks, and then—*yesss*—his erection, hot and hard against her thighs, against her entrance. He had yanked his pants open. Her jeans and panties were down around her knees. She strained upward, her body taut and ready as a bow. He reached between their bodies to the place where she was slick and wet and aching for him. *Now.* He pushed, and she sucked in her breath at the sudden invasion, the startling fullness.

It was too much. It was not enough.

His weight pinned her, trapping her firmly in her body, fully in the moment. She was swimming in sensation, swept away by desire. He hunched into her, working her with long, firm strokes, thrusting into her again. And again. The musk of earth, sweat, and sex rose around them, the slap of flesh on flesh, wet and raw. He pounded into her, deep, deeper. She clenched around him.

His hand gripped her jaw.

Startled, she opened her eyes. His face was dark and intent above her, haloed by the blue, blue sky.

"Come with me," he commanded. "Come."

She was helpless to resist. The tide rose in her body, drowning will, swamping thought. The ground rolled under her like a wave as her crest took her. Above her, within her, Conn's body plunged. Shuddered.

And the dark carried her away.

*　*　*

Conn levered himself from the girl's long body, lying among the green vines and dry husks. Her palm lay curled half-open like a flower. Her scent—sun-warmed skin, soap-washed hair—mingled with the smell of crushed stalks and turned soil.

Gazing down at her pale face and thick, fair lashes, he allowed himself a moment's regret. He would have preferred her cognizant.

And walking, he acknowledged ruefully.

But he had already been gone too long from Sanctuary. He needed her to propagate her mother's line and secure his people's fate. He did not choose to become mired in days of delay and endless explanations, with the risk of her family's interference and perhaps her own refusal at the end.

So.

He had bound her to him by the simplest, strongest means at his disposal. She had not been unwilling. He had experience enough to achieve her seduction, skill enough to compel her response. Magic enough to throw her brothers off the scent should they feel obliged to follow.

Everything had gone according to plan.

Except his own reaction.

Conn frowned. She had moved him. He did not know why. He had enjoyed other partners who were more beautiful and certainly more inventive. Eager partners. Selkie partners.

Not recently, though. He adjusted his clothing, tucking himself away. Perhaps the girl's charm lay in her novelty. Perhaps what he was experiencing was merely relief after a long abstinence.

And yet . . . He glanced down at her quiet face, her fair hair rioting over the ground. When he was in her, when her body rose to meet his, he had felt a power, a control, a hunger to match his own.

Absurd, of course. She was only human, no matter who her mother was.

He slipped off her shoes; reached under her to remove

her jeans. Beneath her garments, she was lovely, clean-limbed and strong, pale and smooth as willow with the bark peeled away.

He laid her back down among the pumpkins, his hands skimming her ribs as he tugged her skimpy top to cover her pink-tipped breasts. Unexpected hunger tightened his belly. Stiffened his cock.

Grimly, he returned his gaze to her face. The children of the sea lived in the moment, following their whims and desires like the pull of the tides. But Conn had ruled for nine hundred years in human form from the tower of Caer Subai. He had learned—painfully—to control his nature, to weigh and calculate and decide. He would not be distracted from his purpose.

He slid his knife from the sheath at his knee.

Corn stood around them in patches, skeletons of summer among the stakes and twine. Conn gathered a sheaf in one arm and, bending, sliced it through in a single stroke close to the ground. He bound the dried stalks together with twine, tying them to form a waist, a neck, legs. The shock at the top he left loose like long, stiff hair.

He laid the corn maiden on the ground beside Lucy, measuring its length with his eyes. They were almost the same size. He dressed the sheaf in the girl's clothing, forcing the jeans over the stalks of its legs, bundling its body into the shirt. He was sweating when he finished. Bits of dust and broken chaff clung to his skin.

Kneeling beside Lucy, he gathered her hair in one hand the way he'd gathered the corn, counting the strands across his palm, *one, two, three . . . seven.* Her face was still, her skin cold and pale.

An unexpected twinge caught him beneath the ribs. He used sex as a tool, a weapon. He did not expect it to turn like a knife in his hand. But his feelings, her feelings, could not be allowed to matter. He did what he must do.

Fisting his hand around the strands of her hair, he yanked it out by the roots.

Her breath escaped her lips in a silent cry. A drop of blood beaded at her scalp, but his magic compelled her to continue sleeping.

He set his teeth, touching his finger to the blood and then to the center of the bundled corn, the *claidheag*, where the corn maiden's heart would beat. If such a creature had a heart. His fingertip burned. He felt the heat flow upward through his arm, power building and pulsing like a headache. He tied the seven strands of hair over the twine at the top.

"Know," he commanded. The pressure hammered at his temples.

He blew into the featureless face. "Breathe."

He pressed the heel of his palm between Lucy's legs, still wet with her essence and his seed. The magic gripped his neck like claws, sinking fangs into his skull, squeezing his brain. He smeared his wet hand over the dry husks of the *claidheag*, anointing it with life. "*Be.*"

He felt the surge, the shock of focused power, leap from him to the sheaf on the ground.

Done.

The power ebbed away, leaving him drained, his head throbbing with the aftermath of magic, and the *claidheag* stiff and still.

Conn inhaled, holding his breath to fill the sudden emptiness of his chest.

Lucy slept, unknowing.

He lifted her body in his arms and carried her away, leaving his handiwork lying behind them in the field.

*   *   *

The dried stalks rattled together. *Know.*

The wind whispered. *Breathe.*

The earth radiated warmth. *Be.*

The breeze teased the bundle on the ground. The *claidheag*'s hair, the pale gold of corn husks or straw, fluttered, smoothing, softening. Beneath the swaddling clothes, its limbs swelled and grew supple, taking on substance, taking on flesh.

From the branches of a spruce, a crow launched, squawking in protest or warning.

The corn maiden opened its eyes, the green-yellow of pumpkin vines. Lucy's eyes, in Lucy's face.

It lay in the field, watching the clouds chase across the sky, absorbing the last rays of the sun, listening to the chatter of the wind.

A catbird landed on a nearby stake, cocked a fierce, bright eye, and flew away again. An ant, wandering the furrows, traced a trail over the *claidheag*'s motionless hand. Slowly, thought formed, a pale shoot from a kernel of consciousness.

It did not belong here, cut down, cut off from the earth. Not anymore.

Sighing, the *claidheag* rose on one elbow and then to its knees. To its feet. It should go . . . The word was buried deep, a fat, round word, moldy with disappointment. *Home.* It should go home.

Following the tug of blood, the stir of memory, it shambled toward the road.

4

CALEB WATCHED MAGGIE STIR ANOTHER SPOON-
ful of sugar into her mug. Less than twenty-four hours after their meeting with the selkie prince, they sat at their
own kitchen table. The night breeze flowed over the sill,
carrying with it the scent of the salt wood.

This was what he'd dreamed of, Maggie in his house
and in his life, sharing their thoughts at the end of the day.
After two months of marriage, he knew her tastes and her
habits, knew she liked her coffee sweet and the windows
open and sex first thing in the morning.

But he didn't know how to give her what she wanted.
Not this time.

"Maybe in a couple of years," Caleb said. "When things
settle down . . ."

She shot him a wry look. "When I am seven hundred
and five?"

He reached to cover her hand on the table. "You don't
look a day over three hundred."

"There's a comfort." But she smiled and turned her palm over, linking her fingers with his. "It's all right, Caleb. I am happy here. With you."

Some of the tension leached from his shoulders. "I'll give Conn our answer in the morning, then."

Margred curled her free hand around her mug. "What about Lucy?"

Caleb felt the stiffness creep back into his neck. "What about her?"

"When I first met her, I thought . . . I felt . . ." Margred shook her head. "She is your mother's daughter, too."

Everything within him rejected the idea. From the time Lucy was a toddler with fat baby legs and a "love me" smile, she had been his. He'd been the one to take care of her. To protect her. To fix her lunch and her scrapes, to read her stories and tuck her into bed.

"Lucy is human," he said shortly. "She never Changed."

Selkies retained the shape they had at birth until they reached sexual maturity. Seals lived as seals for three to six years; humans remained in human form until puberty. When Caleb's brother, Dylan, turned thirteen, he Changed for the first time. His transformation had torn their family apart. Atargatis—Alice, their father had called her— returned with her older son to the sea, leaving her husband, ten-year-old Caleb, and baby Lucy behind.

"How do you know?" Margred asked. "You were not here."

Caleb ran his hand over his short hair. "She called me at school to tell me she got her period, for God's sake. You think she would have mentioned a little something like sprouting flippers and fur."

"Would she?"

Caleb's jaw set. "Lucy's as human as I am," he insisted. "If she wasn't, you would know it. You would have sensed it. Or Dylan would."

"Yes. But she is still of your mother's bloodline. If she were to have a child—"

He didn't want to think about it. His sister was fresh out of college. Barely out of diapers.

"Let's not borrow trouble," Caleb said. "Christ, she doesn't even have a steady boyfriend."

"Neither did Regina before she met your brother," Margred pointed out.

"What are the odds my sister's going to get knocked up by a selkie? As long as Lucy sticks to her own kind, she'll be fine."

Maggie arched her eyebrows. "Really."

Fuck.

He hadn't stuck to his kind. And neither, thank God, had she.

"I only meant . . . You told me yourself most humanmer offspring are human. Lucy's only half-selkie. If she marries a mortal, a human, their kids will probably be human, too. They'll be safe."

"*Lucy's* human children would be safe," Margred repeated.

Caleb frowned. "Probably. The demons have never gone after Lucy."

"Then why do you assume our child would be in danger?"

"Because—damn it, Maggie, you're selkie."

"Not anymore."

"You are. In your blood. In your genes. And I carry my mother's genes. The combination . . ." Fear for her closed his throat. "It's too dangerous."

"Didn't you say we should not borrow trouble?"

"Maggie, if you get pregnant, you might as well paint a bull's-eye on your belly. The demons will come after you. You could die." The thought ripped his insides. His hand clenched hers on the table. "I can't lose you."

"My dearest heart. My love." Her voice was gentle, her eyes dark and tender. "All mortal things die. Now or five years from now or fifty . . . what is any of it, compared to eternity? Yet I would rather have one year with you than a millennium without you. I am human now. Let me *be* human."

She was everything he'd ever wanted. And she wanted a family. With him.

"It's a risk," he insisted stubbornly.

"Life is a risk. I chose this life with you. Let me live it fully."

Her love shook him.

Her faith shamed him.

"Maggie." *Shit.* "I never could resist you."

Her smile was slow and provocative. She was so beautiful, with her wide, dark, understanding eyes and her come-fuck-me smile. "That's what I am counting on."

"You didn't conceive with your mate. What if I can't give you a child?"

"The selkies' birth rate has been declining for centuries. It may be I am barren. If we cannot make a child together, we will do what other human couples do. Adjust. Adopt. I do not expect a miracle, Caleb." Her smile turned rueful. "Or only a very small one."

She ripped his heart.

She tossed back her hair and stood, giving him another of her direct looks. "Do you want to make another list of reasons why this is a bad idea? Or do you want to make love?"

Heat kicked in his groin. Caleb swallowed. He was so screwed. Or he would be, if he gave her half a chance.

If he gave *them* a chance.

"*Life is a risk.*"

"I want you," he said honestly. "I always want you."

Her breasts in his hands, his body in her body. Nothing

between them. Skin on skin, the way it had been the first
time.

"Well, then." Her smile spread. *Come and get me.*

Caleb grinned with love and lust and rounded the
kitchen table.

*   *   *

Bart Hunter fumbled with his front door in the dark.

Something was wrong. Alarm pierced the damp evening mist and the fog of whiskey like a beacon.

No porch light. Lucy always left the porch light burning
for him. The knob turned under his hand before he could
get the key in. She never forgot to lock the door either. She
was a careful girl, Lucy. Responsible. Not like . . .

But his mind winced from the comparison like an old
bruise.

He stumbled into the front hall. So still. So dark. The
smell of the Crock-Pot—tomatoes, maybe, and onions—
permeated the downstairs.

Bart wavered between the empty kitchen and the darkened living room. His stomach rolled with a combination
of hunger and too much Seagram's. Maybe he'd have a
bite, to please her.

But first he'd have another drink.

He lurched for the living room and the liquor cabinet.
Stopped short, his heart banging.

"Lucy?"

She sat upright on the couch, her eyes wide open and
gleaming in the dark.

He covered his start, his guilt, in aggression. He hated
her to watch him drink. "What the hell are you doing up?
You should be in bed."

"I should," she said. Impossible to tell from her tone of
voice if she was questioning or agreeing with him.

Bart scowled. "What's the matter with you?"

She paused, like she was really thinking about it. "I don't know."

He took a reluctant step forward. She looked . . . different. Paler, maybe, though it was hard to tell in the dark. She smelled like she'd been working in the garden after school, a sharp, green smell like summer grass. "What are you, sick or something?"

"I could be sick."

Inadequacy rose like bile in his throat.

He had never known what to do with her, this youngest child, his only daughter. If Alice had stuck around, it would have been different, maybe. Better. Bitterness coated his tongue. A lot of things would have been better.

He rubbed the side of his nose. "Well, did you eat?"

"No."

He waited for her to move, to get off the couch, to jump up and offer to fix them both something like she usually did.

He wanted her to go to bed, out of his way, out of his sight. He wanted a drink, damn it.

But she continued to watch him with wide, unblinking eyes like a doll's. Rooted to his spot on the couch.

Shit.

Bart stomped into the kitchen, burning his hand on the lid of the Crock-Pot as he spooned whatever mess she'd made that morning—chili, he guessed—into two bowls.

He thrust one at her. "Go on. Eat."

She waited until he dipped his spoon and brought it to his mouth before she did the same.

They ate in silence. He didn't know what to say to her. Never had.

She laid her empty bowl in her lap. Nothing wrong with her appetite, at least.

"Well." Bart stood. "I'm turning in."

His daughter regarded him blankly.

"Got an early morning," he explained.

She should know that. Wasn't he out the door before she woke up every morning?

He was relieved when she nodded.

"I should be in bed," she said. "I could be sick."

*   *   *

Something was wrong.

The realization seeped through the fog in Lucy's brain. Blearily, she raised her head, struggling to focus in the dark. She blinked. Her bed was in the wrong place.

Her bed . . . Her room . . . Her stomach lurched. Everything was wrong.

Everything had been wrong for a long, long time.

But her mind jerked from the thought, the way a child learns to jerk his hand from a candle or the stove. If you didn't linger, you couldn't get burned.

Her body felt stiff and weak, as if she'd been lying in one position for too long or had the flu. She'd been sleeping. Dreaming, the way she did when she was a little girl, of her mother's voice. Her mother's voice and the sea. Her head felt stuffed with straw.

What had happened? Was she sick? Where was she?

Where was Conn?

Her mouth tasted foul. She worked a little moisture onto her tongue, trying to swallow. To think. The air was close and smelled like the inside of a locker or the closet under the stairs. Moldy. Still. She felt like she was underwater. As if she couldn't breathe. The ceiling pressed down like the lid of a coffin.

The mattress tilted. Water slapped the wall beside her bed. The lurching of her stomach made sudden, horrible sense.

She was on a boat.

Fear writhed inside her like a big, fat snake. A *boat*.

Moving at the whim of the wind and the water. At the mercy of her fears.

Her heart raced. Her teeth chattered.

Creak. Creak. From overhead.

She pressed her knuckles to her mouth. She hated the water. She was going to be sick. She struggled to hold it in, to hold herself together, to force everything back into its proper place, but her body wasn't hers to control anymore. As if the orgasm that had ripped through her—how long ago? hours? days?—had torn something vital from her.

Scrape scrape. From the direction of the hatch.

Panic swelled her chest, robbing her of air. A whimper escaped her. *Oh, God.*

A shadow loomed at the base of the stairs, broad and black against the dimness of the room. Coming closer. Coming for her.

The tangle inside her rippled and coiled like a snake about to strike. She bolted upright.

No.

Power erupted from her gut, tore from her throat like a scream as the thing inside her launched at the approaching threat. Her control snapped like a thread. Force exploded from her mouth, slammed through the cabin like a shock wave.

Objects hurtled, clattered. Crashed.

Things shattered. Glass. Her mind.

She couldn't see. She couldn't stop. Roaring filled her head.

Like freaking Carrie, drenched in blood and wreaking destruction at the prom.

Stop. Freak.

"Enough." One word, dropped into the raging dark like a pebble into a flood.

She almost sobbed in relief. The wind, if it was a wind,

died. Things settled or slid to the floor. The cabin righted. Her panic shriveled.

That voice.

She knew that voice.

Lucy curled into a ball, gasping, sweating, deafened by the sudden silence.

A light bloomed, soft and round like a marsh light, illuminating a strong jaw, a long nose, a sardonic mouth.

Conn.

He had a cut along one cheekbone, black in the blue light. He didn't wipe the blood away. For some reason, the absence of that simple human gesture chilled her heart.

She trembled, waiting for him to take her in his arms, to say something, do something, to restore her world and her faith.

He glanced at Lucy and then around the cabin. His eyebrows arched. "It would appear," he said, "you are your mother's daughter, after all."

5

‰

LUCY PULLED HER KNEES TO HER CHEST AND hugged them tight, struggling not to lose it. Again. She had survived bad dates before. But this . . .

Conn's face was inscrutable, his eyes shadowed in the odd, pale light.

She'd had sex with him. Unprotected sex with a stranger. Like some stupid freshman who passed out at a kegger and woke up in an unfamiliar bed with no notion of how she got there.

Lucy cringed. She couldn't believe what she'd done. She couldn't believe . . .

Objects hurtling, crashing, shattering in the dark.

She must have lost her mind.

Things like this didn't happen to her. Things like this didn't happen.

The room rocked with the rhythm of the water.

"What . . . Where are we?" she asked. Dim memories clung of being carried, lifted . . . fed? "Was I sick?"

But no one ever fed her when she was sick.

Conn stooped—she managed not to flinch—and fished something from the floor. She caught the gleam of a broken lantern as he set it on the table.

"You will feel better soon," he said, which wasn't an answer. "The sleep took you harder than I expected. But now that you are awake, the effects will wear off quickly."

Not sick, then, she thought. Maybe not crazy either.

She remembered—or had she dreamed?—his arm strong and warm around her shoulders, a cup at her lips.

"You gave me soup."

Had he drugged her? Maybe she was hallucinating. That would explain the things flying around the cabin, the sense of something writhing inside her, waiting to burst out of her chest like the space monster in *Alien*.

She shuddered.

He nodded. "You needed food. Liquids."

The room still rocked. Her stomach churned. Nerves? Or motion sickness?

"How long was I out?"

Conn did not answer.

"How long?" she insisted. Hours? *Days?*

What had he done to her? For her? Under the covers—some kind of fur thing, heavy and warm—she was nearly naked.

She watched his hands in the near dark. A match scraped and flared. Warm, yellow, honest light replaced the eerie blue glow. Stupid to feel cheered by a lamp under the circumstances. But the familiar light comforted her anyway.

Until she saw the condition of the cabin.

Holy crap.

It looked as if a strong wind had scoured the room, or a bomb had exploded. Broken dishes, boat cushions, maps, and magazines splayed like bodies in the wreckage. An empty coffeemaker and a broken bottle rolled together under the table. Red wine, black as blood in the dim cabin, puddled on the floor. The soured fruit smell in the close, still air rose to her head and made her sick.

She ran her tongue over her teeth. She wanted a toothbrush.

Conn lifted a chair one-handed and set it upright. His head brushed the low ceiling. "Do not apologize," he said. "This ship was furnished to withstand storms. The damage is less severe than it appears."

She felt a spurt of outrage, completely ridiculous under the circumstances. Like getting upset over a late assignment when the classroom was on fire. "I wasn't going to apologize. I didn't do anything."

One eyebrow arched upward. "Who else?"

"Um." She stared at him, stunned. "I was *unconscious*. I didn't ask to be brought here. You need to take me home."

He righted another chair, holding it out from the table in invitation. "Come. Sit."

Lucy looked mistrustfully at the chair and then at his face. She didn't want to go anywhere near him. But if she stayed on the bed, he might get the wrong idea.

A hot flush swept her face. Yeah, like doing him in the dirt of her students' garden hadn't already convinced him she was a total slut bag.

She clutched the blanket, the fur soft between her fingers. "Why?"

Conn's gaze rose from her hands to her face. "Explanations will take time. I want you to be comfortable."

"Then give me my clothes."

Something flickered in his eyes and was gone before she could identify it. "They are not here."

"Where are they?"

"I had need of them."

She didn't want to imagine what use he had for women's clothing.

"You promised to take me home," she reminded him.

Right before they'd had sex among the pumpkins. But she didn't want to think about that either. She certainly wasn't going to mention it.

And he better not.

"I said . . ." His voice was cool and precise. "I would take you where you need to go."

She stared at him in frustration. "What kind of a man are you?"

"I am not a man." He paused. "I should say, not . . . human."

The bottom fell out of her stomach. Fell out of her world. For a moment she was back in the dark, with the blood roaring in her head and chaos erupting around her.

She took a deep breath, willing her mind to still, and felt everything inside her slide back into its proper place.

The cabin was quiet. In the silence, she could hear the water rush and gurgle over the hull and the creaking of the rigging overhead.

"Perhaps we should both sit down," he said.

Lucy forced another swallow. At least if they sat at the table, he wouldn't be looming over her. She scooted to the edge of the mattress, reluctant to give up the sleek weight of her blanket. Not that the PETA people didn't have a point, but there was something almost sinfully comforting about the silky brush of fur. And the cabin was cold.

She dragged the blanket off the bed and stood, wrapping it around her like a beach towel or a bearskin rug. The ends dragged on the floor.

She hobbled to a chair. Not the one he held out for her. She didn't want to get that close. Plopping onto the seat, she crossed her arms over her chest like a kindergartner refusing to join in circle time.

Conn's mouth tightened. His eyes darkened. Now that he had her where he wanted her—*ha ha*—he seemed curiously reluctant to begin. Unless this silence was his way of making her talk.

"So." Maybe she should humor him. *Not a man. Not human*, beat in her brain. "What are you?"

"I am selkie." Another pause thickened the air of the cabin. "Like your mother."

The thing inside her leaped, like a child in her womb, knocking the air from her lungs in a big fat whoosh. The blood drained from her head.

The chair scraped behind her as she stood. "No."

His eyebrows rose. "You are unfamiliar with the legend."

"Um." Her mouth was dry. Her skin felt flushed. Feverish. "There was a kids' movie. *The*, um, *Secret of Roan Inish*. About a human woman who turned into . . ."

Her throat closed. The pressure expanded in her chest. She couldn't say it. Because then she would have to take him seriously. She would have to take a lot of things seriously that she was usually very, very careful not even to think about.

Conn nodded. "A seal."

Maybe she was still hallucinating. Or dreaming. "*Your mother was selkie.*"

Lucy shivered, pulling the blanket tighter. The fur whispered against her naked skin.

Fur. Oh, God.

She shuddered and thrust it away. The heavy pelt pooled at her feet.

He watched impassively.

"Was it . . . Is it . . ."

"Mine," he confirmed.

She struggled to breathe. "I was wearing . . ."

"Think of it as borrowing my coat," he suggested.

She blinked. Was he trying to make her feel better? "You're an animal."

He frowned. "An elemental."

"There's a difference?"

"The elementals are immortal, part of the First Creation. Your own mother—"

"You leave my mother out of this. I told you, I don't even remember her."

"You are heir to her bloodline," Conn said. "Her power. You and your brothers."

Her brothers.

She caught her breath.

His explanation burst in her head like a lamp in a darkened room. Like a door opening in her mind. The scene from the other night took on a whole new light. Her family, united against her. Caleb and Margred exchanging long, meaningful looks that for once didn't have anything to do with them being newly married. Dylan, tense and silent. Even Regina had looked at her—avoided looking at her—with tactful sympathy.

She didn't know them anymore.

She didn't know anything.

"They . . . know?"

"Yes," Conn said.

She winced. "All of them?"

"Yes. Your brother is selkie. Margred, too."

She stiffened in rejection, even as the knowledge lumped in her gut. "I don't believe you. Caleb—"

"Not Caleb. Dylan."

She was cold. Naked. Freezing. "That's impossible."

"Is it? Where do you think he was all those years?" Conn's voice hammered at her, relentless as the sea. "Where did Margred come from?"

Lucy's brain whirled. Her tongue stuttered. "She . . . She was attacked. On the beach. Caleb found her."

On the beach. Without clothes, without memory, without any idea of how to get on or any family to report her missing.

Lucy's legs folded like wet string. She sank back onto the chair. *Oh, God.*

"Why didn't they say something? Why didn't they tell me?"

Silence.

"I believe," Conn said at last, "they desired to protect you."

Her anger flashed again. "From what? You?"

"From your destiny."

Her heart pounded. "I don't think it's my destiny to be stranded at sea in my underwear with you."

Stupid. She snapped her mouth shut. She shouldn't have reminded him how naked she was. How vulnerable she was.

Right. Like he didn't know. Like he couldn't see.

"I mean you no harm," he said, almost gently.

She stuck out her chin, resisting the urge to cross her arms over her chest. "Tell that to my brothers. They'll come after me."

Wouldn't they?

Okay, so they weren't all one big happy family. Maybe they had secrets. Maybe they'd even lied. But Caleb would search for her. She could count on Caleb. Even when she was a fourteen-year-old runaway puking her guts out in a gas station stall, her brother had tracked her down.

"They will not find you," Conn said.

His assurance shook her. She was cold. So cold. The fur caressed her ankles. "Caleb will. He's a cop."

"He is not even aware that you are missing. I left a *claidheag* in your place."

She was getting pretty tired of gawking and saying, "What?" So she didn't say anything.

"A *claidheag* is a simulacrum," Conn explained as if she had asked. "A living image created by magic."

"You made an image of me."

He nodded.

She sucked in her breath. "And you think my family won't *notice* I've been replaced by some kind of pod person?"

He shrugged. "Humans see what they expect to see. What they want to see."

She winced. Because, of course, he was right.

That was how she got along. That was how she survived. By fitting in. By blending in. By making damn sure that when people looked at her—her fellow teachers, her neighbors, everybody—they saw quiet, well-behaved Lucy Hunter, who took care of her father and was good with children.

Not the weird kid.

Not the drunk's kid.

Not the superfreak.

Her gaze dropped to the pelt at her feet. Although if Conn was right about all the rest, "freak" barely covered it.

"What about Dylan? And Maggie? They're not human, you said. Shouldn't they be able to, um . . ."

"They have no reason to suspect that you are gone. And the *claidheag* will learn very quickly to be what they want."

"It's not the same."

"But it is. You also pretend." His eyes were sharp as polished steel. His observation cut her heart. "Or will you deny that when your family looks at you, they see only what they want to see?"

"My family loves me," Lucy said, her voice trembling with rage. She hoped it was rage.

"They do not know you."

"Neither do you. You don't know anything about me."

"You are the daughter of Atargatis."

"My mother's name was Alice. Alice Hunter."

"Your mother was the sea witch, Atargatis."

She set her jaw mulishly. "Prove it."

His brilliant eyes softened with what might have been sympathy. "I do not need to prove anything. The evidence is all around you. Within you."

Fur brushed her calves, tempting her to bury her toes in its warmth. She pulled her feet under her chair. "You mean, your pelt."

"I mean your power. Open your eyes. Look at the condition of the cabin. Your gift struck at me to protect you."

"Too late," she muttered. "If I really had some kind of magic force field, it should have kicked in when you jumped me in the garden."

He raised his eyebrows. "It was hardly a rape, my dear. You are no defenseless virgin."

Her cheeks, her face, her whole body burned. She took responsibility for her own actions. But there was no reason to be insulting. "What's that supposed to mean?"

"Merely that you are stronger than either of us imagined," he said coolly. "As you proved again when you flung the contents of the cabin at my head."

"That wasn't me."

"What, then?"

"I don't know. Wind. A whaddayacallit. Poltergeist."

"You believe in ghosts?"

"You believe in selkies."

He laughed. "Indeed."

The laughter made him seem more approachable, almost . . . She bit her lip. Almost human.

Conn regarded her thoughtfully. The lantern warmed the marble perfection of his face, softening the hard line of his mouth. "There was a teacher once on my island, on Sanctuary, who told stories to the children to make them understand. Do you do that?"

"Sometimes," she admitted cautiously.

"Then let me tell you a story," he said. "To help you understand."

He wanted something, Lucy thought. Or he wouldn't be so gentle. *"You can talk to me." "They treat you like a child." "Trust me."*

She shivered.

And yet she had sent for him because she wanted answers. What did she have to lose by listening to him now? Maybe a part of her even wanted to believe . . . What?

"You are stronger than either of us imagined."

And maybe she was an idiot.

The darkness was filled with rising and falling sound, with the rush of wind and water. Ropes creaked. The cabin rocked. The jagged light of the broken lantern danced on the ceiling and spilled like gold coins to the floor.

Apparently her silence was all the assent Conn needed, because he began. "In the time before time, the Spirit of the Creator swept over the waters," he said in his deep, mesmerizing voice. "From the void, He made the domains of earth, sea, and sky. He called the light into being. As each element formed, its people took shape: the children of earth and sea and the children of air and fire. You have this story."

"Um. Some of it." Bart Hunter was not a churchgoing man. But like every other kid on the island, Lucy had attended Mrs. Pruitt's Vacation Bible School. She could still summon hazy memories of Noah's Ark, Popsicle sticks, and glue. She was pretty sure, however, that Mrs. Pruitt's lessons on Creation didn't go exactly like this. "Except God makes Adam out of dust."

"Man was formed later, after the earth flowered and life crawled from the sea. Not all the elementals—the First Creation—were pleased when the Creator turned His efforts and attention toward mankind. The children of air supported Him, in this as in everything. The children of fire rebelled. While those of us forced to share our elements, our territories, with humankind withdrew, the fair folk to the hills and the merfolk to the sea."

She struggled to understand. "You hid."

"We retreated. Yes."

His cool tone needled her. "So, what brought you to World's End? Shore leave?"

His expression grew even colder and more remote. "Not that."

"What, then? What do you want with me?"

"I saw your face," he said abruptly.

She opened her mouth; closed it again.

"In the waters of a tide pool. In a vision. In my dreams." His gaze locked with hers. "I saw you, and I came for you."

Her heart beat faster. It was like something in a fairy tale. Or a dream. She whispered, "Why?"

In the shadows cast by the lantern, his eyes were dark. "There is a prophecy that a female of your mother's line will alter the balance of the elements, perhaps even restore our people to what we have been. We need you. I need you."

Yearning almost robbed her of breath. He was telling her what every child ought to hear, what every woman wanted to believe.

For years, Lucy had been waiting to be wanted. For her mother to come back, for her brother to come home, for her father to look up from his bottle and actually see her. All through childhood, she'd believed there must be something wrong with her, because her mother had left them, because her father was a drunk. All her life, she had wanted to feel a part of things, normal, connected, whole.

And always she had been aware that she was different. Flawed.

There was a knot in her chest, an ache in her throat like unshed tears. Lucy swallowed. What if . . . Oh, God. What if Conn were telling the truth? What if she felt like a freak because she was a freak?

Or her mother was.

Her heart hammered with the need to believe. Panic slithered over her skin.

"I'm not . . . I can't be what you think I am."

"You are your mother's daughter."

She shook her head. "You don't understand. I'm afraid of the water. I get seasick. I can't even swim."

"You have her power. Her lineage. It is enough."

Enough for what? she wondered wildly.

The sealskin lay on the floor between them, the elephant in the room.

"You could have told me," she said, shaken. "You could have explained."

"Would you have come?"

No.

"Maybe not," she admitted. "But I should have had the choice."

His mouth was grim, his eyes bleak. "There is no choice. For either of us."

6

EDITH PAINE, THE TOWN CLERK, STUCK HER NEAT gray bob into Caleb's office. In addition to handling the town's permits, billing, and filing, Edith served as the police department's day dispatcher and the island's twenty-four-hour news source. Caleb never walked past her desk in the outer office without feeling like he should wipe his shoes first.

"You've got a fax from Marine Patrol," she announced. "They want you to keep an eye out for a boat missing from its moorings in Rockland. Caroline Begley from the inn is on line one. And your brother's here to see you."

Caleb pressed a button on his computer keyboard, blanking the screen. "Thanks, Edith. I'll take the call. Tell Dylan to wait."

But Edith stayed in the doorway. She nodded toward his blank monitor. "You're not shopping for cradles already."

Caleb's face heated as if she'd had caught him using the town's computer to surf for porn instead of woodworking plans. "I was thinking of building one."

She gave him what might have been an approving look over the top of her glasses. "Well, a woman does like a man who can handle his tools."

"When you're done sexually harassing my brother," Dylan said from the doorway, "I need to talk to him."

Caleb cleared his throat. "Later. I should take this call."

"Conn's gone," Dylan said.

Adrenaline shot through Caleb's system like a jolt of bad coffee. "When?"

"If you mean Mr. Llyr, he left yesterday," Edith said. "Without paying his bill at the inn. That's why Caroline called. She went to change the sheets today, and his bed hadn't been slept in."

The brothers exchanged a look.

"Thank you, Edith," Caleb said. "Close the door on your way out, would you?"

"But Caroline—"

"Tell her I'll be along to take her statement as soon as I'm finished here."

Edith sniffed. The latch clicked softly behind her.

Dylan propped a hip on a corner of Caleb's desk.

"What do you know about this?" Caleb asked.

"Less than your clerk, obviously. I went to the inn, and he was gone."

"Maggie? Regina?"

"Are fine," Dylan said. "I stopped by the restaurant on the way here."

Caleb released a breath he hadn't been aware of holding. "Lucy?"

"She stayed home sick today."

Caleb frowned. "Again?" Even when they were kids, Lucy had never missed more than a day of school in her life. Caleb sometimes thought the classroom provided the stability their home life had lacked. "Have you seen her?"

Dylan nodded. "This morning. She said she was feeling a little better. Apparently our father made her some tea."

"*Our* father?"

Dylan's lips twisted. "That's what she said."

"So, everybody's accounted for," Caleb said slowly. "Everything's all right."

"Not everyone," Dylan said. "Not Conn."

"He's off my turf. Out of my jurisdiction."

"And it doesn't bother you he left without telling us."

"He's selkie. That's what selkies do."

Dylan lifted a brow. "Still sore about our mother, little brother?"

Caleb's jaw tightened. "This isn't about our mother."

"The prince thinks otherwise. If the prophecy is true—"

"If he gave a shit about the prophecy, he would have stuck around."

"Unless he couldn't," Dylan said. "I would know if the demons broke through my wards. But something must have happened to call Conn back to Sanctuary."

The bad coffee feeling came back to burn in his gut. "That's his problem," Caleb said grimly.

Dylan's flat, black gaze met his. "Until it becomes ours."

*   *   *

The boat flew before the wind, rising and falling with the waves, its sails nearly at right angles to the hull, wing on wing. Conn's hair whipped his face.

He bared his teeth, enjoying the rush and control, the speed as heady as freedom. His presence at the helm was hardly necessary. Magic drove the wind that filled the sails. But he liked knowing he had not lost his touch with the sheets, despite the centuries since he'd last left home.

The island burst from the surrounding sea between the

deep kelp forests and swirling sky, solid as an anchor. Shining like a dream.

Sanctuary.

A possessive ache tightened his chest. He squinted through the strands of his hair, trying to see his home through the eyes of a stranger. Through Lucy's eyes.

The green hills had faded with the passing of summer, but today the sun had pierced the mists and magic to glaze the ancient towers with light. Rock spray sparkled like flung fistfuls of fat diamonds. A cloud of sea birds drifted around the southern cliff face, crying a faint and far-off welcome.

Would the girl sleeping belowdecks appreciate the cold, stark beauty of his island? How could she not?

Unbidden, her words blew back to him. "*I didn't ask to be brought here. You need to take me home.*"

Conn's hands tightened on the wheel, his light mood dropping like the wind. He was as bound by his duty as she was by her destiny. Her fears and his own regret were equally irrelevant. There could be no turning back, he thought bleakly.

For either of them.

He heard her before he saw her, the scrape of the hatch, a soft footfall. He *smelled* her, human, female, sweet.

He turned his head.

Lucy clung to the rail, legs braced against the swell. He had an impulse to go to her, to steady her with a hand beneath her elbow. But the selkie did not touch. Only to fight or to mate, acts of possession as much as passion.

She would not welcome his assistance anyway. In the cabin, she had recoiled from him, from the touch of his fur.

Yesterday she had found an enormous yellow rain slicker and navy overalls in one of the lockers to replace the warmth of his pelt. With the jacket hanging below her knees and the sleeves rolled back from her wrists, she looked ridiculous, appealing, and very, very young.

Old enough, she had said.

For sex? No doubt.

For the rest? He was not sure. He had ruled for nine centuries. He had lived much longer than that. But Lucy was young, even by human standards. To her, even Dylan was old. She could have no idea of real age, no clue what was required of her.

His gaze dropped to her narrow feet, bare beneath her cuffed pants.

And suddenly she was in his head, the air ripe with sweat and sex and the scent of growing things. *Her long body rising from the earth to meet him, mate him, take him. The tiny jewel glinting against her smooth belly. The sun searing his shoulders as he plunged into her, male to female, sex to sex, power to power . . .*

Stunned, he stared, stirred to the heart and the root. His pulse drummed in his ears.

The wind slipped his distracted grasp. The boat veered. The boom swung.

"Look out!" she cried.

The heavy boom swept the cockpit as the wind, freed from the force of his magic, shifted direction. Conn ducked, cursing the sails and his loss of control.

The deck pitched.

He grabbed for the wind and the main sail, pulled the jib sheet on the leeward side. The breeze surged. The sails rattled together and swelled. The boat heeled, collecting itself like a skittish horse, and leaped forward into the waves.

Lucy staggered toward the bench and sat down hard. Water shot over the side. She recoiled from the spray like a cat.

Conn winched the main sail taut. "Thank you."

She stared at him blankly.

"For your warning," he said.

"Well, I could hardly let you get knocked overboard."

He was gratified. "Indeed."

"I mean it," she said. "I can't sail. Or swim."

Ah. He remembered. She was afraid of the water.

Unthinkable, for a daughter of a selkie.

"You must learn to live with the sea," he said.

She straightened inside her bulky clothes. "I'm fine with the sea. As long as it stays on its side and I stay on mine. I only get nervous when the boundaries get crossed."

He recognized her challenge. Very few dared to challenge him.

He should have been affronted. He found himself oddly pleased instead. She was not without spirit, this daughter of Atargatis.

He looked down his nose. "It is only water."

Her throat moved convulsively as she stared over the surging swells running beside the hull. The wind drummed in the sheets. "Right. I guess I should be grateful you bothered with a boat."

"I chose it for you. After . . ." *After he had taken her, among the vines and pumpkins.* "After we met," he amended smoothly.

"Chose it?"

"From your harbor."

Her brows drew together, making her look like her brother Caleb. "You mean, stole it."

Conn shrugged. "The selkie do not hold possessions as humans do. We flow as the sea flows. We accept the gifts of the tide."

"So you just take what you want."

The judgment in her tone annoyed him. He was selkie, one of the First Creation. He did not require her approval. "We take what is needed." He met her gaze, letting the memory of their coupling burn between them. "And what is offered."

Color climbed in her face. But she did not look away. "Where are you taking me now?"

"Home." He nodded to starboard, where the shore moved up and down with the rhythm of the boat. "To Sanctuary."

Her knuckles were white in her lap, but her eyes remained steady on his. "That's not home. Not my home."

He did not wish to antagonize her. But the sooner she accepted her fate, the easier this would be for both of them.

"In time, it will be," he said.

He hoped.

"In time?" There was an edge to her voice like panic. Or anger. "How long are you planning to keep me there?"

He did not answer.

She captured the flying strands of her hair, holding it back from her face. Behind her, the white wake dissolved against the deep blue sea. "How long?" she insisted.

Something stirred at his heart, a worm of scruple or pity. He trimmed the jib, reluctant to meet her gaze. "You are the daughter of Atargatis. You serve the prophecy. As I must."

"Serve it how? I can't do anything."

"Your own actions have proved otherwise."

"What, because I trashed the cabin? That was an aberration. A mistake. Like our having sex."

He narrowed his eyes. His own people would have trembled. This girl met his gaze, her eyes miserable and her mouth resolute. Whatever else she was, she was no coward. And no fool.

"You gave me your body," he explained. In little words, so she could understand. "According to your kind, we are bound."

"We had sex. That doesn't make me your bitch."

Almost, he smiled. "Does it not?"

Her mouth opened. Snapped shut.

"You cannot deny your mother's blood," he said.

"I don't know why you expect me to feel some great loyalty to my mother. She wasn't loyal to me. To us."

"Your mother returned to her rightful place in the sea. It was her nature. Her destiny. As it is yours to follow her."

"I am not my mother."

"Obviously not," he said cuttingly. "Atargatis was a true child of the sea." Restless, vibrant, subject to the whims of the moment and the tempests of her moods, confident of her beauty and her power.

Yet he had never sought the selkie's company, never taken her to his bed.

Never wanted her the way he craved her tall, pale, stubborn daughter. Like the breath in his lungs, like the pulse of his blood . . .

Conn froze. Bloody, buggering hell.

He did not want her. She was merely a necessary means to a desirable end. Through her, he could preserve her mother's bloodline and his people. But she was not one of them. She was not selkie.

The wind splintered against the cliffs and shifted over the water.

He looped the jib sheet around the winch. "We need to come about. Hold this end and pull when I tell you."

Lucy stretched her hand to obey him and then sank back on the bench. "Don't you think that's a bit much? Asking me to assist in my own kidnapping?"

"The jib," he said. "Unless after all you prefer to swim."

He watched her reach for her dignity, drawing it around her like the ill-fitting yellow coat she wore.

"Now," he commanded as they came about.

The jib luffed and then filled. Grabbing the rope, she yanked it taut.

As if it were a noose around his neck.

She cranked the winch, trimming the sail. "So she returned to the sea. Then what? What happened?"

He thought she knew. Surely her brothers had told her? "She died."

"You said the selkie were immortal."

Conn eyed her bent head, pity mingling with his irritation. Had she thought to see her mother again? Foolish, human hope. Even if Atargatis were reborn on the foam, in the manner of their kind, she would retain little memory of her infant daughter.

He adjusted course. "We do not age and die as humans do. But we can be killed."

Lucy removed the winch handle and stowed it carefully away in the cockpit. She claimed not to sail, but growing up in a fisherman's household had clearly taught her how easily items could be lost overboard. "What killed my mother?"

"She drowned. Trapped in a fisherman's net within the year after she left you."

Lucy raised her head, her eyes like the sea on a cloudy day. "Then her destiny didn't do her much good, did it?"

He had no answer to that.

*   *   *

Lucy's hands gripped the rope around the dinghy's inflated sides. Her stomach rose and fell with the gentle chop of the waves. Her feet curled under the seat, away from the seal pelt bundled on the floor. Like a cat in the rain, she kept one eye on the water and the other on the approaching shore.

Dry land. Solid ground.

At last.

The past few days she'd felt trapped belowdecks, breath-

ing stale air, heating canned soup, washing her dishes in
the tiny galley, sleeping in the claustrophobic cabin. Trying to ignore the sealskin she'd folded and stuffed into a
locker. She couldn't lie under it knowing what it was.

What Conn was.

She didn't know where he slept. Or if he slept at all.
When she woke in the morning, she sometimes thought his
scent clung to the sheets. To her skin. But the pillow beside
her was never dented.

The oars dipped, dripped, flashed. Conn reached and
flexed, his knees thrusting into her space, his skin gleaming
with sweat and sunlight. The wind ruffled his hair like a
lover's hand. In Dylan's tight dark suit pants, with his white
shirt open to the waist, he looked like a movie pirate.

Her gaze skimmed his broad chest; jerked away from
his stomach.

She panned the quiet cove behind him, the tumbled shore
of sand and shale, the faded hills climbing in a jagged circle
like the broken edge of a cup. Stark and proud on the cliffs
above rose the round, crenellated towers of a castle.

A white bird with sharply angled wings rose like a kite
on a draft. Sunlight sparkled on the quiet water. A shadow
broke the surface and subsided before she could identify it.
A fish? A seal?

Her lips tasted of salt. She quivered with cold. Fear.
Excitement.

The dinghy rolled as it caught the lip of the surf and
scraped into shore. Conn shipped oars and jumped out, his
bare feet and strong calves splashing in the foam.

She looked at the line of his muscled back as he bent to
the boat and felt another inconvenient quiver in the pit of
her stomach.

She averted her gaze. She knew better. She did.

The last time she'd let down her guard, she'd wound up
unconscious and kidnapped in the middle of the ocean.

She couldn't imagine what Conn would do to her if she let him near her again. Her breath came faster. She didn't want to imagine. To remember. *His breath hot at her ear, his arm hard around her waist, his solid body pulsing, rocking against her* . . .

Her blood pounded.

Oh, God. She *was* a freak. She closed her eyes.

The dinghy wallowed in the shallows, grating against the bottom. Spray shot over the side. At the splash, she flinched and opened her eyes.

Conn tugged the raft toward shore. Not very far. Her weight anchored it in the water.

He held the dinghy steady in the swirling foam. "Get out."

The water boiled and reached for her.

Her heart pounded. Panic dried her mouth. She never went into the water. Never. Not since she was a little girl. Not since . . . "I can't."

He didn't question her. He didn't argue. Letting go of the raft, he plucked her from the bench, grabbed at the seal skin, and strode with them both out of the water.

She cried out in relief and alarm, clutching his neck. He was warm and solid. *Caught between the devil and the deep blue sea* . . . "Wait!"

He looked down his nose at her. "You would prefer to get wet?"

"No, but . . ." She twisted in his arms, casting a desperate look over his shoulder as the dinghy bumped away. "The raft!"

"We no longer need it."

"We might!"

He set her feet on the cold, packed sand. Even in her worry, she noticed he kept his arms around her while she found her balance. "Why?" he asked.

"To . . . get back to the boat," she said. *To go home.*

"Too late," he said.

She stared at him, speechless.

"The northern crossing will be almost impossible in another few weeks," he said stiffly. "Even if—"

But she wasn't listening.

The dinghy drifted and slithered away, trailing its rope behind. Her stomach dropped.

"Oh!" she cried. "Get it. It's floating away."

"Let it go."

But she couldn't.

The water hissed and curled. The dinghy bumped and rattled in the shallows.

She grabbed at Conn's arm. "Please. Hurry. It's getting away."

He stood like stone.

The raft caught a wave and slid out to sea, carrying with it her chance of escape. Her way home.

With a squawk of rage and fear, she plunged into the water after it.

Shock.

Cold. Grasping her feet. Gripping her bones. Twining up her legs and about her torso, big, fat ripples wrapping around her, uncoiling inside her, squeezing her chest. Her gasp slid into her lungs like a knife. She staggered.

The raft bobbed farther out of reach.

She sobbed and set her teeth. She would not go down. She would not. She pushed everything down, shoved it aside, and waded forward. Her slicker flapped and dragged around her. The water clutched her knees. Her thighs. Her hips. The ripples stirred, like a fat snake waking.

There. Just there. She flung out her arm, stretched out her hand, reaching, reaching . . . The rope slid just beyond the reach of her fingers. Something crumbled inside her, hope or a wall, and whatever lurked on the other side pounced on the opening and poured out.

The water sang. A wavelet surged. The rope moved, lifted, floated to her waiting hand.

Got it.

Her flare of triumph crowded out everything else.

She turned in water almost to her hips. She was cold. So cold. Her limbs shook. Her fingers and toes felt numb.

Conn watched from the beach, looking oddly shaken.

Was he worried about her?

The possibility created a warm glow beneath her breast-bone.

She unclenched her chattering teeth enough to call, "It's okay. I'm okay. I, um, got it." She waved the end of the rope.

His cool-as-rain eyes lit from within. "So I see."

She slogged toward him, the raft bumping at her back like a repentant pony.

"You are wet," he observed.

Wet and shaking with cold and triumph.

"I'm freezing," she admitted frankly.

The water sloshed around her ankles. Her feet were blocks of ice.

"Here." Before she knew what he was about, he swung the sealskin up and around her shoulders.

She shuddered in rejection and relief. His pelt was so heavy. Heavy and warm. Her fingers curled into the thick fur even as her insides rebelled. It wasn't desire. Or not only desire. Adrenaline, nausea, hunger . . .

She pressed her legs together to keep them from shaking, to keep herself upright.

He moved closer, tugging the pelt around her. She looked down at his wrists, strong and square. Her breasts tingled.

She drew a sharp breath.

His gaze dipped to her mouth. His nostrils flared. Was he going to kiss her? She didn't want him to.

Her heart banged against her ribs. Did she?

His words drummed in her head. *"It was hardly a rape, my dear. You are no defenseless virgin."*

She took a short, very definite step back, nearly stumbling on the cold sand.

His hands dropped.

They stared at one another. Her breath rasped. The silence rushed between them, cold and insistent as the waves.

She was the first to look away.

7

CONN WAS HOT AND HARD WHEN HE NEEDED to be cool and steady. Shaken. The little witch had shaken him.

Not because of her gift. Though, by God, his senses still stung from the snap of power she'd released when she called the rope to her hand.

He hefted the wet raft and hauled it up the beach, out of reach of the tide, away from the slim girl shivering on the sand. If his body betrayed him, his face, at least, would give nothing away.

He dropped the dinghy at the bottom of the cliff.

She had turned from him. Again.

He bared his teeth like the animal she had called him. Even with the magic still surging through her blood, even with his pelt covering her, she had spurned him.

He had anticipated her rejection. Perhaps, by her lights, he had even earned it. But here on Sanctuary's soil, her un-willingness to accept him had an unexpected sting. A deeper significance. Beneath his injured pride, a profound unease stirred. Sooner or later, she must surrender to her fate. His people needed her.

A thought whispered: *He* needed her.

He did not want to acknowledge the feeling. He did not want to have any feelings at all. But there it was.

"I . . ." Her voice scraped behind him. "Where are we? On the map, I mean?"

Conn stowed the paddles along the dinghy's sides, giving himself time to assume his familiar mask. "West of the *Innse Gall*. The Strangers' Islands," he translated.

He looped the tow rope around a rock. He hoped the damn thing floated away. But remembering her courage in going after it, he could not dishonor her by leaving it untied.

"Ireland?" Her voice was thin.

He felt a moment's pity, ruthlessly suppressed. He had already informed her he would not take her back. What difference to either of them if she was half the world and an ocean away from home?

"Scotland." He turned.

She had tipped back her head to stare up the cliff face, exposing the long, pure line of her throat. In some lights—in this light—she was really quite remarkably pretty. "That would explain the castle."

Even cold and frightened, she refused to be cowed. His lips twitched, his own fears lightening. Perhaps her humor would help her make the best of her new circumstances.

But then his gaze dropped, and his smile faded to a frown of concern. Beneath the sopping cuffs, her feet were the cold, blue color of watered milk. "We must get you inside."

She eyed the cliff again doubtfully.

"There is a path to the tower," he explained.

His private entrance when he walked with the dog in the evening. His escape.

She nodded.

The bushes at the base of the tower rustled. A long, lean shadow appeared, tall as a wolf and graceful as a deer. Its narrow head lifted as it sighted them.

She froze. "What—"

A blue-gray blur streaked down the slope, cutting through the long grass.

"Madadh," Conn warned.

At the last moment, the big hound flung itself on the ground at his feet, spine wriggling, four paws in the air. No dignity at all. Surprise—and something else—tightened Conn's throat. Slowly, he crouched to scratch the beast's wiry belly. Madadh gave him a look of pure adoration before scrambling upright and bolting down the beach.

Lucy's laughter brought a pang to his heart and his gut. The selkie laughed almost as seldom as they cried. The hound coursed in swooping circles, pausing occasionally to dash back and assure itself of his presence. "He's certainly glad to see you."

Yes. Conn clasped his hands behind his back, almost undone.

"I have never been away before," he said stiffly. Never imagined that the dog would miss him. Never realized that the animal's obvious devotion would affect him so. "Madadh, down," he ordered as the dog galloped up with great sandy paws.

It collapsed on its haunches, narrow tail whipping back and forth in the sand.

Lucy's smile lit her face from within. The dog shoved a wet, bearded muzzle into her palm. She rubbed its head.

Conn fought an instant's jealousy. Of her? Of the dog? Either was ridiculous.

"Is that his name?" she asked. "Mad Dog?"

"Ma-dug. It means 'hound.'"

She turned that smile on him and took his breath away. "Very original."

"I used to name them," he said abruptly. *All of them.* "They do not live very long. Nine or ten years. It became easier after a while to call them by the same name."

Her wide gray eyes considered his face, as if she saw a side of him that no one else looked for. That he preferred not to examine himself.

Pride dictated that he not look away.

"How many dogs have you had?" she asked softly.

He shrugged. "Hundreds. After the fourteenth or fortieth, I learned not to become too . . . attached."

She tilted her head, her gaze still fixed on his face. "Then why bother with a pet at all?"

It was a question he often asked himself. Every time he cradled a wasted old body in his arms or stroked a white muzzle. Every time he carried a hound's carcass into the hills to bury it alone and in silence.

"I have always had one. My father always had one. It is tradition," he said. A way of keeping in touch with the past, of staying connected with the father who had abandoned him.

"If you've had—hundreds?—you've had plenty of time to change the tradition," she observed. "I think they're company for you."

His hands tightened behind his back. He stared at her stonily, appalled. Found out. The selkie lived alone, free of human encumbrances and human emotions. They did not require companionship. He did not require it.

"You of course may think whatever you like," he said politely and swung her up into his arms.

He felt the sharp intake of her breath. But she did not struggle.

Progress? Perhaps.

Her tangled fair hair was caught between them. He freed it gently, shifting her weight.

"I can walk, you know," she offered.

"You cannot climb," he said. "Not in bare feet."

"I'm tougher than I look." She smiled ruefully. "And heavier."

Tall and graceful, with skin as pale as willow when the bark was peeled away.

He raised his eyebrows. "I believe I can bear the burden."

As she must tolerate his touch.

He strode with her up the slope. Despite her pale face and cold hands, she felt warm in his arms, warm and damp. Beneath the tangle of sealskin and slicker, he discerned the rapid rise and fall of her chest. His hand was very close to her breast. Her hair tickled his throat. She smelled like woman and faintly of wet dog.

She was not selkie.

But her humanity—messy, genuine, artless—had its own natural appeal.

The track was narrow, worn by his feet and by the dogs. The long grass whispered of home. A bird soared over the battlements, crying in warning or welcome.

Lucy looked up at the bird and down at the path and at Madadh, ranging before and behind them. She looked everywhere, in fact, but at him.

She was pressed against him, angles and curves, long, strong legs and small, firm breasts. Her breath was warm on the side of his face. Her hands were cold.

His blood stirred. He shifted his hold. If he could get her to his room, if he could get her in his bed, he could warm her, comfort her, persuade her, bind her . . .

He frowned. *Because that had worked so well the first time.*

She slid him a sidelong glance. "Are you all right?"

His shaft was hard as stone. "Fine."

"I told you I was heavy."

Long and lean, rather, with a strength to meet his own. "It is not your weight that disturbs me."

"Oh?" She met his hot gaze and flushed. "Oh."

The tower door was ajar. He elbowed it open. The air of Sanctuary rushed to envelope them, cool with mist and magic, smelling of time, stone, and the sea.

She cleared her throat. "You can put me down now."

He did not want to let her go. The longer she submitted to his touch, he felt, the more chance she would accept him. "The stairway is dark. You cannot see."

"Oh, and you can?"

"Yes," he said simply and silenced her.

He carried her up the spiral stairs, his shoulder brushing the rough stone wall, her bare feet suspended over the drop. Tall, narrow chinks of light pierced the gloom. In the stillness, he could hear her breathing and the dog's nails clicking behind them.

The stairs divided, circling to his rooms on the one side, broadening to wide, flat steps and an arch on the other. She adjusted her arm about his neck, pressing her soft breast into his chest. Anticipation pulsed through him. Almost there. He resisted the impulse simply to throw her over his shoulders and take the steps two at a time.

"My lord!" The call rang from the hall.

Madadh growled in soft warning.

Lucy stiffened and turned her head.

Conn tightened his hold.

A broad bulk loomed in the stone archway. Frustration jabbed Conn. But the man who had hailed him was his most trusted warden. No purpose was served by snarling at him. Or by ignoring him either.

"Griffith ap Powell, the castle warden," he said shortly. "Lucy Hunter."

The warden frowned. "Dylan's sister?"

Lucy blinked. "You know my brother?"

Griff spoke over her head to Conn. "What is she doing here?"

"Don't ask," she muttered.

Something in her voice, some subtle alteration of her posture, broke through Conn's lust and impatience. He glanced down. Her shoulders were hunched, her eyes lowered. She seemed almost to have shrunk in his arms.

"My lord, I must speak with you," Griff said, as if the warden had forgotten his own question. Forgotten the girl's very presence.

Conn's skin prickled.

"*Don't ask,*" she had said. Was it possible the words were not simply a comment, but a command?

Unease trickled through him like melted ice. What did it mean, if she could command the castle warden?

"She is the daughter of Atargatis," Conn said, answering Griff's question. "And my guest."

Griff rubbed his grizzled jaw, his dark eyes momentarily confused. "Then she is welcome. My lord, a delegation from—"

"Later," Conn said. "She needs fire, food, and clothes. In the upper tower room. See to it."

And he would see to her.

"My lord." The warden was respectful but firm. "This cannot wait."

"I have been gone two weeks." Conn bit out the words. A blink of an eye in a selkie's long existence. His father had been absent for damn near a millennium and no one was after him to attend to his duties. "Whatever it is can wait another hour."

"Gau knows that you were gone," Griff said.

Conn went still.

Gau was a lord of Hell, an emissary for the children of

fire. Ruthless, humorless, self-important, and dangerous, the demon lord was quick to scent an opportunity or a weakness. He would have seen Conn's absence from Sanctuary as both.

Something dark and fierce rose in Conn. "I do not owe Hell an accounting of my whereabouts."

"No, lord." Griff met his gaze, his expression somber. "But Gau requests an audience."

"Gau can go to Hell."

"He has been to Hell, my lord," Griff said with grim humor. "Now he is coming here. With a delegation."

Madadh's shoulders quivered as the dog responded to the tension in the air. Lucy's gaze darted from face to face.

"He dares much in my absence," Conn said through his teeth.

"Perhaps he knew you were returning," Griff suggested.

"Or hoped I would be gone," Conn said. "Summon the other wardens. Let Gau see our strength."

Such as it was, he thought bleakly.

"Done, lord. Morgan and Enya have arrived already," Griff said. "The others . . . there may not be time."

Strain dug into Conn's shoulders at the combined weight of responsibility and the woman in his arms. "How long?"

"Until Gau arrives?" Griff shrugged. "I cannot map the demonkind as you can. But soon, I think."

Conn's gut clenched. His grip on Lucy tightened.

Gau must not find her was all he could think. The demons had tried to kill Dylan's woman Regina simply because she carried the selkie's child. The children of fire were determined to prevent the birth of a selkie female who might fulfill the prophecy. So far, they had dismissed Atargatis's only daughter as human, unworthy of their notice. But if they knew she had caught Conn's eye, they would swarm like wasps around fruit.

A chill rose from the stairwell and settled in his bones.

Better to keep her hidden.
Even on Sanctuary.

*   *   *

Conn lowered Lucy's feet to the floor. Her toes winced from contact with the cold stone. She clung to him a moment, the only warm and familiar thing in the room, while she got her balance and her bearings.

The hound pressed in beside them and circled the room, its staccato nails loud in the quiet chamber.

The high, curved walls were finished stone. The windows overlooked the sea. If she concentrated, she could hear the hiss of the retreating water and the gulls crying as they dipped over the waves. But unlike the other chambers they'd passed through, this room had actual glass in the windows, veined with lead and filled with tiny bubbles. The carved and gilded furniture looked built for a giant or a king: a vast, empty fireplace, two high-backed chairs like thrones, an enormous wardrobe, a massive carved and canopied bed. Deep blue hangings shivered in the draft.

Lucy shivered, too, cold and overwhelmed.

Madadh yawned and settled in front of the empty hearth.

"Someone will be up soon to build the fire," Conn said. "If there is anything you need, you have only to ask."

How about you take me home?

She swallowed the words before they escaped. He would only say no. And each time she begged and he refused, she felt more helpless, more frustrated than before.

She was sick of feeling helpless, tired of being silent and careful and afraid.

"Is everything all right?" she asked. "This guy that's coming, this Gau—"

Conn's mouth formed a hard line. His eyes assumed the cold, flat sheen of tempered metal. "All will be well," he said. "You are safe here."

Which didn't answer her question at all.

Lucy's heart hammered. Her spine straightened. All her life, she had avoided confrontation. She was the good child, the one who smoothed things over, who made things work. She was used to covering for her father's failures, to denying her own anger and her needs.

But Conn had prized her from her comfortable shell. And however exposed she felt, however naked or afraid, she couldn't crawl away and hide. What was he going to do if she offended him? Throw her back like an undersized lobster?

"Safe from what?"

He released her and crossed to the vast wardrobe, tossing the sealskin carelessly on the bed. "I will answer all your questions . . ."

She blinked. "Really?"

"Later," he finished smoothly. He laid a hand on a carved panel of the wardrobe, swinging it open to reveal a flash of red, a gleam of gold, a fall of black as rich as midnight. Shrugging out of his shirt, he dropped it on the floor.

Because holding a conversation wasn't hard enough. No, she had to push for answers while he was stripping.

She jerked her gaze from his hard-planed, hairy chest to his face. "When?"

His hard mouth softened. "Tonight. Over dinner. Right now, more urgent matters require my attention."

He thrust his hands into his waistband and shucked his pants.

No underwear. He was naked except for a long black knife strapped to the inside of his left calf.

She sucked in her breath. Okay.

He was broad and hard. Her gaze skimmed the ridges of his stomach to the dark hair between his thighs, down to the knife, and up again. All of him stood broad and hard.

Her mouth dried. His gaze locked with hers.

Arrogant asshole. As if she would take one look at his magnificent manhood and beg him to take her.

Oh, wait. She had.

In fact, she admitted wretchedly, if she weren't so worried that she was committing more than her body, she would be tempted to again.

She moistened her lips. "How urgent?"

His eyes had darkened to gray smoke. But instead of reaching for her, he pulled a long, loose shirt from the wardrobe. "The wardens wait. I cannot stay. Not even to satisfy your . . . curiosity," he added softly.

Hot color whipped into her face.

She stood there while he dressed with swift, easy movements, apparently undeterred either by his impressive hard-on or her presence. Soft black pants—ha, that took a moment—loose white shirt, a tunic the same deep purple as the inside of an oyster shell. And instead of looking ridiculous, which might have soothed her confused feelings at least a little bit, he looked comfortable. Masculine. Assured. As though he wore velvet every day of his very long life. As if . . .

Lucy frowned. "He called you 'lord.'"

Conn shot her a quick look. His hands were busy fastening a heavy gold belt low on his hips. Something in the gesture, something in his eyes, reminded her of Caleb strapping on his gun, preparing to go on patrol.

"Dylan did, too," she said slowly, remembering. "When you came into the restaurant. 'My lord.' I thought he was just saying it because he was surprised. Like, 'My God' or something. But he wasn't, was he? I mean, he was surprised, but . . ."

Conn gave a final tug to his belt. "I must go."

She stood there with her frozen feet and yellow slicker, realization seeping into her tired brain. "Who are you?" she whispered.

His eyes were cool as burnished silver. "You know who I am."

"No, I don't," she said, amazed by her own audacity. "Or I wouldn't have to ask."

Did he hesitate, for just a moment? His face was hard as marble. "I am Conn, the son of Llyr, prince of the merfolk and lord of the sea. And Gau must learn that I protect what is mine."

The hound rose from the hearth, its gaze fixed on his face, its small round ears erect.

"Madadh, stay. Guard," Conn commanded.

And before the girl or the dog had opportunity to react, he was gone.

8

STAY. GUARD.

Standing in the middle of the cold stone floor, Lucy eyed the big, hairy dog blocking the door. "Are you supposed to keep me safe? Or keep me in?"

The hound gave her a long, level look and turned its head away.

"That's what I thought," she muttered. "Who does he think he is anyway?"

"I am Conn, the son of Llyr, prince of the merfolk and lord of the sea."

Prince. The word crashed on her like a wave, robbing her of balance and breath. And she was what, Cinderella? She paced. Alice in Wonderland. Beauty in the castle of the Beast.

She wanted to go home. Longing swept her for her brother's smile, her father's querulous voice, her students with their quick hugs and straggling garden plots. She squeezed her eyes tight as if she could shut out the castle, as if she could make everything go away, go back to what it had been. Like Dorothy after the tornado, waking to find her journey had all been a terrible dream. A nightmare.

Her nightmare.

She had always dreamed of the sea. The sea and drowning. In her dreams, the oceans came for her, a hungry wall of water that swept everything, destroyed everything, killed everyone she loved.

Her mother had drowned. *"Trapped in a fisherman's net within the year after she left you."*

The sea took everything.

Pressure crushed her lungs. She couldn't breathe. Roaring filled her head, louder than the ocean. The sound of loss. Of fear.

She trembled. She *remembered* . . .

Standing in her crib, crying in the dark, holding out her arms. And Caleb, kind and bleary with lack of sleep, trudging in to pick her up. A boy forced by circumstance to be a man. Patting her back, bringing her water, whispering that everything was going to be all right. She had allowed herself to be comforted then, only to learn as the years passed that her life would never be all right.

When she was nine, Caleb went away to college. *"Be good,"* he'd said. *"Take care of yourself and Dad."* So she had, while the dreams came back, worse than before. She could pretend to control them, put them off with bedtime reading or hot milk or sex, but she'd never completely outgrown them.

Alone before the empty fire, she hugged her elbows. So what? Everybody had bad dreams. She wasn't that little girl anymore, crying for her mother.

Conn called her the daughter of Atargatis. But she was more. She was Caleb Hunter's sister, New England born and bred of hardy Yankee stock. Stubborn as the beach roses that bloomed along the cliffs, tenacious as the goldenrod that sprang among the rocks. She had endured island winters when the pipes froze and the harbor froze and the ice ran like a waterfall down the porch steps and had to be hacked with an axe. She had struggled to adulthood in a house haunted by her mother's ghost and the specter of her father's drinking.

"You are stronger than either of us imagined," Conn had said.

Maybe.

Yes.

She released a shuddery sigh. Time to start acting like it, then. She could begin by getting dressed. Something in that wardrobe had to fit her.

She approached the tall wardrobe. Beauty at the castle of the Beast. Too bad there were no friendly spirits, no motherly teapots, to pick out something for her to wear.

Madadh raised his head; pricked his ears.

Something bumped and clattered below.

"Bollocks!" cried a voice on the stairs.

Lucy jumped, pressing a hand to her mouth.

"Watch it! You nearly took my fingers off." A second voice, young, male, aggrieved.

"Well, if you weren't so fucking clumsy—"

"Shh. She will hear us."

The hound gave a soft woof and lurched to its feet, its big paws scrabbling on the stone floor.

"I can hear you now," Lucy said.

Silence.

And then a scrape. A thump.

"Ma'am?" The voice cracked. A boy's voice, she thought.

"I . . . Yes?" she called.

"We cannot pass the dog."

Obviously not. Madadh guarded the doorway, shoulders hunched, head lowered, tail stirring from side to side. Good sign? Bad sign? She had never had a dog.

"Um. Madadh," Lucy said, feeling foolish. "Here, boy." Would it obey?

She forced more authority into her voice. "Madadh, *come*."

The hound's narrow, bearded head swung in her direction. Slowly, slowly, the tall hips and long body followed. Padding to her side, Madadh sat with a thump. The dog's head came to her elbow.

She clasped her hands tightly at her waist. "You can come in now."

A grunt, another thump, and a man—a young man's legs—appeared as he backed over the threshold, carrying one end of a large trunk. His companion followed, carrying the other. Setting their burden down, they turned to face her.

Boys. She released her breath. They were just boys—sixteen? seventeen?—in long white shirts and ragged shorts, one big and broad with a shock of dark hair and a belligerent expression.

Tough guy, Lucy thought with a teacher's instincts and a smothered smile.

His companion was wiry and lean, not quite grown into the strength of his wrists or the size of his feet. Beneath a mop of blond-streaked hair, his eyes watched her, guarded and golden as the dog's.

He nudged the trunk with one foot. "Warden said you needed clothes."

She swallowed. "Yes. Thank you."

The bigger boy shifted his weight awkwardly. "There's more."

"Other clothes. If these do not fit you." The tawny one frowned in apparent concern. "You are taller than Miss March."

"Miss March?" Lucy asked cautiously.

"She was our teacher."

Was? "What happened to her?"

"She got old." A girl spoke from behind the two boys.

Their age, Lucy thought, *or maybe older.* With girls, it was hard to tell. She had sleek, dark hair the color of mink and a wide-lipped, sulky mouth.

"She died," said the big, dark boy.

"I'm sorry," Lucy said.

The girl shrugged, her eyes cool blue and disdainful. "She was human."

Her casual dismissal chilled Lucy. *She* was human. Did that mean . . .

"Are you a teacher?" asked the tawny-haired boy.

"I . . ." Lucy dragged her scattered thoughts together. "Yes."

"We don't need a teacher anymore," the girl said.

The boy shot her a look. "Speak for yourself."

"Suck-up," taunted his companion.

The wiry teen clenched his fists. "Stupid."

"Fisheyes."

"Tell me your names," Lucy said. As if this was the first day of school, the first fight on the playground.

The tough guy scowled, unwilling, maybe, to back down in front of the girl.

"Iestyn," said the other boy, the one with the strange, pale eyes. "This is Roth."

The girl tossed her head. "Kera."

She looked like a model, a girl made up to look like an adult. A beautiful almost adult in a short silk tunic the color of apricots that left her arms and most of her legs bare. Beside her, Lucy felt like a scarecrow. She resisted the urge to pull the slicker tighter.

"I'm Lucy."

"Warden said to call you Miss Hunter."

She smiled easily, encouragingly. "I think we can drop the 'Miss.' I'm not that much older than you."

For some reason that made the bigger boy laugh.

Iestyn poked him to shut him up. "Warden said anything you want, you can ask us."

Anything you want . . . She would have killed for a shower. A long, hot one. But she suspected enchanted castles didn't run to indoor plumbing.

"Maybe . . . A fire?" she suggested hopefully.

Iestyn nodded. "We brought wood. And water for your bath."

"The prince said you would want one," the girl—Kera—said.

Conn had ordered her a bath.

Something softened in the center of Lucy's chest. That was thoughtful. It didn't make up for kidnapping her, of course, but she could still appreciate the gesture.

Roth came back with a bundle of driftwood and dumped it by the empty fireplace.

Lucy roused. "I can do that." She nudged Madadh out of the way to kneel on the cold stone hearth.

While she arranged wood and kindling, Kera drifted from the room, delivering an armload of towels before disappearing again. Iestyn and Roth trudged in and out, dragging in a copper tub big enough to sit in and buckets of clear, hot water. A faint sulfur smell rose with the steam.

Lucy shivered with cold and anticipation. "Did you have to boil all that?"

Iestyn grinned and leaned down to strike a spark to the fire. "No, there's a spring deep in the cliffs under the castle. Where all the elements meet, earth and air, fire and water. But—"

"It's a bitch of a climb," Roth said.

"But my lord thought you would appreciate some privacy on your first night," Iestyn continued.

Roth snickered.

Blood surged in Lucy's face. They weren't talking about

the bath anymore. Conn's clothes hung in the armoire.
This was his room. She sat back on her heels, hoping the
boys would blame her sudden flush on the fire. She cleared
her throat. "I bet you enjoy that. Having your own hot
springs, I mean."

"Oh, aye," Roth said darkly. "If you don't mind demons
looking at your butt."

Iestyn's bucket slipped, splashing water out of the tub.

Roth jumped back, cursing. "You great wanker!"

"Here." Lucy got between them with a towel, reassured
by their squabbling, glad for something to do. They were
just boys after all.

She mopped up the mess while the fire crackled and the
boys trudged in with more buckets and went out again.
Red shadows danced on the hearth. Under the slicker, a
line of sweat traced down Lucy's back. She glanced from
the half full tub to the open door and sighed. She was not
getting naked in front of the boys. Still she was beginning
to relax, lulled by the fire and their uncomplicated wran-
gling, soothed by the promise of the bath and the possibility of clean clothes.

To pass the time, she opened the trunk.

A long red buttoned cloak lay on top. She lifted it carefully, shaking the scent of lavender from its folds. Below
were neat piles of thin drawers and thick socks, tidy stacks
of yellowed shifts and bright shawls, sturdy dresses of no
particular color or style. She looked dubiously at some of the
dresses. The waists were so tiny, the shoulders so tight. Several pieces she was sure would fit: a hooded cape in deep
green velvet, a padded turquoise robe, a sheer silk nightgown that whispered of seduction.

Everything was clean and creased, as if it had been lying unused for a long time. Lucy frowned. A very long
time.

When the boys came back, Lucy was smoothing the

wrinkles from the green cape, trying not to notice how her hand trembled against the velvet. "Your teacher, Miss March . . . How old was she?"

Iestyn looked surprised. "Almost a hundred, I guess."

Lucy's heartbeat quickened. Her suspicions grew. "And how long ago did she die?"

"I don't . . ."

Kera reappeared and set a silver hand mirror on one of the chairs. "Fifty years ago."

Iestyn nodded. "Maybe more."

"But you knew her. She taught you." Her mouth dried. *Over fifty years ago.*

"Aye." Roth's grin revealed strong white teeth. "The prince said he was not having us grow up as little savages."

"But we were the last," Kera said. "Or almost the last."

Iestyn set another bucket on the hearth. "There was Dylan."

"But he had already gone through the Change before he came," Roth said.

"We were the last on Sanctuary," Kera said.

Lucy moistened her lips. Her pulse drummed in her ears. "The last what?"

Iestyn regarded her with wide gold eyes. "Why, the last children."

* * *

Conn's tower overlooked the sea. But despite the western views of the sunset, the eastern views of the purpling sky, the drafts that slid over the thick stone sills and skittered along the floor, the air was thick and hard to breathe. He felt the pressure in his chest. The tension in the room was palpable.

Half a dozen wardens gathered around the map spread across his desk. His gaze rested on them in turn. Griff, solid as a castle wall. Morgan of the northern deeps, in the black and silver of the finfolk. Enya, her breast as white and round as the pearls twined in her hair. Brychan. Kelvan. Ronat. They crowded without touching, protecting their personal space with planted feet and angled elbows. Even gathered in council, the selkie were solitary. Territorial.

The bloodied sun cast pink rectangles on the floor and across the desk, but the map needed no illumination. The heavy parchment glittered with pinpricks of light like constellations fallen from heaven. Each glowing dot represented an elemental's energy.

The angels' white brilliance was lost in the great gray swathes of humanity that covered the continents. But all the other elementals twinkled and winked, their energies coaxed to sparks by Conn's magic: green for the children of the earth, the fair folk, clustered in the wild places, woods and mountain ranges; red for the children of fire, flickering along fault lines; blue for the children of the sea, scattered across the oceans like a smattering of stars.

Ignoring the headache pulsing in his temples, Conn spread his hands over the map, focusing his concentration, until he felt the demon lord Gau's presence like a burning coal against his palm.

Opening his eyes, he tapped the map with one finger. "Gau is there. Coming from the fault lines of *Yn Eslynn*."

"When?" Ronat asked.

"Soon." Conn rubbed his burned palm absently. "Tomorrow, at a guess. Post a guard on the spring and another on shore to meet him when he comes."

Enya frowned, flipping her red hair back over her shoulder. "Why the shore? Do you think he will come in human form?"

Unlike the other elements, fire had no matter of its own. Lacking physical bodies, demons could move with the

speed of thought. However, to speak, to act, the children of
fire needed to assume corporal form. Most demons resorted
to possessing living hosts. The powerful ones, like Gau,
could borrow enough matter from the elements around
them to present at least the appearance of living things.

"He has no need of a human body on Sanctuary," Griff
said.

"Not if his intention is merely to talk," Morgan coun-
tered. "But if he is looking for a fight—"

"He would not seek it on our soil," Conn said. "I believe
he will manifest, for convenience and as a demonstration
of strength."

"And what of our other visitor?" Enya asked.

Conn stiffened.

Morgan, the golden-eyed, silver-haired lord of the finfolk, frowned. "What visitor?"

"She is none of your concern," Conn said.

Enya's smile showed all her teeth. "Then why bring her
to Sanctuary?"

"What visitor?" Brychan repeated.

"Our prince has brought a human female to Sanctuary,"
Enya said.

"Nothing wrong with that," Griff rumbled.

Enya touched the warden's mark among the pearls on
her bosom. "Of course not. Anyone might enjoy a human
liaison. But to bring her here—"

"She is the daughter of Atargatis," Conn said.

They knew the prophecy. A daughter of the house of
Atargatis would change the balance of power among the
elementals.

Ronat rubbed his jaw. "I thought the only offspring was
a son. Dylan."

"Dylan is the only selkie," Conn said evenly. "Nevertheless, the girl carries her mother's blood."

"But she is human," Brychan objected.

"Her children might not be," Griff said.

"Assuming she can have children," Enya said, her voice as tight as a sail.

Conn heard her resentment with regret. Long ago, the warden had offered her body to bear him an heir, a child to secure both their futures. He had used her for a time with all his considerable patience and skill. But their union was barren, and after repeated failures, Enya had chafed at staying at Sanctuary to breed. Her return to the sea had been a relief to them both.

"We cannot predict what her children would be," Conn said smoothly. *Our children. Mine.* His surge of possessiveness shook him. "But she is heir to the prophecy."

"Then you have put her at risk by bringing her here," Morgan said. "You put us all at risk. Gau is coming. If he discovers her presence—"

"Who's going to tell him?" Griff growled. "You?"

Conn leashed his own fury and fear to speak calmly. The leader of the finfolk accepted Conn as liege in his father's place, but among his own people Morgan was a prince, with a prince's pride. He gave Conn fealty; Conn tendered respect in return. "So far the demons have not considered her a threat."

"If she is not a threat to them, then she is of no use to us."

"She has power. More than they know." Almost to himself, Conn added, "More than she is aware of herself."

"Then how do you know she will not use it against us?" Morgan asked.

Six pairs of eyes turned to Conn with varying degrees of accusation and trust. He was strangely reluctant to share what had happened between them. And yet his wardens had the right to know.

"I have bound her," he said bluntly.

Ronat grinned.

Morgan's golden eyes glinted. "At least I understand now why you brought her here."

"Sex?" Enya's voice was shrill with scorn. "You could have sex with anyone."

And have, her tone implied.

Conn looked at her without speaking. It was true. He could have anyone. But he did not want anyone else.

He only wanted Lucy.

*   *   *

The cold beat against the windows like the sound of the sea. Inside the stone chamber the fire pulsed like a heart, pumping heat into the room and through her veins.

Lucy had washed her bra and panties in the tub and draped them over the back of one of the thrones to dry. Her damp hair hung over her shoulders. Despite her layers of clothing—padded turquoise robe, fine silk nightgown, thick wool stockings—she felt ridiculously underdressed.

She tightened her sash around her waist. Her stomach growled.

She glanced at the table set by the fire. Iestyn had carried away the bath and brought her dinner on a tray. As if she were sick. Or in jail. Her gaze lingered on the covered silver serving pieces and heavy-footed tureen. Definitely not prison dishes. There were knives.

And two wineglasses.

Nerves danced in her stomach. The high-backed chairs stood empty. Waiting. Where was Conn?

Madadh's tail thumped lazily on the threshold. Lucy's heart beat a little faster. She looked up.

Conn filled the doorway, broader than Caleb, taller than Dylan. The firelight gleamed on his sleek, dark hair, slid greedily over his proud, strong-featured face.

She felt a pull in the pit of her belly and dropped her gaze.

"You have not eaten." An observation, not a question.

She fidgeted with her belt. "I was waiting for you."

"*I will answer all your questions,*" he'd said. "*Tonight.*"

He strolled forward. "I was detained."

He did not apologize. Did not explain what had detained him. The fire crackled. The quiet hummed like the silence in her father's house, thick with secrets and resentments.

Lucy took a deep breath. She was a big girl now, she reminded herself. She could ask whatever she wanted. "You said we would talk," she reminded him.

He gestured toward the tray. "Over dinner."

She wanted food almost as much as she wanted answers. She surveyed the array of fancy silver dishes, the tall crystal pitcher full of water, the dusty bottle of wine, and offered him a smile. "It'll be a treat to eat something I didn't fix myself."

He gave her an unreadable look. "Let us hope you think so after you have eaten."

Puzzled, she lifted the lid of the scrolled and scalloped tureen. A cloud of steam escaped.

Lucy blinked. *Oatmeal?*

She set the silver cover down again. And . . . She uncovered another dish. Apples. A whole fish, gutted and grilled, and a dozen orange mussels gaping from their shells.

"You will want wine," Conn murmured, raising the bottle.

She was afraid the combination of the firelight, the alcohol, and the man would go to her head. She perched cautiously on one of the thrones. "Water's fine, thanks."

Conn's lips curved as he handed her a glass. "The wine will compensate for the meal."

She sipped. The wine went down like liquid sunshine. "It's good."

"I am glad you approve." Conn transferred fish to a plate. The smell of grilled seafood teased her appetite. Her mouth watered. "The room is to your liking?"

Her sense of unreality grew. She wasn't used to making civilized conversation over a glass of wine in front of the fire. At home, she ate alone, with the television on for company. When she'd dated in college, her boyfriend usually spent the evenings with his video games before joining her in bed.

She swallowed. Not that this was a date. Her gaze slid to the giant bed, the deep blue curtains falling from its carved canopy, the sealskin draped at its foot, and jerked away.

"It's very beautiful."

"You are warm enough?"

She felt lapped by warmth—the food, the flames, the interest in his eyes.

Steady, Lucy.

"Sure. Well, the floor's a little cold, but—"

"I will bring you a rug."

What was he going to do? Hijack another yacht? "That's not necessary. I—"

"Lucy." Her name, softly spoken in his deep voice, brought her gaze to his strong, pale face, his silvery eyes. Inside her thick socks, her toes curled. "This castle is full of treasures lost and found under the sea. Over the centuries, I have had plenty of time to indulge my tastes. My senses. Let me indulge yours."

Oh, boy. She was tempted by more than the rug. She broke eye contact, poking at her fish with a fork.

"This is good," she said after a few bites.

Conn leaned back in his chair, watching her over his wineglass. "Griff will be relieved to hear it."

Lucy pictured the big, gruff castle warden. "He cooks?"

Conn looked amused. "Among his other duties. He has not had anyone to cook for—or to cook for him—in some time."

Lucy ate oatmeal while she pieced together scraps of information. Who else ate the warden's cooking? "Miss March," she guessed.

Conn's brows rose. "You know of her."

"The boys told me." The oatmeal was thick and saltier than she was used to. She washed it down with more wine. "She was their teacher."

"Yes." He selected a small, dark apple from a bowl and began to peel it.

"They said she died. Fifty years ago. But they are—"

"Older than they appear," Conn finished for her.

"But . . ." Confused, she watched as the peel fell in a thin red ribbon.

"I did tell you we do not age as humans do," he reminded her gently.

Part of her mind had accepted the teens were selkie—like her mother, like Dylan, like Margred—without really recognizing what that meant. "But . . . they're kids. Teenagers. Dylan grew up."

But not old, she realized. Her breath caught. Dylan looked younger than Caleb, even though he was older by three years.

Conn quartered the apple and put a piece on her plate. "Dylan spent the first thirteen years of his life among humans. And much of the time since then on an island your mother bequeathed to him."

Dylan had an island? She took the apple. "What difference does that make?"

"We do not age in the sea," Conn explained. "Or here in Caer Subai. Only when we live as humans, away from Sanctuary and in human form."

She bit into the apple. Crisp, tart flavor exploded on her tongue. "So, how old are you?"

He hesitated. "I was blood born to my father, Llyr, three thousand years ago."

Lucy inhaled. Choked.

Conn handed her a napkin and waited politely while she coughed into it.

"What . . ." She wheezed. "What about your mother?"

"I do not know her."

She lowered the napkin to stare. "You don't know who your mother was?"

"I mean I barely met her. I do not remember her." He handed her a glass of water. "If you are born in the sea, you live in the sea until your first Change, the first time you take human form at seven or eight years old. If you are born on land, you live on land—again, until you mature and Change at eleven or thirteen. I was born in the sea and weaned when I was two years old. By the time I came here, to Sanctuary, I had not seen my mother in years."

She gripped the glass tightly. "That's terrible."

"Different, perhaps."

"Kids need their mothers." She spoke from experience and deep, buried longing.

"They need someone to teach them how to survive and occasionally how to behave."

She tried to remember what he'd told her about his childhood. "*I received instruction—what there was of it— from my father.*"

"So you hired a teacher."

"Not exactly."

"Miss March."

"She was not only a teacher," Conn said. "She was Griff's wife."

Her head hurt. Lucy set down the glass, pressing her

cold fingers to her temples. "They were married? A selkie and a . . ."

"Human." Conn shrugged his elegant shoulders. "It happens. Your mother married your father."

She pushed away from the table, her appetite gone. "My mother left my father."

"Because the choice was taken from her." Conn topped off her glass. "Griff was devoted to his mate until the day she died."

"Uh-huh. How did she feel about living on Sanctuary?"

"She was happy here. Fulfilled."

"So you got lucky," Lucy said. "When they got married, I mean."

Conn sipped his wine and did not answer. His eyes were shadowed in the firelight.

She stared at him, his words niggling at the back of her mind. *"They need someone to teach them how to survive and occasionally how to behave."*

And Roth's voice. *"The prince said he was not having us grow up as little savages."*

A fissure opened in her chest. She opened her mouth to breathe. "Not lucky. You brought her here, didn't you?"

Conn's face closed, cool and smooth as ice. "She was happy," he repeated. "She chose to stay."

"But she didn't choose to come." She balled the napkin in her lap. "What did you do? Take her like you took the ship?"

"The whelps needed a teacher. I do not apologize for doing my duty for my people."

Her mind whirled. Her mouth was dry. "Is that why you . . . Why I . . . But Iestyn told me there aren't any children anymore."

"That is why," Conn said.

Her heart slammed into her ribs. "I don't understand."

But she did. Oh, she did.

"I need children," Conn confirmed. His gaze collided with hers. "I need you. Your children. Ours. Your blood and my seed to save my people."

9

≈

"*CHILDREN,*" LUCY REPEATED. SHE STARED AT him, shocked. Angry. Dismayed. He couldn't want . . . He couldn't mean . . . "I haven't even agreed to have sex with you."

"Again."

She flushed hotly. "*Ever.*"

His brows arced upward. "You cannot deny there is passion between us."

Deny it? Even now, with her heart burning in a sheath of ice, she was aware of him. Attracted to him. Her weakness where he was concerned infuriated and scared her.

"Passion's not enough," she said stubbornly. Desperately.

Conn watched her from his chair, as still as a cat at a mouse hole, his silver eyes molten in the flames of the fire. "There is no shame in pleasure."

She remembered the feel of his warm, sleek hair under her fingers, his mouth suckling her breasts, the startling fullness of his invasion as he moved on her, as he plunged into her. Her body remembered and wept for his.

No shame . . .

"And no future," she said.

Look at her parents.

"On the contrary," he said. "I can give you a better life than the one you left. I would be faithful to you. There would be no other partners for either of us as long as you live. You would be honored here."

Emotions churned under the ice, threatening to break through her shell of composure. She could smell the clean burning wood and the scent of her own arousal.

"Honored?" Her voice cracked.

"Of course. You are the daughter of Atargatis," he said and shattered her heart.

"I don't want to be honored." She flung the words at him. "I want to be . . ."

"What?" His eyes were as sharp and brilliant as glass.

She took another deep breath, almost a sob. "All my life, I imagined being needed. Waited to be wanted. Dreamed of being loved for myself, for who I am."

She raised her gaze to his. "Not fucked because of who my mother was."

Her deliberate crudity hit him like a slap. He was out of his chair and over her before she could draw breath. Not touching. Never touching. But leaning close, caging her with his arms on the arms of her chair, overwhelming her with his closeness, sucking away her will.

"I want you," he said between his teeth. His hard face loomed over her, mesmerizing in its intensity. "Never doubt it. I want to put myself in you as deep, as hard, as often as I can. I think about taking you on the boat, on the beach, on the bed, against the wall. I want to feel you come apart around me as I fill you with my seed."

His images made her weak. Hot. She swallowed hard and lifted her chin. "You want sex."

"Not just sex." His tone was dark with threat or promise.

"Right. You want to knock me up."

He drew back, his light, penetrating eyes searching her face. She forced herself to hold his gaze as the fire ate all the oxygen between them. She could not breathe.

"I want to give you children," he said. "Children who would love you. Need you, as I need you."

Her heart constricted. She squeezed her hands together in her lap to contain her desperate longing. He could not give her what she wanted. She could not be what he needed. "Because of some story about my mother."

"Because my people are dying." His tone was harsh. The stark look in his eyes pierced her heart. "You promise life."

He pushed up on the arms of her chair and strode to the window. The shape of his head and the lonely set of his shoulders were framed in stone and outlined by the night. The uncompromising line of his back made her want to weep.

She swallowed hard. "I thought you were immortal."

"Yes. But the cumulative years away from Sanctuary weaken our human bodies. Fear of aging drives us to the sea until we lose the will and finally the ability to Change. The oldest can no longer speak, act, think as rational beings. My own father . . ." He broke off, staring out the darkened glass.

Her mind struggled to comprehend. "Your father?" she prompted softly.

Conn's shoulders were rigid against the dark glass. "My father, Llyr, abdicated rather than rule any longer from Sanctuary. He went beneath the wave, never to return. That's what we call it, that's what we say, when one of our own is seduced by the sea. And every time it happens, our numbers diminish by one more."

His bleak tone opened a chasm in her chest. So they'd both been disappointed and abandoned by their parents.

That didn't mean that she could help him. Or even that she should try.

"Then you're, like, the king now."

His back appeared to stiffen even more. " 'Like' the king?" he repeated. "Yes."

"So there must be something you can do. Something else." *Besides get me pregnant*, she thought.

"We could do more once," he said, still without turning. "In the time before my father's time, when our blood was thicker and our gifts were stronger, before the sea sickened and our people declined. This is the fading of our season. We do not have such power anymore." His voice was bitter. "I do not have such power."

Which didn't stop him, apparently, from taking responsibility. She wanted to resent him for what he was prepared to put her through. But she admired him, too.

"Can't you . . . You could have other children," she said.

"Few, too few, conceive. Our numbers dwindle as our magic ebbs. No children have been born of selkie parents in a hundred years." He turned, his face hard-edged as winter ice. "I gathered the human fosterlings, the children born of human mothers or raised by human fathers, and brought them here. There are not enough to ensure our survival. Not nearly enough. Your brother was the last."

Dylan, the brother she barely knew, the selkie brother who had only recently returned to World's End. He had moved back into the room he once shared with Caleb. Although now that he was engaged to Regina, he spent most of his time with his new family.

His *family*.

Lucy blinked. "Dylan is having a child."

"Indeed."

"So why don't you talk to him? Why don't you ask him to . . ."

Oh.

Her brain stumbled. Her gut churned. She stared at Conn, remembering. "You did," she said slowly. "That night at the house. You came to talk to Dylan."

His eyes were wary now and cool. "I offered them a chance to raise their child on Sanctuary."

She pressed her hands to her stomach. "You offered them more than a chance. You gave them a choice."

"Lucy—"

"Which is more than you gave me."

Conn clasped his hands behind his back. "Your brother knew what he risked and what he rejected. You do not."

"I heard you talking on the stairs." She sorted through the jumble of memories and emotions, picking her words. "You said I carried the bloodline. My mother's bloodline. You said I had the right to choose."

"They should have told you."

"Well, they didn't." Her lips trembled and then firmed. Her family's failure to include her, to trust her, still hurt. "And neither did you."

And that hurt even more. It scared her, that he had the power to hurt her emotionally.

"I'm telling you now," he said evenly.

"Telling me." She stood on shaky legs. "Not asking me. What happened to *my* right to choose? I'm entitled to say no."

"You said yes." His voice was clipped and precise. "In the garden."

His hand gripping her jaw, his face dark and intent above her, haloed by the blue, blue sky. "Come with me," he commanded. "Come."

She shuddered a little in longing and reaction. "I don't remember saying anything."

"Your actions were assent enough."

Her cheeks burned. "I agreed to have sex with you. Not have your babies."

His jaw bunched. "Humans do conceive after sex. Or did that not occur to you when you were under me?"

He might as well have punched her in the stomach. All her breath went. Her knees wobbled. She hadn't even considered the possibility she might be pregnant.

Stupid, stupid, stupid.

"I got carried away," she mumbled. "I won't again."

He flowed across the room to her in two quick strides. "You will."

She threw up her hands, panicked. If he touched her, she was lost. "I can't. You can't make me."

He stopped dead. Their eyes locked.

Her heart hammered under her breastbone. He could, she realized. Who would stop him? Who would even blame him?

"*My people are dying,*" he had said with a look. With *such* a look. He wrenched her heart.

Oh, God. She could feel herself slipping, feel her resolve eroding like sand. What should she do?

They faced each other across a foot of bare floor. Tension hummed between them. He was so close, so big and male. If he reached for her, would she scream? Fight him?

Or would she let him do anything he wanted?

Everything she wanted.

"I will not force you," he said coldly.

Relief rushed through her. Of course it was relief. That crash of feeling couldn't possibly be anything else. Letdown. Disappointment.

She sucked in her breath, aware of the rise and fall of her breasts under the padded silk. "Okay," she said cautiously, waiting for the "but." She was pretty sure there was a "but."

"Neither can I let you go. You belong here. In time you will come to accept that."

The tension spilled as anger. "I'm not some homesick kid at summer camp. I won't wake up one morning and suddenly decide to get with the program."

"Nevertheless, you will stay." His austere face looked hard and worn, like a stone carving of a medieval king or a saint. "You will sleep here tonight."

She twisted her sash, holding on to her self-control. She felt restless, itchy, disagreeable.

Dissatisfied.

"This is your room," she said.

"Yes. You are safe here."

"Really." She hardly recognized that hard, provoking voice as her own. An itch built in her blood and crackled under her skin. "Who's going to protect me from you?"

His gaze moved over her face. "Is it me you must defend against?" he murmured. "Or yourself?"

Her hand flew to strike him. He gripped her wrist, letting her feel his strength. Held her, while her pulse beat a frantic tattoo in her throat and the air throbbed thick between them. His eyes darkened. His grip shifted.

She felt the beat of his blood through his fingers on her wrist, pounding through her, overtaking the rhythm of her heart. Her pulse slowed to match his. His heart drove hers, one pulse, one beat. He pulled her close, closer, until his face was an inch from hers. She was surrounded by him, his scent, his heat. Her lungs clogged. His breath skated over her lips. She parted them in anticipation, almost tasting the wine of his kiss.

And still he didn't close the gap between them. His mouth hovered over hers, daring her participation, taunting her control.

Frustration vibrated in her throat. She lurched on tiptoe to meet his mouth. Her teeth scraped his lower lip. Her body registered the jolt of his before he plunged into the kiss with her, taking her, tasting her, in soft, hungry bites. Her muscles tensed at the shock of heat and then the surge of delight like slipping into the bath before everything went fluid and warm. Response seeped through her blood and rose in a flood to her brain. *More, yes, now, again . . .*

She suckled his tongue. She wanted to eat him alive. All her life she'd been starving for him, for this. He slid his hand under her hair, holding her head still while his mouth plundered hers and her heart threatened to beat its way out of her chest. Swamped by need—to touch, to take—she tugged against the grip on her wrist. His fingers tightened and then released as he swept her up, as she wrapped both arms around his neck. His knee pushed between her thighs. His broad hand molded to her bottom, pulling her roughly against him. He was fully, hotly aroused, thick and long against her. He dragged her toward the bed.

Panic reared out of the fog of emotion, the wave of need. Panic and reason.

She surfaced, gasping. "No."

"Too late." His mouth claimed hers. His touch was hard and branding. "Let me have you. Give yourself to me."

Oh, she was tempted, horribly tempted and afraid. He was too strong for her. If she let him take her, if she once gave herself up to him and her need, he would consume her, body, mind, and heart. Her pulse raced. The back of her knees hit the bed.

"You said you wouldn't force me," she reminded him breathlessly.

"Not force." His lips were warm on her cheek, her ear, the side of her neck. "Persuade."

His skill weakened her knees. Her will. But inside, a small, hard kernel of her Lucy self remained, stubborn as a seed in winter. She shook her head. "It's the same thing. It's the same if I can't walk away."

His hands stilled. He raised his head. "Bollocks. You want this. You want me."

She fought not to squirm. "Maybe." *Yes.* "But I won't have sex with you as long as I'm your prisoner."

His eyes narrowed. He was angry, she realized. Anger—strong emotion of any kind—had always terrified her. But losing herself, losing control, scared her even more.

"You would use your body to bargain for your freedom?" he asked.

Heat whipped into her face. "It's my body. We can't have any kind of equal relationship, we can't have sex, if I'm not free to choose."

"Equal." A snarl of fury and frustration tore from his throat. "I am more your prisoner than you are mine."

If the bed hadn't been behind her, she would have wobbled. Retreated. She took refuge in confusion. "I don't know what you're talking about."

"I am selkie." He ripped the sealskin from the foot of the bed and thrust it between them. The fur spilled between them, heavy, enveloping. "I gave my pelt into your keeping. I gave myself, my freedom up to you. You hold my life in your hands as surely as you hold the fate of my people."

She felt battered, bewildered, assaulted. Trapped against the bed, she faced him, bristling like a small, cornered animal. "I didn't ask for your life. Or your pelt. I didn't ask for any of this. I don't want it."

His silver eyes blazed. "You do not have the courage to take it," he said coldly.

He dropped the fur at her feet and walked out.

*   *   *

Conn sat in the dark in the antechamber that had once served as the selkies' schoolroom, away from the wardens still gathered in the hall. Most had gone to bed, their own or others', in pursuit of sleep or fruitless coupling. The last conversations—of politics and pair bonding—sank to murmurs like the fire.

Conn frowned into his whiskey glass. He had taught himself from his father's failures, determined not to repeat his father's mistakes.

Never surrender to impulse.

Never admit emotion.

Never reveal weakness.

Tonight he had done all three, with predictable and disastrous results.

A footfall alerted him he was not alone. His heartbeat quickened. He raised his head, hoping . . . what? That she had come after him?

Griff stood in the room's archway, outlined in the red glow of the great hearth.

Conn's disappointment was sharp as the whiskey in his mouth. He raised his eyebrows. "If you're seeking a partner for the evening, warden, you have come to the wrong place."

The castle warden entered the schoolroom, avoiding the scattered tables and chairs in the dark. "I found my partner over a hundred years ago. This was her place. I come to sit and remember."

The man's unabashed devotion to his dead mate made Conn ashamed of his ill humor. Ashamed and almost jealous. "Were there no selkie females in the hall to provide distraction for the night?"

Griff smiled wryly. "I shepherded half of them into the sea at their first Change. I am too old for them."

"Younger than I am."

Griff eased his big body into a little chair, stretching his long legs toward the empty hearth. "It's not the years, my prince. It's what you do with them."

Conn inclined his head, acknowledging the point.

"I am surprised to see you here," Griff continued. "Or indeed, at all tonight."

Conn turned the glass in his hand. "My plans for the evening met with an unexpected . . . obstacle."

Griff straightened. "Gau?"

"A human obstacle," Conn clarified.

Relaxing, Griff eyed the amber liquid in Conn's glass. "So you are applying a human solution?"

"It seemed appropriate." Conn let the eighteen-year-old Scotch roll on his tongue. "Whatever their other limitations, humans make good whiskey."

Griff gave him a level look. "And is it those 'other limitations' that have you drinking alone in the dark rather than enjoying your lady's company?"

Conn stiffened. He did not discuss his personal life with his wardens. But neither could he permit Griff to lay responsibility for his present dilemma at Lucy's door. "The fault was not hers," he said shortly, "but mine."

They sat in companionable silence.

Griff cleared his throat. "Sometimes women—human women—need work to warm to things."

Conn raised his eyebrows. "If you are thinking to advise me on my sex life, I'll need another drink."

"I am not talking about bed play. Or not only about that," Griff said. "The girl has been on Sanctuary less than a day. She needs time to adjust."

Time was something selkies had in abundance. Over the course of his long and careful existence, Conn had grown used to thinking in terms of years and centuries. But the demons' murder of the selkie Gwyneth and the news of Gau's visit had kindled an unfamiliar urgency in him.

The demon lord's visit and his own impatience.

Driven by necessity and lust, he had spoken too soon, pushed too hard, expected too much. Griff was right. Lucy needed time to grow accustomed to the island before she accepted her place here. Before she accepted him.

"How long?" he asked.

"That depends on what you did to piss her off," Griff said.

The warden's tone was heavy with humor and knowledge—the consequence of loving a human, Conn supposed. Griff had taken his Emma from the wreckage of her ship on Conn's orders, lived with her for more than three score years, sired and raised two human children with her.

And in the end, had seen those children grow up and away, had held their mother's hand and watched her die. That, too, was a consequence of binding your life to a mortal life. A mortal love.

The memory of Conn's own words haunted him. "*I would be faithful to you. There would be no other partners for either of us as long as you live.*"

He pushed the thought away.

"How long before your mate . . . adjusted?" he asked.

Griff rubbed his jaw. "Weeks, it was. It would help your cause if you could find the lass something to do. Something useful. Make her feel needed here."

Lucy's image, Lucy's words, rose to accuse him. "*All my life, I imagined being needed. Dreamed of being loved for myself, for who I am. Not fucked because of who my mother was.*"

Conn took another sip of whiskey to wash the memory away. "I explained the need. She wants no part of it."

Or me.

"Something else," Griff said. "We do not need a teacher, but—"

"She's not taking over the cooking," Conn interrupted. "She had enough of that where she was." He looked at the whiskey glass in his hand and set it down. "Let her train with Iestyn and the others."

Griff's brow pleated. "She is not selkie."

"But she has power. Let us see what she can learn to do with it."

"If you want to please her, there are easier ways. Maybe a gift . . ."

Conn waved the suggestion away. "I already told her she can have anything she asks for."

"Except her freedom," Griff said.

Their eyes met. Conn smiled bitterly. "Except that."

"Then it must be something she cannot ask for," Griff said. "Something she wants."

Frustration snapped through him. "How do I know what she wants if she does not ask?"

Griff shrugged. "You must pay attention. Listen. Women like that."

"Anything else?" Conn asked dryly.

"You might try a cold dunk in the ocean."

"No."

"I did not mean the swim will persuade her." Griff grinned. "But it might help you."

Conn stood and stalked to the empty fireplace. *Never admit emotion. Never reveal weakness.* With his back to Griff, he said, "I cannot."

"My lord." Griff's tone was understanding. Sympathetic. "You cannot deny your nature forever. A dip in the sea now and then will not turn you into your father."

Conn clasped his hands behind him. "She has my sealskin."

Silence crackled.

"You gave her your pelt." The warden's voice was ripe with disbelief.

Conn fought a spasm of irritation. "She could not take it."

"No," Griff agreed instantly. "But . . . You need the swim even more, then. If not to cool your blood, then to clear your head. To give her your pelt . . . What were you thinking?"

He had not been thinking at all.

At least, he hadn't been thinking about her.

Only of himself, his people, his people's needs.

Somehow, against all reason and every instinct he had for self-preservation, he must find another way.

"*Pay attention,*" Griff had urged. "*Listen.*"

Unbidden, another voice whispered in his mind, soft and broken as the sea. "*All my life, I dreamed of being loved for myself, for who I am.*"

Conn curled his hands into fists. He could try. What did he have to lose?

Except everything.

* * *

She had the moon and the dog for company and the wine for consolation.

They were not enough.

Lucy paced from the window to the fire. Inside the robe's padded sleeves, her hands were shaking. Her throat was raw. Her eyes burned with unshed tears.

If she were home, she would have gone for a run or escaped into her garden, grabbed a book or turned on the TV. Anything to dull the edge of her desire and drown out the busy chatter in her brain. Anything to numb the pain, to blunt the sharp memory of Conn's words.

"*My people are dying. You promise life.*"

And the look in his eyes when he said it, that look . . . How could she bear it? He was killing her. He had kidnapped her and now he was tearing her apart, stripping away her defenses. When they were gone, what would be left?

If you peeled a crab from its shell, it died.

She pressed the heel of her palm to her chest, as if she could hold the pain inside or push it away.

She wasn't brave like Regina or confident like Margred. She was twenty-three and all alone, and she wanted to go home.

She felt the thud of her heart against her hand and remembered Conn's body pressed to her body, his desire rising to meet her desire, his heart driving hers. One breath. One beat. One pulse. One heart.

He made her feel things, he made her go places she had not visited for a very long time. Places she'd avoided for most of her life. She was terrified of losing herself in him. Even more afraid she would discover things inside herself she could not bear to live with.

If she did what he wanted, if she submitted to him, how would she ever find herself again?

How would she find her way home?

She shivered and walked to the window. Through the bubbled glass, she could see the wavering shadow of the boat rocking at anchor, a black splinter caught in the silver-webbed sea. The only boat in the harbor. Her only escape off the island.

She didn't kid herself that she could handle a forty-foot sailboat in a rough winter crossing. But as long as she had the boat, she had options. She had hope. They were near the coast of Scotland, Conn had said. If she drifted out to sea, there was a chance she would be spotted and rescued. All she needed was an opportunity.

An opportunity and the courage to trust herself to the sea.

"*You do not have the courage,*" Conn had said.

The memory rose hot in her face, burned in her breast.

She drew a shaky breath. She needed air. She needed . . . She fumbled with the window's iron latch. Pushing open a square of leaded glass, she craned to catch a glimpse of the dinghy on the beach below.

A movement on the rocks dragged at her attention. She

looked and looked again, and the breath she had taken hitched in her throat.

Conn stood at the meeting of sea, stone, and sky, a lonely figure sculpted in taut, clean lines of marble and moonlight. Naked. His shoulders gleamed. His muscles were fluid as the waves, his hair as black as night, as he gazed out to sea. Something in his posture, some shadow on his face, pierced her heart. She closed her eyes, but she could still see him burning at the water's edge, weary, proud, and alone.

So alone.

He was shattering everything she believed about herself, everything she had built or tried to hold on to.

He was breaking her heart.

Blindly, she turned from the window, turned from him.

And nearly tripped on the sealskin at her feet. Her heart jumped into her throat.

The pelt gleamed in the firelight, dark as night with hues of amber and gold.

Lucy bit her lip. She couldn't leave something so personal lying like a rug on the floor. Conn had urged her to think of it as a coat, but she knew better now. Tentatively, she stooped and took the sealskin up, bundling it into her arms.

The fur whispered against her breast. *"You hold my life in your hands as surely as you hold the fate of my people . . . I need you."*

Her chest tightened. Her fingers flexed. Her gaze went back to the window.

She thought she could summon the courage to go.

Could she find the courage to stay?

10

THE MORNING WAS HEAVY WITH FOG AND FORE-
boding, slicking the old stones like rain, echoing through
the corridors and courtyards like a gathering army.

Lucy, hurrying after Iestyn, felt as if she were drowning,
swallowing lungfuls of cold, damp air. Her feet slipped.
Her heart pattered. She was *so* in over her head. Madadh
slunk ahead of them along the curtain wall, a lean gray
shadow.

Iestyn had told her nothing when he appeared at her
door earlier with a cup of hot tea and another bowl of salty
oatmeal. Only that after breakfast she was "wanted in the
inner bailey." Whatever that meant. Wherever that was.

"This way," Iestyn said.

Her heart pattered in nervous anticipation. A great dou-
ble archway opened onto a square of short, dense grass.
The walls rose smooth and gray all around, punctuated by
towers. Water flowed from a curved pipe in the wall and
splashed into a deep, round basin of stone.

She recognized Roth on the low stone bench, legs apart

and knees on elbows like a football player sitting on the sidelines. Waiting with him was a man.

Her heart stumbled.

Not Conn.

The castle warden, Griff Somebody.

Lucy deflated like a day-old party balloon.

He inclined his head. "Lady."

She nodded back, unsure what she expected or what he expected of her.

"I trust you slept well." His eyes were tired and kind, with laugh lines at the corners.

In that great empty room, in that vast empty bed, with the sea snarling below her window all night . . .

"Yes." Her voice was scratchy. She cleared her throat. "Thank you. Where is, um . . ."

"The prince asks your leave," Griff said, mercifully anticipating her question. "Important matters require his attention this morning."

Which put her, of course, in the not-so-important category. Should she be offended? Or relieved?

She attempted a smile. "So you're my babysitter."

"Something more than that." His voice was dry. "I am overseer of Caer Subai. I serve at the pleasure of the prince."

Oh, dear. Had *she* offended *him*?

Around his neck he wore a silver chain and a flat silver disk like Dylan's engraved with three connecting spiral lines. What had Margred called it? The warden's mark.

"I didn't mean your work isn't important, too," she said hastily. Whatever it was. What did wardens do anyway? Was he like a prison guard? "Just that you're stuck with me."

Roth snorted.

Griff silenced him with a look. "It is our privilege to have you join us."

"Where's, um, Kera?" she asked.

"Kera's talent is beyond my training," Griff said.

Lucy moistened her lips. "Training for what?"

"Magic," Iestyn said.

"The prince thought we might help you become more familiar with your gift," Griff explained.

Yes. A surge of instinct, sharp as hunger, lurched in Lucy's gut.

No, no, no. Fear and memory smothered her lungs, tightened her throat. *Force exploding through the cabin. Objects hurtling, clattering, crashing. Things shattering. Glass. Her mind.*

She drew a deep breath. Held it, until everything inside her was forced back into its proper place. "Thanks, but I'm not . . . I can't really do anything."

His eyes were kind and dark and fathomless as the sea. "Magic is not something we do, lass. It is what we are."

She swallowed. "I don't know what I am."

"Perhaps it is time to find out."

Her panic resurged. Maybe her life B.C.—Before Conn—wasn't all that great, but it was *her life.* Over the years, she'd whittled and shaped herself to fit her family's expectations, to take her place in the close-knit island community. If she learned too much, if she changed too much, could she ever go home again? What if her family and neighbors couldn't accept her? Would she be able to reinsert herself back into her old life, like a square peg forced into a round hole?

Would she even want to?

"I can't do anything," she said again. And then, more honestly, "I don't want to do anything."

"You could watch," Iestyn said.

In the silence, the gurgle of the fountain seemed very

loud. Outside the castle walls, a sea bird cried. Lucy's heart hammered in her chest.

Griff and the boys regarded her with varying degrees of interest and expectation.

No pressure there, she thought.

She didn't owe them anything. She was here because Conn had kidnapped her. And however disappointed she had been not to see him this morning, whatever claims he made about her mother or their highly unlikely future children, she didn't owe him anything either.

His voice drummed in her ears. *"Your brother knew what he risked and what he rejected. You do not."*

Lucy frowned. Maybe she owed this to herself.

If she had no magic, would they let her go?

Her gaze met Griff's. "Show me."

* * *

"Weather working is the simplest gift and the most common," Griff lectured in his deep, easy voice. The boys sprawled on the bench and on the grass, clearly bored with a lesson they'd heard too many times before. Lucy perched on the wall bordering the fountain, out of reach of the water, her hands folded in her lap. "The first to come and often the easiest to master."

"Except for sex," Roth said.

Griff shot him a sharp look. "Which no woman will be learning from you, laddie. Seeing as you haven't mastered the art yourself."

Iestyn grinned.

The bigger boy flushed to the roots of his dark hair.

"Water," Griff continued, "is our element. So sensing water, feeling it, affecting it, is our power on the earth and over the earth and underground. There is the water you can see and touch—liquid water, rivers and rain and clouds.

But it is the water you cannot see that creates the rain and clouds, that cools and warms the earth and sustains all life. This is the water you must know and control if you want to work the weather."

His explanation sounded oddly like a fifth grade science lesson on the water cycle, Lucy thought. No wonder the boys looked bored. She was having trouble concentrating herself. The day was so gray, and Griff's voice droned on. "*Rising air . . . absorbing heat . . . energy . . .* "

She shook her head. Not enough sleep.

"Feel the pull from the earth," Griff urged, quiet as a mourning dove murmuring from the trees on a long, slow, summer afternoon. "Feel the flow of rising water."

The sky brightened and darkened. A peculiar little wind swirled the waters of the fountain and disappeared. No one else spoke. Nothing happened.

Lucy leaned her head against the stone and closed her eyes. Tired. She didn't have to do anything. She didn't want to do anything.

"Follow the vapor, feel it cool," said Griff.

She shivered, cold. Too cold. Too wet. Behind her closed eyelids, she pictured Maggie standing in the hall the morning after Caleb brought her home, the wind blowing through the front door and her arms outstretched to the rain. Remembered the tingle of electricity in the air and along her skin, the feeling of fullness in her chest, the heaviness in her head. She felt high, dizzy, as if she floated miles above the earth. Currents flowed, droplets flashing like a shoal of silver fish. She opened her mouth to breathe. Pressure *there*. A push.

A *pop*.

A warm shaft of sunlight fell on her face.

"Well done," Griff said softly.

Lucy opened her eyes. Blinked.

The waters of the fountain sparkled. They all looked at

her: Griff with an arrested expression, Roth wide-eyed, Iestyn with open admiration.

She shivered. Not with cold this time.

"What?" Her voice was shrill. "I didn't do anything."

"Well, it was not me," Iestyn said. "I was trying to make rain."

"I wanted sun," Roth offered.

Griff's eyes narrowed. "Did you, now." Not-quite-a-question.

Her heart thudded. *It wasn't me, it couldn't be.*

Could it?

The possibility gnawed at her insides. She felt like that Spartan boy who stole a fox and hid it under his tunic. Either she exposed herself or she let herself be torn apart. Neither seemed like a very good option.

"Nothing happened," she said. "Not really."

Griff's forehead creased. "Likely not. This being your first time and all."

She sat very still, barely breathing, trying hard not to remember Margred in her wet blue dress, standing in the blowing rain.

Griff sighed. "I must go."

He paused, as if he was waiting for her to say something.

Lucy bent her head, studying her clasped hands in her lap as if she'd never seen them before. As if they belonged to somebody else.

Maybe they did. She bit her lip.

Roth stood.

"Stay," Griff said. "I do not want to see any of you anywhere near the hall while the delegation is here."

The delegation.

A chill silence settled over the small courtyard, unrelieved by the singing, sparkling fountain. Lucy's peace fled. She had forgotten the demons were coming.

Maybe she wanted to forget. Not that anyone had asked her to face demons.

Thank God.

Roth apparently did not share this perfectly healthy attitude. "I can handle myself."

"You cannot handle Gau," Griff said. "The demons are coming here as a show of strength. We do not respond by exposing our youngest and weakest."

"But we are at peace," Iestyn said.

"For now," the warden responded grimly. "That did not stop them from murdering our Gwyneth."

Lucy sucked in her breath. Conn had said the selkie could be killed, but . . .

"*Murdered?*" Her voice rose. She bit her lip again, from embarrassment and because she really didn't want to know.

Griff gave her another long, assessing look. "This summer. On your island, on World's End. I thought your brother must have told you, seeing as he was so involved."

"No." She felt numb, absorbing this fresh shock. She knew the case, of course. It had been all over the news, all over the island. An unidentified tourist from Away had been tortured, killed, and dumped on the beach.

Not a tourist, she realized now, sickly.

A selkie.

And her brother knew.

"Dylan and I never even spoke before Caleb's wedding," she said.

Griff nodded. "Caleb, he's the one. He and Margred bound the killer."

"Caleb?" Dismay was turning her into a parrot.

"Aye. It was well done, too, for all your brother's human and Margred's lost her pelt."

Her mind struggled to come to grips with the fact that this summer, while she was writing lesson plans and waiting tables and working in her garden, her family had apparently been acting out episodes from *Buffy*. She wanted to go home. She wondered now if the home she missed, the family she thought she knew, even existed outside her imagination. "What do you mean, lost?"

Griff shrugged. "Gone. Destroyed. The demon that killed Gwyneth burned Margred's sealskin."

Lucy tried to reconcile his words with the fur at the foot of the bed, with her memories of her sister-in-law. She summoned an image of Maggie, bloodied and dazed on the night Caleb brought her home. But overlying that was the picture of Maggie smiling up at Caleb on their wedding day. What was real? Which was true?

"And what happens . . ." Her throat closed. Conn's harsh face haunted her. His fierce accusation echoed in her memory. "*I am more your prisoner than you are mine.*" She wet her lips. "What does it mean? When a selkie loses its sealskin?"

"They cannot Change," Iestyn said promptly.

Lucy blinked. "That's it?"

"That's frigging everything." From Roth.

"Ask my lord what it means," Griff said. "And stay away from the hall."

Before she could frame another question, he had turned away through another arch to another courtyard where the grass gave way to cobblestones. For a large man, he moved very lightly. Even on the stones, he barely made a sound. Beyond him, Lucy glimpsed more tall, curved stone walls and a big door bound in iron, standing open. The hall?

She looked at the two boys. "What now?"

They exchanged glances. "You do not know?"

She felt like a student teacher on her first day of school. Not a good feeling. "Well, he's going to join Conn and the other wardens, right? To meet this . . . demon person."

Iestyn nodded. "Gau."

"Do you know why they are meeting?" Roth asked.

She didn't have a clue. She shook her head.

He scowled. "We thought you would."

Iestyn uncurled from the grass.

"What are you doing? Where are you going?" Lucy asked.

"To get a look at them."

She was not their teacher. She had no authority over them at all. But she didn't need authority to know this was a Bad Idea, like being trapped in a house with a serial killer and going alone to investigate a noise in the basement.

"Griff told you to stay away from the hall."

"He said he didn't want to see us," Roth said.

"And he won't. We can get a good view from the barbican," Iestyn added.

They turned on her with identical smiles of pleased challenge. "*They are older than they look,*" Conn had said. They were selkie. Maybe they knew what they were doing.

But they looked like a couple of ten-year-olds on World's End planning to dive off the rocks into the quarry pool.

She watched them climb the broken, narrow stairway to the battlements. They were only halfway up the wall when the castle shuddered like a horse tormented by flies. Lucy's heart lurched. The vibration rose through the stones under her feet and shivered in her bones. Madadh pressed against her leg, shoulders bristling.

She patted the hound with a shaking hand, taking comfort from his warm, wiry bulk. "What was that?"

Iestyn turned, his face pale and his eyes brilliant with excitement. "The demons are here. In the caves under the castle."

Roth called down. "Hurry, or we'll miss them."

* * *

From his seat on the dais, Conn watched as the delegation from Hell drifted across the great hall, escorted by a rigid Morgan and the northern wardens. The finfolk shimmered in silver and black. The children of fire shifted like pillars of smoke, transparent and opaque by turn, their number and their countenances constantly changing. In the shadows of the hall, their eyes glittered like sparks.

The demon lord Gau was the solid center of this entourage. Lacking matter of his own, he adopted illusions to suit the mood of the moment, bending light and imbuing particles of earth, water, and air to sustain the form and function of a diplomat. Today, indulging a sense of humor or perhaps merely a flair for the dramatic, he had assumed the aquiline visage, flowing robe, and laurel crown of an ancient Roman. *Virgil*, Conn thought. Dante's guide through the *Inferno*. The wise elder statesman, the virtuous pagan.

Gau was fond of misrepresentations. Even his name meant "lie."

Gau stopped in front of the dais, the focus of all eyes. "Lord Conn."

Conn inclined his head a bare fraction. He did not stand. "Lord Gau. You have come far from Hell to trouble our company."

The demon smiled, his teeth only slightly pointed. "All places are Hell, my lord. It is only a matter of perception."

Conn raised his eyebrows. "You are here to debate philosophy."

"I come to offer my respects," Gau said, "and in acknowledgment of the long history between us."

"I see no respect in your recent violence against our people," Conn said coldly.

"My prince, we are not your enemies. For centuries, the children of fire have watched in sympathy as your numbers, powers, and territories decline, as the humans despoil your oceans and abuse your patience. The demon Tan sought merely to bring your attention to an existing problem."

"Through murder." Conn kept his voice level and his hands still on the arms of his chair. *Never admit emotion. Never reveal weakness.*

"Tan's methods were perhaps extreme," Gau admitted. "But his intentions were good."

Enya leaned forward, displaying her bosom and her teeth. "We all know where the road of good intentions leads."

Gau's smile was sharper and more predatory than hers. "Through personal experience, I am sure. How many years did you sacrifice the sea's embrace for the tepid lovemaking of your prince? With the best of intentions, of course."

"Careful, demon," Conn warned softly. "I will not tolerate attacks on my own. Any attacks."

The demon stared back at him, his eyes black, blank and shiny as dead beetles in his borrowed face. "But you do it all the time," he protested. "You watch as humans overrun the earth, pollute the water, violate the very air, and you do nothing. What does it take to exhaust your patience?"

"You are very close to finding out."

"Am I? Am I really? And what of your people's patience? What of the finfolk? Your father wasted centuries in dreams and denial. Do you expect them to follow you while you do the same?"

What *of* the finfolk? Morgan had escorted the demons from the caves and through the castle's outer defenses. Had Gau used the opportunity to undermine the finfolk lord's loyalty? Or did the demon seek to sow trouble now by stirring up Conn's own doubts?

Conn looked at Morgan. The warden of the northern seas returned his stare with expressionless golden eyes.

Doubt slid under Conn's calm surface, quick and stealthy as a shark, a cold shadow on his soul. "The children of the sea are neutral in your war on Heaven and humankind," he said evenly. "We will not side against the Creator."

Gau watched him with cold calculation. "Even though we are here to offer ourselves—again—as allies in protecting all of creation?"

Anger constricted Conn's lungs. He forced himself to breathe. "Was it an alliance you offered Gwyneth?"

Gau's eyes flickered. He waved a hand. "One selkie. One, among—how many is it now, prince? At least she wasn't clubbed by humans, her sealskin stripped from her living body. She has a chance to be born again on the foam. Her pelt was returned to the sea."

"Not by you," Griff growled.

"Not by me personally," Gau admitted. "But nonetheless, returned. Let's not be shortsighted."

"I see you clearly," Conn said. "Liar. Torturer. Murderer."

Beside Gau, Morgan stirred. "Killing one of us does not inspire trust."

Gau spread his hands, stretching his mouth in a parody of astonished innocence. "Did I say I had killed her?"

"Your master, then," Ronat said impatiently.

"My master is also displeased by this unfortunate development. Was not the victim also one of us? A fellow elemental. Tan acted completely without Hell's knowledge and approval. No, I am here . . ." Gau's black gaze traversed the circle of wardens and lit again on Conn. "To offer Hell's regrets."

Conn drew another careful breath. He did not believe a word of the demon's protestations. "You go to great effort to make an apology," he said dryly.

Gau showed his teeth in another smile that skittered

around the chamber like dead leaves in an alley. Enya looked away. "Is not your goodwill worth my poor effort?" His voice was dangerously close to sincerity. "We do not want a conflict, my lord. You cannot afford a conflict."

His face was a mask. His voice was a lie. But what he said, Conn realized bleakly, was true.

Conn did not have the numbers or the power or the support to force a quarrel with Hell. He could not fight and win. He could not surrender and survive. All he could do was cling to his duty like a barnacle to the rocks and pray that Lucy turned the tide before they all dried up and died.

If she had his children . . .

He pictured her lean, quiet face, her eyes like the sea in the wake of a storm. But it was not that.

Not only that.

Gau was waiting for his response.

"In the interest of peace, we accept Hell's apology," he said formally.

Gau bowed with only a trace of mockery. "We are grateful for your wisdom, sea lord. My master would be disturbed if anything interfered with the present delicate balance of power."

Despite Gau's distinguished mask, despite his diplomatic phrasing, Conn knew very well he was not being thanked.

He was being warned.

*　*　*

Lucy sat with her hands in her lap, listening to the gentle sound of the water, feeling the sun on her face, trying hard not to think of anything at all.

"*You belong here,*" Conn had said to her last night. "*In time you will come to accept that.*"

Was he right?

She wondered how Dylan had adapted, coming here for the first time when he was thirteen, leaving behind his family and friends, the only life, the only world he'd ever known. But Dylan was selkie, and he'd had their mother with him.

She wondered how Griff's wife, Emma, had adjusted, the only human, the only mortal on Sanctuary. Conn said she had been happy here. Fulfilled. But Emma's husband had been devoted to her until the day she died.

Lucy pleated the red wool in her lap and wondered how it would feel to be loved. How she would feel if Conn loved her.

She remembered the look on his face as he gazed out to sea, his body carved out of moonlight and marble, and her heart ached in her breast.

Madadh growled and rose to a crouch.

Startled, she glanced down. The dog's small ears laid back along its narrow skull. Its yellow eyes blazed. She followed its line of sight to the empty arch and beyond to the cobblestoned keep. Her chest tightened in apprehension.

"It's okay," she soothed, without any idea whether everything was okay or not.

Madadh took a slinking step forward.

She reached—*no collar*—and put her hand on the dog's shoulders, feeling its muscles bunch beneath the fur. "Let's not be silly."

Something was going on in the outer courtyard. The tall iron-bound door swung silently open. No footsteps. No voices. She still had time to retreat to her room. Assuming she could find it in this pile of stones.

She stood. "Come on," she urged Madadh, sounding unconvincingly cheery. "Let's—"

The dog bolted from under her hand and tore across the courtyard.

"*Crap.*" She took off after him.

At the arch, she stopped, catching herself against the cold, finished stone, her heart hammering against her ribs.

A phantom company of—people?—poured like smoke through the open door. Not people. Ghosts. Ancient soldiers, senators, centurions, like extras from an old Bible movie, like visions from a nightmare. Something about the shape of their skulls, the set of their shoulders or eye sockets, wasn't quite . . . right. Their robes and bodies flowed and faded in the sun. Through their booted feet, their sandaled legs, she could see the stones of the courtyard standing out like bones.

Her blood chilled.

Madadh launched like a rock from a catapult through the shifting, shimmering crowd. The air swirled and sparkled in the dog's wake.

"Madadh, no!" Lucy shouted as one figure—tall, robed, with leaves of some sort circling its dark head—turned and raised one hand.

The hound dropped like a stone.

Lucy pressed her hands to her mouth.

The man, if it was a man, looked from the dog whimpering at its feet to Lucy cowering against the wall. Its eyes glowed like the embers of a dying fire. They scorched her soul.

She felt the brute thrust of its invasion like an ice pick in her skull, like a broom handle between her legs. Jabbing. Burning. Tearing. *Wrong.*

Instinctively, she recoiled into the shadow of the arch, her heart thumping in her chest and the taste of ashes in her mouth.

11

BART HUNTER CAME HOME TO THE SOUND OF the TV and the smell of burning food. He dropped his boots by the front door. "Lucy?"

No answer.

Where the hell was she?

He didn't want to be here. He didn't want to be home. Usually at this hour he was at the inn. A man deserved a drink after putting in a day on the water. He shouldn't have to chase after his grown-up daughter. She was too old, he was too old, to put up with this shit.

But while he was in line to sell his catch—young lobsters, shedders, to stock the co-op's pond over the winter—that jackass Henry Tibbetts had joked, "Where'd you bury the body, Bart?"

Like his daughter was dead instead of just taking a couple days off sick.

Like she'd run off.

Like her mother.

"Lu!" he bellowed.

It wasn't like her to skip work. Even when she was a little girl, she'd never missed more than a day of school. Never gave any trouble, he thought with pride and regret.

The TV chattered—some woman with big lips and small tits leaning over a stove. Bart snapped off the set and heard noises from the kitchen. Running water. Scraping sounds.

He found Lucy in the kitchen, standing in front of the sink, chipping away with a spatula at some godawful black mess in a frying pan. Cupboards and drawers stood open. Dirty cups, bowls, and spoons littered the counters among splotches of flour, grease, and tomato. Under the smoke and char floated a sharper, fresher scent, like a mowed lawn.

Lucy's head jerked around as he entered the kitchen, her shock of blond hair flying. Something—tomato sauce? chocolate?—smeared her cheek. Her eyes were wild.

Bart halted. He didn't ask her what was wrong. They never asked. There were too many possible answers he didn't want to hear. "What the hell are you doing?"

She lifted the pan half out of the sink, slopping water to the floor. "I wanted to make dinner."

His gaze went from the wet floor to the hard, blackened remains of . . . whatever it was, stinking in the sink.

He frowned, bothered. Bewildered. "Why didn't you just throw something in the Crock-Pot?"

"I don't know," she said, her lower lip trembling. "I don't know anything."

Her eyes welled with tears.

Bart recoiled. But under his worry and aggravation, a memory stirred: Alice, right after she'd come to live with him, struggling in the kitchen. *"But I want to cook for you,"* she'd protested when he came home to another ruined dinner. *"Like a regular wife."*

"*I didn't want a regular wife,*" he would tease her. "*I married a mermaid.*" Maybe he'd fry up some eggs, then, or boil lobsters. Sometimes they'd skip dinner altogether and go upstairs to make love.

In the old days. In the good days. In the days when she still loved him enough to please him, and he'd loved her enough to trust her.

The old, familiar pain ripped at him.

He looked at Alice's daughter, her flushed face, her tear-filled eyes, and shifted his weight uneasily.

He'd never been a good father to her. Hadn't needed to be. Caleb had raised her since she was in diapers. By the time the boy left home, she was pretty much taking care of herself. And him, too. Doing the laundry, doing her homework, opening cans of soup for dinner. A good girl. No trouble, he thought again.

But she was in some kind of trouble now. Henry said she hadn't been into work all week.

"Maybe we should go out," he said. "To eat. Give you a break."

Her green eyes—green as grass, greener than he remembered—widened. "Why?"

"You've been sick," he said gruffly. "Not yourself."

"Not myself," she repeated.

He wouldn't take her to the bar at the inn, he decided. They'd go to Antonia's. "Get a good meal inside you, you might feel better."

Her tears dried up as if by magic. "I will feel better."

He was unaccountably pleased with himself and her. "And tomorrow you get yourself back to school."

She stared at him, her face a blank.

His mouth dried in panic. Had something happened to her at the school? Something she couldn't tell him? She was fired, maybe, or . . . His mind skittered away from all the things that could happen to a girl, all the dangers he'd never been able to protect her from.

"School," she said suddenly and smiled. "To learn."

He jammed his hands in his pockets. "To teach."

"To teach and learn."

"Right." Well, why not? "Better than brooding around the house like your old man."

She smiled, a hint of mischief in her face. "Get a good meal inside you, you might feel better."

He chuckled, already feeling better than he had in a long time.

*   *   *

Conn's gaze swept from Madadh's body, limp on the cobblestones, to Lucy's white, stricken face. For one second his heart simply stopped, frozen in terror.

Across the courtyard, Gau smiled, taunting him. Playing him.

Fury slammed through Conn like a storm surge, sweeping everything in its path.

His lips pulled back in a snarl. "Hold him."

Gau's form flickered. Perhaps it was an effect of the sunlight, but the demon lord appeared almost shaken. "I am an emissary. You do not have the authority to hold me."

"My realm," Conn said. "My rules."

A sigh rippled through Gau's cohort. The stench of demonkind lay over the keep like smoke. In that shifting, shimmering crowd, any one of them could have slipped away. Any one of them could have seized a second's opportunity, a moment of human weakness, to slide into Lucy's mind and possess her, to settle into that long, lean body, to rape her of her will.

Conn reached out with his senses, all his senses, but he could find no taint of demon in her, no fingerprint of Hell. Whatever had been attempted, she was not possessed.

His fear abated. His fury did not.

Gau bent his borrowed features into an expression of pained surprise. "You would not jeopardize our détente for . . . a dog?"

"My dog," Conn said.

My woman.

He did not look again at Lucy. He would not draw the demon's attention her way. But he was achingly aware of her shrinking into the shadow of the arch, her fingers pressed to her mouth.

"You do not have cause to hold me," Gau objected.

"Pray you are right, demon," Conn said grimly. "Or even Hell will not protect you from me."

"I acted in self-defense," Gau protested.

"Bollocks," Griff said. "The animal cannot bite a ghost."

Madadh.

Now that his greater fear was soothed, Conn could spare thought for the dog. He reached the hound in three long strides, barely noticing the wardens who squeezed out of his way. The hound was young, strong, only three years old. Only three . . .

Conn dropped to his knees.

Gau sneered. "Your concern is touching. I did not expect such feeling from the great lord of the sea."

Conn ignored him, his hands doing a rapid check of the dog's heart, limbs, lungs. Madadh cocked an anxious yellow eye upward and whined. *Alive.*

Conn's lungs relaxed enough for him to draw breath.

"You see? The animal is merely stunned," Gau said. "I would not do anything foolish to upset the balance of power."

Did the demon's gaze slide to Lucy?

"Bugger the balance of power," Conn said through his teeth. "Touch what is mine again, Hell spawn, and I will snuff you."

Gau hissed.

Conn found Ronat among the wardens who had followed him from the hall. "Water and blankets for the hound."

"Yes, my prince."

Conn smoothed a hand over the dog's head and rose to his feet. The hound's tail thumped weakly on the stones.

"What shall we do with Lord Gau?" Morgan asked.

Conn wanted to send the demon lord back to Hell. But he would not release Gau until he had confirmed Lucy was intact.

She still stood in the shadow of the bailey wall, outside the wardens' protective circle. Her face was ravaged. Ashen. The delicate skin beneath her eyes appeared bruised.

Conn's face set. His gut churned. He needed to get her to himself. Somewhere he could hold her, touch her, assure himself of her safety. Anger still pounded in his temples like a headache, but controlled.

Or nearly controlled.

He stalked across the courtyard.

She had lowered her hands, holding her elbows tightly across her midsection as if she had taken a mortal wound. Conn gritted his teeth. She could hold on to him. Wouldn't that be the normal human female response to an attack? She should throw herself in his arms. He would not mind.

But first he must get her away from Gau. From all of them.

He moved on her, close enough to see the sweep of her thick, fair lashes and the part in her springy hair, near enough to smell her skin and her fear. He searched her gaze. Her eyes were wide with shock, but it was her spirit that looked out of them.

She was safe. His heart, which had been clenched as tightly as a fist, relaxed enough to beat. She was herself.

Ronat spoke from behind him. "My prince? Lord Gau?"

"He can go to Hell," Conn said without turning. "Escort him to the caves."

Lucy's tongue came out to moisten her lips. His entire body clenched in response.

"Upstairs with me," he commanded softly. "Now."

She craned her neck to look over his shoulder, apparently oblivious to her danger and his need. "The dog . . . Is Madadh all right?"

He wanted to shake her. Did she fail to realize how narrow an escape she had just had?

"The dog is in shock," he said curtly. The vision of Madadh stretched on the cobbles, of Lucy with her hand to her mouth, struck him again with bruising force. "But it will live. Perhaps this will even teach it to listen."

A tinge of color returned to her pale face. "It wasn't Madadh's fault."

"He should have obeyed."

Her eyes were wide and desolate. "Are you mad at him? Or at me?"

Conn drew a short, sharp breath. He was furious at Gau and at himself, for not anticipating her danger, for not moving quickly enough to protect her. But he had no intention of debating his feelings with the entire court looking on. He was not discussing his emotions at all. His fear was too new, his need too raw.

He gripped her arm above the elbow. "Upstairs."

She regarded his hand on her arms as he propelled her across the bailey toward his tower. "Did you know you only touch me when you're hauling me somewhere?"

She did not sound accusing. Her tone was almost wistful. It filleted him like a knife.

His hold tightened. So did his jaw. He did not know how to touch to give comfort or reassurance. Only to fight or to mate. "I touch you. I have been inside you."

They were almost to his tower.

"Sex doesn't count," she said.

Temper and need erupted inside him. His control shattered. "Then it doesn't matter if I do this."

He spun her through the doorway, backed her against the wall, and covered her mouth with hot, hungry urgency. The kiss was rough, almost savage. Fury and fear pumped through his blood, drummed in his head.

She was his to claim.

His to protect.

His to take.

*   *   *

Lucy absorbed the shock of his assault, feeling his hunger, feeding it, needing it.

Gau had caught her in the open, unprepared. She hadn't had time to find shelter behind the wall she'd been building her entire life.

When the demon attacked, she'd struck back instinctively, throwing up barriers to protect herself, her defense less like building a wall and more like dumping a load of bricks on the demon's head.

At least, that's what it felt like to her. She didn't know how it felt to the demon.

But the alien presence in her mind was gone, extinguished like a campfire under a shovelful of dirt, leaving her empty in the rubble and the ashes, with gritty eyes and coated tongue. Her chest felt hollow. Her mind was bruised. The taint of smoke and char caught in the back of her throat and lingered in her sinuses.

She needed Conn's taste to wipe it out. She needed his touch to feel alive again and safe.

She welcomed his hard, urgent mouth, his rough, claiming hands. He leaned into her, his heavily muscled body a bulwark and a refuge. She rested her hand on the back of his neck, the edge of her little finger riding that line of smooth, exposed skin, and felt his groan vibrate in the back of his throat, in the pit of her stomach.

He could fill her. He could take her to a place where she wouldn't have to think. His hands closed over her breasts, and she quivered in reaction and relief. She craved the warm oblivion of sex like her father craved his bottle. She wanted to feel something other than lonely. Something besides numb.

Conn made her feel. He trapped her against the wall with his body, his breathing quick and hard. The storm inside him swirled around them, charging the air, sending lovely electric thrills sliding along her skin. She was squashed between the bite of stone at her back and his muscled weight all along her front, breasts, belly, thighs. His erection pulsed against her, thick with life. He bent his head, and she felt the rasp of his jaw and then the warm suction of his mouth on her throat. Her eyes slid shut.

Dust and ashes and despair.

She opened them again hastily and Conn was there, warm and real, hard and urgent. She threw her arms around his neck, fisted her hands in his hair. *Take me. Save me.*

He growled and lifted her into his arms, plunged with her into the cool, shadowed tower, hauled her up the stairs. Round and round they climbed, darkness and light playing over his hard face, her gasps and his footsteps echoing in the enclosed space. She could feel the urgency in him, violent as an approaching storm. Her head spun. She was breathless, dizzy, drunk with anticipation.

It was sex. Just sex.

It was life.

It was everything.

She licked the hollow of his throat, savoring the taste of salt and man. He carried her to his room and dropped her on his bed. She bounced once before he came down hard on top of her, taking his weight on his elbows, caging her legs with his thighs. His mouth covered her mouth. She parted for him eagerly. His tongue plunged inside.

Her hips hitched upward—*there, please*—seeking pressure, seeking relief. The blunt, hard ridge of his arousal rubbed the juncture of her thighs. She struggled to open her legs, to capture his, but he straddled her, his knees on the cloak, pulling the wool fabric tight across her body. She was trapped and itchy. Desperate.

Panting, she struggled to throw him off. He rose up—*not enough, not nearly enough*—and grabbed her hips and turned her facedown into the mattress.

Um, no. Not like this. He was too strong. It was too much. She was wary of his total dominance, and even more alarmed by her own response.

In any contest of passion, she would lose. Had lost already.

And she didn't even know the stakes.

She twisted to face him.

But he pinned her down, his arms enclosing her arms, his thighs restraining her thighs, his strength surrounding her. With one hand, he pulled up on her cloak and her skirts, bunching the material around her waist. The wash of cold air on her bared legs was distraction and relief. His hands shaped her bottom, measured the span of her hips, tugged the elastic of her panties down her thighs. She shivered, open to him, vulnerable and wet and open. She turned her face on the pillow as he reached under her, as his long-fingered hand splayed over her belly, toyed a moment with her piercing, dipped into her navel. His touch moved down, slow, seeking, deliberate. She moaned and then bit her lip, the pain a tiny punctuation point to pleasure.

He was so close behind her, hot and solid behind her, his body controlling her body, his hands compelling her response. She was drunk, dizzy with the mingled, musky odors of his sweat and her arousal. She felt him shift to adjust his clothing, and trembled in anticipation. Her breasts tightened. Her boundaries blurred.

His knee shoved her legs wider apart. She writhed. He stroked, his hand teasing, skimming over her slick, sensitive flesh. Swaying on her knees, she ground against him, a willing accomplice in her own surrender.

He kissed her nape.

She made a muffled sound of frustration into the pillow and *bit* him. His arm. Like an animal.

His breath was hot in her ear. "You want this."

She felt the hair at his groin, the smooth, hard jut of his cock rubbing the crack of her buttocks. He took himself in hand, positioning himself, sliding the thick head against her wet opening. She melted for him. Moaned. His skin was hot and silky. Her womb softened and clenched.

She panted and tipped her hips upward, helpless to deny him. "Yes."

"Then take it." He thrust. "Take me."

Deeper.

"Take my seed."

Her body jolted. Her mind rebelled. But mind and body were taken up, taken over, by the feel of him inside her, pumping inside her, filling her to bursting. She was blinded, breathless, caught in a current she could not control. She cried out and convulsed, her orgasm ripped from her, tumbling her over and over like a shell trapped by the tide. Wave after wave racked her, wrecked her, her contractions milking his until he plunged, until he shuddered and groaned and released deep inside her.

His big body sprawled over hers, damp. Spent.

Lucy closed her eyes, absorbing the pounding of his heart, the sound of his labored breathing.

"Now," Conn said, his voice deep with satisfaction, "you will stay."

12

≈

"Um." Lucy's mind floated somewhere above the bed, anchored only by the knot at her heart. Her head still reeled from the force of Conn's possession, from the fullness of her own surrender. Her body felt swollen and achy. Loose, as if Conn had taken her apart and put her back together without using the manufacturer's instructions. "I didn't say I would stay with you."

The smell of sex, sharp and musky, hung in the air and clung to her skin. The covers were a tangled mess. So was she. And Conn, instead of rolling over and falling asleep or jumping in the shower and out the door, seemed content to lie beside her, his hand resting lightly, possessively on her hip, his gaze on her face.

"I do not require the words. This is enough." He tucked a strand of hair behind her ear, the back of his knuckles brushing her cheek. She almost wept at the tenderness of the gesture. Unexpected from him. Unprecedented for her. "This is better."

Her heart kicked in her chest. Her mouth was dry. "This doesn't solve anything."

He lowered his hand. His dark brows drew together. "I gave you my seed."

Yes. She moistened her dry lips, uncomfortably aware of the tenderness in her belly, the wetness of his semen between her thighs. He had pushed himself so firmly, so deeply inside her, she was afraid she couldn't tell anymore where he ended and she began.

"Uh-huh. And do you make a lifetime commitment to everybody you have sex with?"

He frowned. "Of course not. I am selkie."

She swallowed. "Well, I'm human. And humans take time to get to know one another before they . . ."

"Fuck?" he suggested very softly.

He was angry, she realized. Hurt? But that was ridiculous.

"Make a commitment," she said.

"You said 'yes,'" he reminded her. "In words, this time."

She felt her face turn red. "I would have said anything you wanted to have you inside me."

His nostrils flared. His eyes were deep and dark. "Then—"

She was miserably embarrassed. But she was even more determined to finish, to make him understand. "I would have done anything. Given you anything." She took another deep breath, forcing herself to his gaze. "And that scares the crap out of me."

He frowned. "Did I hurt you?"

"What?"

He examined her face. "I was rough. Did I hurt you?"

She was braced for his impatience. His unexpected consideration shook her heart. "I'm fine. You were . . ." *Relentless. Overwhelming.* "Incredible. But it's not enough."

He gave her a long, considering look. His mouth curved with wicked intent. "I can give you more."

All the air left her lungs. Desire pinched her breasts, stabbed her womb. The temptation to give up, to give in to him, almost overpowered her.

She curled her legs under her and sat, smoothing her skirt over her thighs so she wouldn't have to look at him. "Last night you accused me of not having the courage to take what you offered me."

"I was angry."

"You were right. I am afraid. I'm afraid I'll give myself to you, and I'll be left with nothing."

"Lucy." He laid his hand over hers, stilling her restless picking at the fabric. His hand was warm. Her heart turned over in her chest. "I gave you my pledge."

"Because of the prophecy."

"I gave you my pelt."

"I don't know what that means." Which only proved her point. "We're too different, don't you see? There's too much I don't know about you. That we don't know about each other."

Conn released her hand and left the bed. She felt his loss like the pain of a missing limb, as if something warm and vital had been severed. The mantle of the fireplace framed the proud set of his shoulders. Today he wore gray velvet and lace at his throat. He looked like a portrait of an aristocrat in a book of eighteenth-century paintings.

Or like a king.

"The selkie are the children of the sea," he said with his back to her. "We take our life and our power from the ocean. A selkie who gives up his pelt gives his power and life into another's keeping." He turned, tall, stern, and forbidding as ever. "And a human who takes a selkie pelt holds that power over its owner. As your father held your mother."

Lucy stared at him, a terrible suspicion rooting in her brain. "You mean, against her will."

He did not answer.

Her heart pounded as the foundations of her world rocked again. "My father *loved* my mother."

Conn's face was without expression. "He would say so."

She didn't know how to respond. What would it mean if all these years, all her father's choices, hadn't been governed by grief at all, but by guilt?

"And she . . ." Lucy's voice shook shamefully.

"Cared for him, I believe. For a time."

"Then Caleb . . . And Dylan . . ."

"Margred made the choice to live as human for your brother's sake. As Dylan chooses to stay with Regina."

But Maggie loved Caleb. No one who saw them together could doubt it. And Dylan was devoted to Regina.

Lucy's heart beat faster. "What does that have to do with you and me?"

Conn's face became, if possible, even colder and more remote. "I took your freedom. I gave you mine. What more do you want of me?"

Her throat ached.

Your love.

But of course she couldn't say that. He had given her what he had. All he could. Could it be enough? She didn't want to be like the little girl in the fairy tale, crying for the moon.

What did she want?

"I want to be part of a normal couple," she said. "I want a regular relationship. Somebody to talk to and laugh with and care about. Somebody who is with me because he cares about me. Not because of a prophecy or a sealskin or anything else."

He gazed back at her steadily with those cool-as-rain

eyes. "I cannot change what I am or what I have done. I would not if I could. There is no going back for us."

"I'm not asking to go back. I just want to slow down."

"To what end?"

Doubt lodged like a splinter in her chest, pricking old insecurities. She couldn't entice her live-in boyfriend to go out for pizza. Did she seriously think she was going to sell the three-thousand-year-old lord of the sea on the concept of dinner-and-a-movie?

"To get to know each other."

"I know you."

Sexually.

Yes.

The red marks of her teeth scored his arm.

She flushed and looked away. "You only know part of me. You don't know my favorite color or my favorite flower or if I leave the cap off the toothpaste or whether I like Chinese food. You don't know if I go to church or what side of the bed I sleep on or the name of my first boyfriend."

"And you think these things are important."

She stuck out her chin. "What they demonstrate—the trust, the closeness—is important. Yes."

"Very well. Tell me."

She was surprised into a laugh. "You want a list?"

"Yes."

He was serious. The realization was at once completely ridiculous and oddly reassuring. "Getting to know someone doesn't work that way. It takes time."

He clasped his hands behind his back. "How much time?"

He was pushing at her, always pushing. Tentatively, she pushed back. "Worried about how many childbearing years I have left?"

His eyes glinted. "Not as long as I can spend them in your bed."

Her pulse jumped. Desire was a whisper against her skin, a throb in her blood. How could she slow her rapid slide into dangerous dependence when he could arouse her with a look, a word?

"We need to compromise. I'm willing to give you— us—a chance. You need to give me space."

He raised his brows. "This room is not enough for you?"

Haha. "I meant emotional space."

"Agreed. During the day, you may take all the time and talk and emotional space you require. But at night, we share the bed."

Her pulse beat in her throat and between her legs. "That's your compromise?"

His lips curved. "Yes."

She sank her teeth into her lower lip to contain her answering smile. She wanted to sleep with him, yearned for a body beside her in the dark to provide an illusion of intimacy and keep her dreams at bay. She wanted more than that. Even now, with her body slick and tender from his assault, she craved him in ways and places that shocked her. That would probably shock him, if he knew.

Her gaze flickered to the bite on his arm and away, sliding over him like a hand, greedily gathering up impressions: the column of his throat, his long, strong, broad body, the pillars of his thighs. She recognized the slow uncurling of desire in her stomach with delight and despair. His rough possession had released her sexual appetite like a genie from a bottle. How would she ever wrestle it back under control?

I wish . . . I wish . . .

"Tell me his name."

She jerked her attention back to his face. "What?"

"The name of your first boyfriend. The one you think of when you look at me."

"Oh." Hot blood flooded her face. "It's not important."

Conn regarded her steadily, immovable as his tower, inexorable as the sea. "The trust is important," he quoted softly back at her.

Her heart raced. *Trapped.*

"His name was Brian."

Conn waited.

Crap.

"He, um . . . We met my sophomore year. At a party?" She snuck a look at him to see if he understood. Just a typical Saturday night, open doors and open bottles at a friend of a friend's apartment. Watching other people get wasted usually didn't appeal to Lucy. She'd had too much of that growing up. But Caleb had recently deployed to Iraq, and she had felt anxious and itchy, cut off and almost unbearably lonely. So she'd let her roommate nag her into going.

"You had sex with him," Conn said.

"That night?" Lucy winced. "Yeah."

Hookup sex. Her first time. Brian was drunk and she was nervous. She recalled fumbling and hunger and pheromones trickling like a cocktail through her veins, heady and addictive. She'd stumbled home giddy with hormones, almost believing in love at first sight.

"And after?"

"Sometimes." She cleared her throat. "Actually, we, um, lived together for a while."

She'd never told Caleb. She never told anybody, except her roommate. She had visions of her brother coming home from Iraq and field dressing her boyfriend. So there had been no one to confide in, no one to advise her. Fermented by time, the words spilled out like acid, thick and corrosive.

"Sometimes he couldn't . . . He didn't want to . . . Well, look at me." She hunched her shoulders in irritation and embarrassment. "I'm hardly a supermodel. And he was taking some really hard courses, he was too tired to . . ."

"What are you, some kind of freak?" Brian had protested sleepily, irritably, when she reached for him the fourth—or was it the fifth?—time. "Get away from me."

Lucy winced at the memory. "He didn't like it when I made demands."

* * *

"Made demands"?

Sodding angels. Blood flooded Conn's brain and his cock. He'd like her to make demands of him. He wanted to throttle the young fool who had taught her to devalue herself, who had cheapened her sensual selkie nature.

"Look at me," she had said.

He did. He saw her thick, springy hair, her lean, strong face, the thick sweep of her pale lashes. She was not an exotic beauty, not an obvious one, but subtle, clean-limbed, and lovely. Her clear eyes reflected the moods of the sea. Right now they were the color of storm, gray washed with moisture.

Lust transmuted to tenderness, flooding his chest and tightening his throat.

"I see you," he said.

She braced.

"I want you." He held her gaze, held his arms away from his body, palms upward. "I am at your service. Command me."

Her lips parted. He saw the possibilities work into her imagination and bloom in her eyes, deep, disturbing, exciting. But she did not have the confidence to command or even to ask. Not yet.

So he crossed to the bed and bracketed her face in his hands. Her skin was warm and faintly flushed. With his thumb, he smoothed the thick, stubborn line of her brows, the subtle indentation of her chin. She closed her eyes, and he kissed her quivering lids and the slope of her cheekbone and the corner of her mouth.

Her breath escaped on a sigh. Carefully, watching her, he moved his hands to the fastenings of her cloak, undoing the long row of buttons one by one. His knuckles brushed her breasts. She trembled.

"Beautiful." His whisper vibrated between them.

She opened her eyes, the gray depths swirling with yearning and denial.

"Like the sea at dawn," he said.

She snorted in disbelief.

Anger stabbed Conn's gut. Anger at her human lover, who had taken her and left her in such doubt.

Anger at himself, for doing the same.

Yet for all that he had taken, he could give her this. He continued to undress her, taking time, taking care, pausing to admire each part. His sex words made her blush and squirm, so he told her without words how exquisite she was, how firm, how fine, how delicately made. He set his lips to her shoulder, inhaling the perfume of her skin, tasting her salt. He traced the velvet tips of her breasts and bent to suckle them.

She made a sound of impatience low in her throat and reached for him.

He stepped back from her urgent touch. "Lady, I am yours. At your service."

Her drowning eyes were lost. Confused. They tore his heart. "So?"

"You wanted to slow down," he reminded her wickedly.

A smile trembled on her lips. Her hands dropped to her sides.

Tension shivered through him. Not only to have her, but to return to her a measure of her feminine power. He shucked his own clothes hastily, tunic, leggings, and shirt. His cock jutted, rock hard and rampant, but he ignored his own arousal to focus on hers, brushing his hands up and down her arms, letting his touch drift from the angle of her hip to the curve of her belly. The tiny jewel, caught in gold, glittered against her skin.

He touched it with one finger. "What is this?"

She looked down. "Um . . . aquamarine, I think."

"I mean, why do you wear it?"

"You don't like it." Her voice was flat.

What could he tell her? That it excited him? That it repelled him? Both were true.

"I have never seen anything like it," he said honestly. "The selkie do not alter or adorn their skin. It is pretty," he added.

"Gee, thanks."

He traced a line from the piercing at her navel to the soft thatch below. "This," he said, "is beyond gold to me."

Her breath caught, a tiny betrayal. Her eyes were fathoms deep and dark. Outside the tower, the wind murmured and moaned.

He moved in, gliding his lips along her throat, feeling the beat of panic and desire, down her beaded breasts and the fragrant hollow between, down, down, following the line of his finger to the place where she was wet and waiting for him. She made a choked exclamation in her throat and fisted her hands in his hair, swaying closer, jerking away. Sweet. Hot. Her response maddened his blood.

The wind rattled the glass in the windows, sending shadows chasing across the floor. He was drunk on her. Her need became his need, her pleasure his desire. He eased her back on the bed, coaxed her to lie on his pelt. Her hair spilled over his sealskin, blond on black. Kneeling on the floor, his head between her long, smooth thighs, he harrowed her with lips, teeth, and tongue, feeling her response, feeding on it, until she undulated against his mouth and her breath came in sobs. Her beauty almost drowned him.

He dragged her up and held her hard against him as he reversed their positions, as he sat with her on his lap. Rain lashed the glass. The storm drummed in his ears, raged in his blood. Seizing her hips, he pulled her to straddle him there on the edge of the bed. Her knees pressed his flanks. Her breasts brushed his chest. Her gaze locked with his.

Shock held them both still.

They were touching but not joined, his body poised and probing, hers open and wet.

"Take it," he said, his voice thick, and the words meant something different now. A benediction. A plea. "Take what you need."

He watched her slim throat move as she swallowed. His neck was corded with strain. The room grew dark. She braced her hands on his shoulders and slowly, slowly, sank onto him, taking him into the heat and the wet. His teeth clenched. His breath hissed. He stretched out his legs as she wiggled to take him deeper, feeling her muscles flex and relax, feeling her body clench and release, a fierce internal milking of his shaft. Her eyes were bright and blind as she moved in awkward rhythm, her fingers digging into his shoulders, her body tight around his.

Lightning shattered the shadows as she gathered the storm, owned it, rode it. Rode him. Power pulsed inside and out. She shuddered. He groaned. He felt the crackle and surge as she closed around him, rising and falling like the sea.

His heart contracted. "*I am yours,*" he had told her.

But he had not believed it until now.

When the wave came, the swell took them both.

13

❦

PALE YELLOW LIGHT FLOODED THE WESTERN wall of the inner bailey. The short turf dissolved in a tumble of rock and weed like a green wave breaking on shore.

Lucy lifted her face to the sun's caress, incandescent with happiness. Every moment of the past three days that Conn had not been with the wardens, he had spent with her—most of them in bed. There was nothing he wouldn't do and little they hadn't tried. She felt exquisitely sensitive, achingly alive, her skin burnished by his constant attentions. She glowed, inside and out.

"Stones, it's hot," said Roth from the bench.

Lucy started, her attention jerked back to their lesson. The temperature in the courtyard eased a degree or ten.

Griff rubbed his jaw with one large hand. "Aye. Too hot to concentrate anymore today. Go enjoy yourselves."

Three males looked at Lucy, their eyes dark with animal awareness. They knew, she realized. Even the boys.

She felt plunged in boiling water, scalded pink. "It does seem warm for October," she offered.

Roth choked.

Iestyn dropped his gaze.

"It's the current," Griff said kindly. "Coming from the south. The island never gets so very cold."

"Or so warm," Roth said. "Usually."

Iestyn kicked his ankle.

Lucy cleared her throat. "Good growing climate."

"Good for oats and apples," Griff said.

"Wild onion, too," said Iestyn. "Under the orchard trees. And mint."

Lucy's gaze wandered back to the strip beneath the sun-drenched wall. Not that it was any of her business, but . . . "Wouldn't it be more convenient to grow inside the walls? The herbs anyway."

"Aye. Emma planted some bits of things by the kitchen, years ago." Griff smiled ruefully. "They are not doing so well now."

"By the kitchen?" Lucy frowned, picturing the outer bailey. "Not much sun there."

"You could move them," Griff suggested. "In the spring."

Lucy jolted. Spring was months away. When she'd asked Conn for time, she hadn't thought so far ahead.

"Or now is good," she said. Now was very good. Why screw things up? "Fall is the best time to transplant."

"Is it?" Griff's dark eyes assessed her. "You might have a look, then."

"I will."

Why not? Conn had told her he would be meeting with the remaining wardens through midday. One thing she'd learned growing up was that you couldn't sit around waiting for somebody to pay attention to you. Conn cared for her, her comfort, her pleasure. It was just that he had other responsibilities to occupy him and she had . . .

The back of her neck prickled. *Very little.*

Time to do something about that.

"Well." She stood. "Thank you."

"Iestyn here will bring you your lunch," Griff said.

"I can get it. I'm usually very competent."

Griff and the boys regarded her with blank, male, uncomprehending stares.

Lucy sighed. "I'm going by the kitchen anyway."

And by the great hall, she thought. Conn was in the hall. Not that she would actually get to see him, but even the chance proximity was enough to make her heart skip. Like she was ten years old again, pedaling her bike past Matthew Miller's house, sweaty and breathless with anticipation.

But when she approached the arch to the outer bailey, her footsteps faltered. She hadn't actually walked this way since her encounter with the demon lord. The memory thrust into her mind, invasive, painful. She blocked it the same way that she had blocked Gau.

"He sensed that you were human and therefore vulnerable," Conn had said during one of their time-outs to talk. Last night? The night before? He rose to put more driftwood on the fire, the firelight sliding over his strong features. Lucy had pulled the covers over her breasts. She was cold without his warmth beside her—and even the memory of Gau made her shiver. Conn's voice was deep, with an edge like an axe. *"Now he knows you are under my protection. He will not violate the sovereignty of Sanctuary again."*

Lucy was pretty sure she had protected herself last time, but she liked the way Conn's concern made her feel. Safe. Cared for. Also, Conn was naked. The whole time he was talking, she was focused on the hard slope of his shoulders and the curve of his haunches as he stooped to the fire.

She crossed the cobblestones.

The long, low building opposite the keep was the

kitchen, with the well beside it. Lucy didn't see any raised beds or weeded plots, but creeping among the stones was a tiny-leaved plant she recognized as thyme and a taller shrub that might be sage, straggling in the shade. Near the kitchen door sprouted a clump of gray-green foliage with dried-up spikes. Lavender? She rubbed a velvety leaf between her fingers and sniffed. Marjoram. Good on chicken and fish. She would have to talk Griff into allowing her to take over some of the cooking.

Planning a garden, planning meals . . . She was remaking her old life here, with Conn as the new center.

Something about that thought struck her as not quite right. She pushed the feeling away and opened the door to the kitchen.

The interior was dim, cluttered, and cool, more storeroom than kitchen. The air smelled of apples and onions, fish and peat. Shuttered windows admitted bars of light, revealing stone stained with smoke, shelves thick with dust, casks, bags, and barrels piled against the walls.

Well. Lucy turned slowly. If she wanted something to do, she had come to the right place. As her eyes adjusted, she saw a long, wide table covered with what looked like treasures from a flea market, silver, crystal, and china. A wide open hearth and a cold iron stove anchored one end of the room. A deep trough with a pipe dominated the other. The walls were lined with open shelves.

Lucy stepped closer and blinked in surprise at rows of cans. All sizes and shapes of tins and cans, labeled in all languages, with faded pictures of tomatoes, peaches, beans.

"*We accept the gifts of the tide,*" Conn had said.

If she could get them open, she could prepare a feast. *A feast for one?*

A frown formed between her eyebrows. If she wanted to eat alone out of cans, she could go back to Maine.

Not that she could actually go back. Not that she wanted to now. Conn wasn't in Maine.

She smoothed her brow and straightened her shoulders, and began to search among the bone-handled knives and silver tongs for a can opener.

A male voice drifted through the slatted windows. ". . . more pressing concerns occupying his attention."

A woman laughed without amusement. "Occupying his bed, you mean."

Lucy froze, gripping a spatula.

"I take it you do not approve of the prince's liaison," the man said coolly.

Oh, God. They were crossing the courtyard, a man and a woman walking together. Wardens?

"I forfeited my right to approve or disapprove when I left the prince's bed," the woman said. "And you, Lord Morgan?"

Lucy held her breath. Concealed by the shutters, she edged closer to the window to see them better. To spy, she admitted to herself with a lurch of shame and discomfort. A tall man dressed in black, silver-haired and smooth-faced. That must be Morgan. And the woman with him, with the red hair and the large pink pearls, had shared Conn's bed.

She was very beautiful, Lucy observed.

She tried not to mind. What had she expected? Conn must have learned all that technique somewhere. She knew going in he wasn't the three-thousand-year-old virgin.

"The ice shelves are shattering in the northern deeps," Morgan said. "The seals lose ground day by day. Under the circumstances, I find it difficult to sustain interest in Conn's new broodmare."

Ouch.

Lucy's throat closed. They didn't know her. How could they judge her?

"You have my sympathies. If not, it seems, Conn's help?" The woman's tone made the statement a question.

"He does what he can," Morgan said grimly. "Which is not enough to counter the humans' depredations. Perhaps when the oceans rise and drown them, we will have some relief."

Lucy swallowed. Apparently she wasn't the only human these two selkies disliked. They were being mean. Hateful.

Conn's broodmare.

She cringed.

"You agree with Gau, then?" the woman murmured.

Morgan's long strides checked. They were very close to the window. Lucy huddled in the shadows, her heart beating against her ribcage like a trapped bird. "You heard the prince," he said without expression. "The children of the sea are neutral in Hell's war on humankind."

"Not so neutral while that human *galla* shares his bed." The scornful tone made translation unnecessary.

"Her mother was selkie," Morgan said.

"Her mother was a bitch."

"But a fertile one," Morgan pointed out. "Conn wants a child."

The red-haired woman bared her teeth. "You presume to tell me what Conn wants?"

"I presume nothing," Morgan said harshly. "Were it otherwise, Hell might have had a different answer."

They walked away. If the woman said anything in reply, Lucy didn't hear. Her blood drummed in her ears. Her stomach churned.

She needed to see Conn. Obviously the council meeting had broken up. He would come looking for her soon. She needed the reassurance of his strong arms and encouraging words. *He* didn't hate her because she was human. He thought she was beautiful. He had agreed to give her time.

As long as she continued to have sex with him.

"Conn wants a child."

She closed her eyes against the pain. Yeah, he did. *"Your blood and my seed to save my people,"* he had said.

He hadn't lied to her. Maybe it would have been easier if he had. Because now she couldn't even take refuge in anger. She couldn't blame him for deceiving her.

She had deceived herself.

She set the spatula back on the table, her hand shaking. She needed time to think before she faced him again.

*   *   *

"Where are you going?" Iestyn's young voice caught Lucy at the postern gate.

Lucy swept a longing glance beyond the castle walls, where the green slope wandered down to lose itself in the orchard before swooping to peaks and crests. Rocks heaved from the turf like whales from the ocean. The ridges glimmered in the afternoon sun. She wanted to be out there. She wanted to be gone, away from the towers and expectations that pressed down on her and made it hard to breathe.

She turned and gave Iestyn a tight, teacher-to-pupil smile. "For a walk."

His brow furrowed. "I thought you were getting lunch."

She swallowed past her aching throat. "I'm not hungry." That much, at least, was true.

The boy's gaze passed over her and lingered on Madadh, tongue lolling, at her side. "I will come with you."

"No," she said sharply. Too sharply. A wildness reared inside her. She was desperate for escape from this place. From her pain. "I'll be fine. I have Madadh with me."

Iestyn's face hardened in a curiously adult expression. And then she remembered. He only looked like a teenager. "The dog did not protect you when Gau attacked."

No, she had protected herself.

"I'll be fine," Lucy repeated. The Hunter family motto, used to guard secrets and deflect concern. She frowned, curiosity momentarily winning through her longing to be gone. "How much did you see, spying from the wall?"

"Enough to know you should not be wandering outside the walls alone."

His concern was sincere and touching. "Conn said I was safe here."

"You could still get lost or turn an ankle. And then I'd be in trouble. I cannot let you go."

She raised her chin. "You can't stop me."

Iestyn grinned at her, a boy's grin, teasing, daring. "Will you put it to the test?"

Um, no. For all his wiry build, he was as tall as she was and as leanly muscled as a high school runner.

"How old are you?" she asked.

Another grin. "I'll tell if you let me come with you."

She blinked. Was he . . . Could he be trying to flirt with her? There was a complication none of them needed.

But his friendly smile was balm to her bruised ego.

"That's okay. I'm not that interested," she said and set off down the hill.

Madadh ranged ahead, his long tail gently waving like the flag on the back of a bicycle. The wind plucked at Lucy's hair and stirred the high weeds of the orchard. The heavy-sweet scent of apples carried on the breeze.

Iestyn fell into step beside her. "I was twelve when the prince brought me to Sanctuary."

That caught her attention. "Conn brought you?"

Iestyn nodded. "He paid my father in gold."

"How did your mother feel about that?"

"I do not know. My mother is selkie." He slid her a sideways glance. "Like yours."

"But . . . Didn't you see her after you came here?"

"No. She did not want me," he explained simply. "I was conceived in human form, so all the time she carried me she could not go to sea. She gave me to my father as soon as a nurse could be found. I do not remember her, and I doubt that she remembers me."

Like Conn, Lucy thought with a pang at her heart. Poor boy. Poor lost boys. "It must have been hard for you to leave your dad."

Iestyn shrugged. "He was sorry to lose me just as I grew big enough to help around the farm. But my lord gave him enough gold to hire many men."

They waded through the orchard grass, threaded with wild strawberry vines and jeweled with tiny blue and white flowers. Fruit still clung to the low branches, dark as garnets, golden as moons, and under each tree a ring of windfalls lay like a necklace.

"I mean, it must have been hard for you emotionally," Lucy said.

"I could not stay," Iestyn said.

"Why not?"

"I was near my Change." He raised his head to watch the hound, trotting out of the trees and up the slope on the opposite side. "The first time is hard, even when you are prepared. You must generate your own skin from the inside. It hurts. Like your guts being torn out."

"But you don't have to Change," Lucy said before she could stop herself.

Her lungs squeezed in her chest. Her heart pounded. For a moment she was a fourteen-year-old runaway again in the seedy gas station outside Richmond, puking her guts into the dirty washroom toilet, dying on the cold tile floor.

Iestyn turned and regarded her with narrowed golden eyes. "Of course you do. All selkies Change. We cannot help it. It is our nature."

Lucy forced herself to breathe. All selkies Change.

She was not selkie.

They hiked up the hill after Madadh, now scrambling through and over the rocks. The climb pulled the over-worked muscles of her thighs, eased the tightness in her hamstrings. The sun poured down like honey, edging the shadows. The breeze carried the faintest trace of smoke from this morning's fires.

"So you need somebody with you?" she asked.

Iestyn nodded. "It helps for the Change. And after. The pull of the sea is strong and hard to break. You need a guide with you the first time out, to help you find your way back."

"And without a guide?"

He shrugged again. "You stay beneath the wave. Forever, maybe. Unless it occurs to you to come ashore."

She tried to guess what would bring a selkie ashore. "Like for food?"

"Er." Iestyn's face reddened. "For sex, mostly."

"Oh." She swallowed. Of course. Her own mother . . . And Maggie . . .

A long, low howl echoed from the rocks ahead and then another and another in an eerie chorus that quivered up her spine.

Madadh crouched, ears flattening, hair raising along his shoulders.

Lucy shivered. "What was that?"

"Wolves."

She stopped dead. "*Wolves?*"

Iestyn flashed her another grin, his embarrassment forgotten. "They are harmless."

"Harmless," she repeated in disbelief.

"Aye. Unless you're a silly sheep."

He was plainly teasing. She didn't care. She looked at Madadh, quivering like an arrow in a bow, and then at the track ahead, winding through the rocks. "So I'm a sheep," she said. "Let's go back."

"*Baaa,*" Iestyn said.

She stuck out her tongue at him. They turned to begin their descent.

And froze as a great gray wolf glided from the shadow of the rocks and blocked their way.

Madadh whimpered.

Iestyn paled. "Shit."

Fear raked claws down Lucy's throat. "You said the wolves were harmless."

"They are." Iestyn reached down cautiously, never taking his eyes from the wolf, and drew a long black knife like Conn's from a sheath at his knee. "These are not wolves. Not anymore."

Oh, God.

She worked moisture into her mouth. "What—"

"Demons."

Panic, blinding, bright, went off in her head. She blinked to clear her vision and saw more shapes slinking, circling on either side, sticking close to the rocks. She clenched her empty hands.

"Behind me," Iestyn ordered, his young voice strained. "Do not run. They attack from behind."

She stumbled to obey. Stones littered the track at her feet. She stooped, grabbing one in each hand, and faced the head of the path.

The wolf confronting Iestyn snapped and snarled. Threatening. Testing. Lucy almost turned.

And would have missed its two companions as they drifted into sight, silent as smoke.

Her knees shook. Her arms trembled. Madadh growled low in his throat.

Iestyn shouted. "Go! I command you!"

The wolves in front of Lucy bared their teeth, laughing. Madadh bristled and shook.

"Conn," Lucy whispered.

Regret opened like a chasm in her heart. Her palms were slippery with sweat. She gripped the stones tighter. She didn't want to leave him. Not like this, with so much unspoken and unresolved between them.

The shadow in front of her leaped. She screamed. She had a confused flash of heat, teeth, and eyes before Madadh lunged to meet it, their bodies colliding with a force that sent them rolling over the ground, jaws snapping, claws raking.

She heard Iestyn grunt, felt him stagger behind her as he absorbed another attack. Everything was noise and fear and confusion. She threw a rock and missed. Threw another and watched it bounce uselessly off the wolf's side. The circling wolves edged closer. Behind her, Iestyn lurched and thrust. Something warm spurted over her foot.

She looked down. *Blood.*

Madadh yelped.

And Lucy got mad.

Rage flooded her gut, filled her chest, flowed through her trembling legs to stiffen them. She felt it coiling, writhing and rising within her, broad, slippery ripples of fury rolling through her body to her brain, too much to control, too huge to contain. Pain knifed her brain, shards of brightness behind her eyes. Flinging out her empty arms, she shouted, "Enough!"

The word went out from her like lightning and struck the snarling, writhing knot that was Madadh and the wolf. She heard a cry from Iestyn of pain or surprise, smelled scorched meat and burning hair, watched horrified as both animals jerked and collapsed.

Oh, God. Oh, God. Her hands fell. Her breath sobbed. *What had she done?*

The hound staggered bleeding to its four feet. The wolf stayed motionless on the ground.

Iestyn drew a sharp breath behind her.

She turned.

The boy swayed above the slumped carcass of the first wolf. Beneath his tawny mop, his face gleamed pasty white. Blood crawled from a jagged bite on his arm. His knife dangled uselessly at his side.

As she watched, he grinned shakily and switched the bloody blade to his other hand.

"That's two," he said.

Lucy swallowed and nodded, trying hard not to throw up.

More shadows boiled out of the rocks. More wolves lurking, circling.

Waiting.

14

≈

THE LONG BLACK SHADOW OF THE KEEP CRAWLED
across the cobblestones, measuring time like a giant sun-
dial.

Impatience surged thick through Conn's veins. He did
not want to be here in the shadows of the courtyard listening to Griff.

Lucy burned in his brain as she had in his visions, her
long wary body and lean, composed face, her hair as ripe
as grain. He carried her image in his mind—Lucy, waking
and sleeping, naked and coming. With him. Under him.

He was lost in her, as captivated by this mortal woman
as his father had been by the sea.

The comparison made him grit his teeth. He was not
Llyr, to shuck responsibilities along with his clothes.

And if he had not been so obviously preoccupied this
morning—*obsessed, besotted*—perhaps Griff would not
be carrying tales of his wardens conspiring in corners.

"You think Morgan would negotiate with Hell behind
my back?"

Griff's dark eyes were somber. "I do not know if he would go that far. It may be his pledge to your father still holds him."

"His loyalty must be to our people. Not the king."

"Which people? Morgan is finfolk."

"The finfolk are as much children of the sea as the selkie. If he serves one, he serves us all. We cannot survive if our loyalties are divided."

"Are you speaking of Morgan?" Griff asked steadily. "Or yourself?"

Conn drew a short, sharp breath. "My loyalties are not in question. We need children. A child, a daughter of Atargatis, to fulfill the prophecy."

"Morgan is concerned a pregnancy would provoke further conflict with Hell."

The children of fire would not welcome a shift in the present balance of power.

Conn's hands clenched. His head throbbed. "I will not give her up."

"Because she carries the bloodline."

Because he could not contemplate his existence any longer without her, her quiet tenacity, her fierce sexuality, her eyes, deep and secret as the sea.

"I will not give her up," he repeated more quietly.

Griff sighed. "Then you must speak with Morgan."

"Very well." Another delay to keep him from Lucy. Damn it. "And you can talk to Enya."

"Enya, lord?"

"Yes." Conn smiled thinly. "Since you understand women so well."

"Not that one." Griff cleared his throat. "Why not let your lady win the wardens over? Surely if they met her—"

"They despise her because she is human," Conn said. "All the meetings in the world will not change that."

"No human in the world can do what she can do," Griff argued.

"I will not subject her to—"

"*Conn.*"

His name. Her voice. The whisper sailed on the wind, snagging like a barb in his brain.

He jerked, a fish on the line.

Lucy?

His heart hammered. He felt the spider touch of trouble on the back of his neck, a crawling fear inside his skin, as his gaze swept the courtyard.

"My prince? What is it?" Griff asked.

Conn's head pounded. The shadows beneath the towers were empty. But the sound of her voice was fixed in his mind, a jagged silver hook connected to a line as fine as filament.

His tongue felt thick. "Where is she?" he asked hoarsely.

"Enya?"

"My lady."

Griff's face creased in concern. "In your solar, I assume."

No.

Lucy.

Something was wrong.

Conn's lungs constricted. He stepped into the slanting sunlight, into the warm current of air, following the tug of his whispered name. The line stretched over the castle walls and away, floating on the wind like a strand of Lucy's hair. Fragile. Golden.

Where are you?

His questing thought spun along the bright thread, drawn from the marrow of his bones, spilling like blood from his heart.

She was out there somewhere. Beyond the castle walls. He felt her trembling like a kite in the grip of the wind, a vibration in his fingertips and his mind.

Griff stirred. "My lord."

The interruption almost yanked Conn back, but he clung to that spark of connection, pouring himself along the filament, spooling out his power, trying to reach her, desperate to touch . . .

The thread snapped.

His breath went. *No.*

The contact broke.

Lucy.

She was gone.

Conn's blood roared in his ears.

"My prince?" Griff's voice, worried. "My lord, are you all right?"

*   *   *

"Are you all right?"

Iestyn's strained voice penetrated the roaring in Lucy's ears, pierced the fog in her head.

The last attack had almost done them in. Done her in. She was reeling with shock, bone-weary with fatigue.

"Don't run," Iestyn had ordered.

Not a problem. She couldn't move her legs. Could barely raise her arms. Her shoulders were on fire, her vision hazy with exhaustion.

"Fine," she croaked.

Alive, anyway. Breathing. At least, she told herself the whimpering gasps that escaped her throat qualified as breathing.

Madadh made the same sounds at her feet. Her nails curled into her palms. Somehow the hound had crawled to her, smearing an ominous dark trail behind him in the dirt. She had blasted the wolf that ripped open the dog's belly, but she could not kneel to care for or comfort him, could not take her eyes off the snarling, snapping pack prowling the perimeter of their dead.

She shifted. Trembled. Wolves attacked the weak. She had to be strong.

But the evil they faced sapped her strength and drained her will. She felt its malice like a weight in her chest, a pressure in her head, pushing, always pushing against her mind's defenses, poking cruel fingers through the chinks, searching for an opening, probing for a weakness.

She blocked it out. Blocked everything out, the grief and the fear and the stench of blood and burnt flesh. She could no longer smell the orchard or the sea.

Soon the pressure in her head wouldn't matter. Each rush drew the circle tighter like a noose. Soon there would be no room left to strike, and she and Iestyn would go down under a mass of thrashing bodies and rending white fangs.

Her eyes stung with sweat. With tears. Her shoulders ached. What more could they do, a bleeding boy and an exhausted girl against a pack of wolves? Her legs shook. How long could they stand?

She blinked. Too many teeth. Too many eyes. Circling, with all the menace and none of the grace of wolves.

She had never been a fighter. Caleb was the fighter, steadfast and strong. Like the lead soldier in the fairy tale he used to read to her. She would have liked to see Caleb one more time. Caleb and his gun. The thought made her smile. She would have liked to say good-bye.

Her smile faded. Would her family even know what had happened to her?

And Conn. She would have liked to . . .

No.

Her resolve was a lump in her stomach, plain and cold

and about as heroic as oatmeal. But she was not ready to say good-bye to Conn.

She licked her cracked lips. In her life, in her world, the cavalry didn't ride to the rescue. Her prince never came. That hadn't stopped her from trying.

From surviving.

She uncurled her bloody palms. She stiffened her wobbly knees. When the demons sprang again, she was ready for them.

*   *   *

Conn smelled smoke.

Seared flesh. Scorched earth. The sizzle of ozone. All carried on the wind like the stench of branding or the plume of a funeral pyre.

Griff coughed.

Brychan swore.

They were already breathing hard, running hard. In the sea, they were all power and grace. On land, they ran, feet pounding, legs pumping, weapons hastily belted on, bouncing against backs and thighs. Sweat trickled down faces and chests.

Conn had sacrificed stealth for speed, numbers for readiness. It took time to assemble; longer to arm. Time he did not have.

Barely a dozen wardens followed as he bolted out the gate, as he trampled the orchard flowers and thundered up the slope, following the broken whisper of his name.

The air felt viscous. Thick. Conn floundered like a mortal in the sea, carried on a wave of dread.

The acrid smell of smoke and blood drifted from the rocks like the reek of a human battlefield. A bird cried in outrage, rising like a black flag in the sky.

Air knifed his lungs. *Please, God . . .*

The selkie did not pray.

Please God, let her be safe.

A wolf—*not a wolf*—materialized snarling underfoot, hot fetid breath, red, wet gullet, eyes filled with flame and hate.

Demon.

Conn caught the flash of teeth, the threat of claws as he swung, taking off its head in a single stroke. Blood spurted from severed organs. The wolf's body fell, twitching, the spirit within extinguished.

He heard an ululating cry, not animal, torn from an animal's throat.

Conn leaped over the corpse, aware of other shadows, other battles around him, growls, howls, the clash of bone and steel. *Please, God.* He ran up the track, between the standing stones.

And froze at the tableau between the rocks.

Lucy. And Iestyn. They were propped back to back like a pair of stick figures, looking as if a hard wind would blow them over. Their faces were sallow with fear or loss of blood. The boy's right arm dangled, dark and useless.

Conn inhaled. The smell of sulfur and singeing hair scored the back of his throat. Lucy's torn hair rippled in the wind like a battle standard. Blood stained her skirt. She stood awkwardly, straddling a crumpled rag, a toy dog with the stuffing torn out.

Conn's chest tightened.

She swayed like a tired horse, her naked hands raised. No weapon. Yet ringed around them, like the fallen apples under the trees below, was a black and bloody harvest of dead wolves.

And beyond that . . .

The rocks boiled with darkness.

Conn shouted and charged up the hill.

The scene wavered and dissolved in a rush of noise and heat. Adrenaline pumped. Time slowed. Conn swung and struck, slitting throats. Windpipes. Fast, hard, bloody work. Demons were immortal, but like the fire they sprang from, they needed oxygen to survive. They could not stay in a host that could not breathe. Around him he heard grunts, growls, and thuds.

The wolves retreated.

The wardens plunged in pursuit.

Conn stepped over the ring of dead and pulled Lucy into his arms, desperate to touch her, to assure himself she was safe. She lunged at the same time, wrapping her arms around his neck, her body pressed tight to his. She was shaking hard enough to disguise his own tremors, her damp face buried against him. Her tears scalded his throat.

His shaking hands raced over her, shoulders, back, ribs. She was whole. Unbleeding. Unbroken. *Thank you, God.*

"I'm sorry," she mumbled against his neck. "So sorry."

What was she apologizing for?

"Ssh." He petted her. "You are safe now."

He raised his head and met Morgan's eyes. The fin lord's lip curled. Conn was suddenly conscious of embracing his human lover in full sight of his assembled wardens. His hands tightened. He returned Morgan's stare without expression. *I will not give her up.*

His small force drifted back by ones and twos, the wolves slaughtered, the demons dispatched.

Conn looked down at the top of Lucy's head. How had she and Iestyn held off the wolves so long?

"Iestyn . . ." she said.

"Is all right. Everything will be all right. Brave girl."

She drew back. "I wasn't brave."

"You fooled me," Iestyn said behind her.

"I'm sorry," she repeated, her eyes huge in her white face.

Was she possessed? *No.* Then . . .

Her gaze dropped to Madadh, motionless at her feet.

Ah. Comprehension slid into Conn like a blade, scoring his ribs, piercing his heart.

"It's all right," he lied gently.

All things mortal died. At least he had not lost her. This time.

He crouched beside the dog and laid his hand on Madadh's head. The bones were sharp beneath the blood-matted fur. The dog's breath rattled, warm and weak, its golden eyes already glazed. Its rear paws twitched, as if the hound dreamed beneath his master's desk in front of the fire.

Conn's eyes stung, dry and gritty. He did not cry. The selkie did not weep. Only a dog, he told himself fiercely. One of hundreds over the centuries, loyal and replaceable.

His throat closed with grief.

He could not heal its wounds. That gift had been lost to his people since before his father's reign.

This much he could do.

He stroked the stiff fur. He sent his power through his hands, through twisted entrails, torn flesh, and tortured nerves, taking the hurt into himself, easing the dog's pain and its passage.

Lucy kneeled beside him, her hair falling over her face and his hands, weeping the tears that burned at the back of his throat.

"Good-bye, friend," he whispered hoarsely. "Sleep in peace and dream of rabbits."

Lucy sniffed. A single tear dripped onto the back of Conn's hand.

And sizzled.

He caught his breath in pain and surprise as the heat of that single drop pierced his hand like a nail and burned in his palm. Beside him, Lucy glowed, radiating waves like warmth. He grabbed her hand and set it on top of his, their fingers tangling in the dog's bloody fur. He felt the magic pulse through their link, the scalding current that rose in her roll through him in long, low, billowing breakers, flooding all the arid, empty recesses of his parched spirit. He was drenched, drowning in power. It poured into him, stomach and lungs, mouth and eyes, flowing, filling, surging, spilling in a great golden wave. Dimly, he heard shouting, like rescuers calling from shore, as the flood of power caught and carried him away. He fought to channel the stream that thundered through him, shunting it along the paths of Madadh's pain, feeling it foam and churn amid the welter of ruined tissue and failing organs.

The dog yawned, shuddered, lurched. More shouts, more shadows, a flurry of movement along the edges of the current. Magic roared in his head, poured through his veins.

The wave crashed and shattered in dazzling, jewel-bright splinters of azure and topaz. Lucy cried out and slumped. The ripples of magic drained away, leaving Conn blind and breathless in its wake, the hound whole and the girl unconscious on the bloody ground.

*   *   *

Consciousness returned in chinks and chunks, like light fitting itself around a window shade. Lucy sighed. Her bed was lumpy. Her cheek pillowed against something hard. Hard and surprisingly comfortable.

She didn't want to move. Heck, she wasn't sure she could open her eyes. She felt weak, light-headed, and empty, as if she had been in bed for days with the flu.

"Shall we build a litter for the *targair inghean*?" someone asked.

"No." The deep voice stirred her hair. She smelled grime and sweat and the wild salt tang of the sea. "I will carry her."

She knew that voice. Conn's voice. She was sitting on his lap, cradled in his arms. His hard chest moved with his breath, up and down, like the ocean.

"My prince . . . your hand . . ."

"I will carry her," Conn repeated in his arrogant, don't-mess-with-me tone.

She smiled against his shoulder.

The arm that was her pillow tensed. "Lucy." A single word, hoarse with hope.

She found she could open her eyes after all.

His silver eyes blazed in his hard, haggard face.

Her heart squeezed. Something had happened, she thought. Good? Bad? She remembered kneeling beside him, and the dog . . .

She moistened her lips. "Madadh?"

Conn's expression flickered. "Here," he said.

The hound pushed forward, wriggling. Instinctively, she put out her hand, accepting soft, wet kisses on her palm. She rubbed the dog's hard skull, patted its filthy, blood-encrusted side.

She blinked. Its intact hide.

"I don't . . ." *Understand.*

"You healed them," Conn said, watching her closely. "Madadh and Iestyn both."

Her chest hollowed. Her blood drummed in her ears. "I didn't . . ."

She stopped, remembering the great golden wave, the rush of power, too huge to contain or control.

"Iestyn reached for you when you fell," Conn continued, his face impassive. "And when he touched you, his wounds were healed."

Her mouth dried. She couldn't speak.

Iestyn knelt before them, his face white with emotion. He took her limp, damp hand in his uninjured right arm—

she noticed the black half moons of blood under his fingernails—and pressed the back of her fingers to his forehead.

"*Targair inghean*," he said in a choked voice.

Lucy bit her lip. "Um."

Iestyn's words rippled outward, magnified by the rocks, picked up and repeated by several people—wardens—standing around. Waiting. What were they waiting for? She recognized Griff, who smiled at her with cautious pride, and the tall man with silver-blond hair who had called her Conn's broodmare.

She lifted her chin. He met her gaze. His eyes were gold, like Iestyn's. An odd little smile touched his lips before he bowed his head.

She tightened her fingers in Madadh's wiry coat.

Griff came forward. He didn't kneel, as Iestyn had. But he, too, bowed, raising her hand and touching it to his forehead. "*Targair inghean*."

"Don't you start," she begged him.

"He does you honor," Conn said behind her.

She turned her head to look at him. "Why? What are they saying? What does it mean?"

"You are the daughter of Atargatis."

"So?" she asked, bewildered. "We knew that."

"The promised daughter," Conn explained gravely. "The *targair inghean*. The one foretold by the prophecy who will alter the balance of power and save our people."

15

≈⊛≈

LUCY PULLED THE TURQUOISE ROBE TIGHT. SHE
didn't like the way Conn was looking at her—not as the
woman he wanted to take to bed, but as if she were a puz-
zle he hadn't quite figured out.

He sprawled in the thronelike armchair on the other
side of the bedroom hearth, watching her from beneath
thick black lashes.

Earlier, he had disappeared while the members of his
household had bustled around her with hot water, towels,
and tea. They addressed her as "lady" and "*targair inghean*,"
but she did not know them. Kera appeared shaken, and
Roth was subdued. None of her attendants comforted her
as Conn might have done or teased her like Iestyn or
answered her questions like Griff.

She understood Conn's need to closet himself with his
wardens. Understood and resented it.

Now that he was finally here, she felt like one more item
on his To Do list.

Outside the tower windows, the sky glowed pink and orange, bright as the beach roses back home.

She had asked him for time.

But there was no time. The past few days had slipped through her fingers like a rope of fat pearls, each one precious, perfect, glowing, whole. Now the string was cut, and she could only grab after what they had shared before it was lost.

What they had shared . . .

She was not his broodmare, whatever those wardens had said. She was . . . what? How did he see her now? What did he want from her?

His hair was black and shiny from his bath. His face had fallen into its usual, inscrutable lines. Despite his stretched-out legs and half-closed eyes, she could feel tension emanating from him like the heat of the fire.

"How old were you," Conn asked quietly, "when you learned to fear the sea?"

The dispassionate gentleness in his tone tore her apart. She hugged her elbows. "I don't . . ."

Remember. The lie died on her lips.

Today she had faced down demons. Surely she could confront a few memories?

She looked at Conn's face, hard with kingship. She could at least try to be worthy of him and of her new title.

"Eleven," she said abruptly. "I was eleven."

"A difficult age."

She blinked, trying to picture the immortal lord of the sea as an eleven-year-old boy. "You remember?"

A glint appeared in those silver eyes, so that for a moment he looked like her lover again. "We have—we *had*—children on Sanctuary," he reminded her. "Many of them came to us then."

"So you know preteen girls."

He did not answer.

"I took childhood development," Lucy said. "I know adolescence sucks. But while everybody else was experimenting with nail polish and training bras and sneaking cigarettes in the woods, I was trying to cook dinner and make good grades so I could go to college like Caleb. And he was gone and my friends were changing and I hated it."

"You do not like change."

She twisted the sash of her robe. "Not really. I mean, as long as things stay the same, you know what to expect, right? You're kind of in control. Even if you're miserable."

"You did not want to Change."

"That's what I just . . ." She dropped the ends of her sash, realization opening like a chasm in her chest. "Oh."

Oh.

"We bring our young to Sanctuary so they will have someone to guide them through the Change," Conn said. His eyes were deep and dark. She wished he would take her in his arms again. But he sounded like a psychiatrist rather than her lover. "You had no one to prepare you. No one to guide you through your woman's changes or your first Change as a selkie. You were afraid."

Anger, unacknowledged, unexpressed for years, burned in her chest. "That wasn't my fault."

"Of course not."

His dismissal only fueled the fire raging at her heart. "It was her fault. My mother's. She could have stayed. She should have stayed with us. With me."

"She was selkie."

"She was selfish." The accusation burst from her aching throat with the force of pent-up grief.

"And you do not want to be like her."

"No."

"In any way."

"I . . ." Lucy closed her mouth. Opened it. "No."

"She would have come back for you," Conn said, and his voice was so gentle she almost didn't care if he lied. "If she had lived. She would have come back for you and Caleb both at the appropriate time."

"When you're a kid, you don't get the concept of 'the appropriate time,'" Lucy said bleakly. "You just want your Mommy."

"It is different for us."

"Not that different. You miss your father."

Conn flinched as if she'd stuck him with a harpoon. "My father did not die. He went beneath the wave."

"And mine went out on his boat and got drunk. Gone is gone. There's more than one way to be abandoned."

"Lucy . . ." Regret weighted his voice.

She shook her head. Her eyes were dry. Gritty. "It's all right. I'm all right. I'm all grown up now."

"It may be that your power focused on suppressing your Change," Conn offered carefully. "And the exercise of that power, the discipline of your gift, day after day, year after year, has made you strong."

She swallowed past the lump in her throat. "Well, that's what you want, isn't it?" she managed with only a trace of bitterness. "For me to be strong. For me to be the *targair inghean*." She stumbled over the unfamiliar phrase: *tar-guhr een-yen*.

His eyes darkened. "I want you to be yourself."

"Then you should have left me alone!"

Her words reverberated between them. She would have snatched them back if she could.

She stood there miserably. This was not her fault.

Or his either, she admitted fairly. Sometimes being able to see both sides sucked.

"I cannot," he said grimly.

She nodded, resigned. "Because of the prophecy."

His eyes blazed. "Because that was not *you*," he snapped.

"Cautious, fearful, unfulfilled, eking out some dutiful half-life. You are more than that. You deserve more than that."

"It wasn't that bad," she muttered.

Conn flowed out of his chair with a ferocious grace that made her pulse jump. "It is *intolerable*. To deny your nature . . . To give up your freedom . . ." He broke off.

She gaped at him, and she knew. She knew, and her heart cracked.

"*There is no choice*," he had told her. "*For either of us.*"

She had not understood then. He was as isolated in his world as she was in hers. As bound by his duty. As trapped by his destiny.

If she had been his broodmare, then he was, what? The king's stud?

She set her teeth. He had made her role as easy on her as he could.

Now she could return the favor. She could release him from at least one of his responsibilities.

"Intolerable for me?" she asked softly. "Or for you?"

His face was hard as arctic ice. "I beg your pardon?"

"You're as stuck as I am. You said so yourself." "*I am more your prisoner than you are mine*," she remembered. "But at least you don't have to have sex with me anymore."

She waited for him to protest, prayed for him to object.

He did neither. Only watched her with narrowed eyes.

She hugged her elbows, heartsick and determined in the face of his silence. "I'm the promised daughter, right? The one in the prophecy. So you don't need to get me pregnant."

"Are you barring me from your bed?"

His tone was still measured and even, but there was a turbulence in his storm gray eyes that raised the tiny hairs along her arms and made her hope.

"Not if you want to be there," she answered.

"You called my name," he said unexpectedly.

She blinked.

"Before," he explained. "When you stood with Iestyn. You called, and I sensed you needed me."

"I did," she whispered.

I do.

"There is a connection between us. I do not know what to call it. I have never experienced such a bond before." He prowled across the room, stopping in front of her, close enough to touch. "I only know when the demons attacked and the connection snapped, when I believed that you were taken or dead, the sun was blotted from my sky and the oceans ran dry."

She opened her mouth, but nothing came out, not even air.

"And then I saw you, fair and valiant, pale with fear and shining with power." He stood so close his breath stirred her hair. His deep look sizzled along her nerves like lightning. "You fill me. You restore my sun. You replenish my spirit. You know . . . Lucy, you *know* what I want."

Her heart shook. Did she?

All her life, she had dreamed of being wanted for who she was. She had never believed in her own desirability, never felt herself loved.

Never imagined herself the way Conn saw her.

She moistened her dry lips. She had never initiated their lovemaking before either. "Maybe you could show me."

"Indeed." A smile warmed his voice and lingered in his eyes.

His long fingers traced her cheek, cupped her chin. She shivered in anticipation and desire, prepared for him to claim her. His mouth settled on hers gently, almost delicately, his lips warm and persuasive. The tenderness of his

kiss stole the breath from her lungs and drew her heart
from her chest.

He raised his head. "This is not fair."

Her eyes opened. Her arms tightened around his neck.
He couldn't stop now. Could he?

"What?"

"You should have what you want, too," he murmured
against her lips.

His teasing was new and sweet, but her body had moved
beyond laughter. Her blood raced warm and urgent. She
arched against him, feeling his desire hard against her
stomach. "I'd say you're about to give it to me."

"This rug, for instance," he continued as if she hadn't
spoken. His hand on her hip caressed her lightly through
the slippery silk. He was only touching her with one hand,
but every nerve in her body was dancing and alive.

She glanced down, distracted, at the rich blue patterned
Oriental. "What?"

He brushed his lips over hers. His body was hot and
broad and close. "I had the rug delivered for you. To keep
your feet warm against the stone. But it serves me as
well."

"Um. Great." Why was he still talking?

"For example, when I do this," he said, and knelt in
front of her.

He slid open her robe, breathed her in through her gown,
nuzzled between her thighs. His breath seared her through
the fabric. Her knees trembled as he drew up the hem.

Long minutes later, her hands fisted in his hair, warm,
damp silk beneath her fingers. She was panting, twisting,
breathless, blind.

"Oh, God," she choked out.

He licked into her again, making her moan, and then
pressed a kiss low on her stomach.

"Don't stop," she begged.

"You haven't told me if you like it."

"I love it."

"The rug."

She stared at him wildly.

"It's blue." His gaze fixed briefly on the aquamarine at her belly before traveling up to her face, his expression pure male and smugly satisfied. "Your favorite color."

"I'm crazy about it," she said, shaking with laughter and need. Crazy about him. "Would you fuck me, please?"

His face was suddenly serious. "I want to make love to you."

Her breath went. Her heart stopped. "Yes. Now."

"On this rug," he said.

"Anywhere."

He pulled her down and loved her, rode her, until she cried out and came apart in his arms.

That night the sun went down over the sea in banners of scarlet and gold.

*   *   *

Conn rose on one elbow, watching Lucy's profile in the pale light of morning. His other arm draped across her waist. His hand curved over her thigh. Even in sleep, her face never relaxed completely. Her long, mobile mouth was closed and composed. Faint lines scored the wide space between her brows.

Only in sex, only with him, did she release her customary control.

The thought swelled his morning cockstand, nestled against the sweet curves of her bottom. He bent his head to sniff her thick, fair hair rioting across their pillows. She smelled of sweat and sex. Musky scents, earthy and arousing.

A wave of gratitude and lust washed over him.

He nuzzled her neck. She murmured and hunched her shoulder, making the covers slip, exposing the strong, smooth curve of her arm, the upper slope of her breast. Her skin was so smooth, so soft and damp and lovely to him. His cock twitched impatiently. He had to have her again. He had to have her.

Last night he had used her well and ridden her hard. It did not seem right to wake her.

He grinned against her tickling hair. So he wouldn't.

He bent her forward, so he could see the delicate bumps of her spine, and lifted her leg over his thigh. He cupped her small ripe breasts, brushed her velvety firm nipples, explored the curve of her belly and the dangling jewel at her navel before stroking down, down, to where she was still warm, wet, and swollen from their play.

He sucked in his breath. Perfect. She was perfect for him. She shivered and stirred as he slid a finger through her slick folds, swirling, sliding, making her wetter, hotter still. She moaned his name. He kissed her shoulder. She pushed back against him, eager, reaching. He nudged her forward, bending her over his arm. Her hand flexed, digging into his thigh. And then he slid home, sheathing himself in smooth, sleek heat. He felt her jolt as he thrust, heard her soft, panting breaths as he ground and rocked against her, *hot, perfect, his.*

"*Conn.*"

"I have you," he assured her.

He would never let her go.

Her contractions took her, shook her, seized them both. He gripped her hips as she convulsed, absorbing her sweet shudders as she bit the pillow and came over and over again. He wrung her orgasm from her before he groaned and slammed himself all the way inside her, emptying himself inside her, hotly, deeply inside her.

Slowly the room settled. His breathing returned.

He stroked her hip, his heart expanding in his chest. "Ask me for something."

She yawned and smiled all at once. "You mean something else?" Her voice was slurred.

He smiled fiercely over her head. "Anything you want."

She wriggled to face him, her hair catching under her. "Do you mean it?" She sounded almost awake now. Alert.

"Yes," he said certainly.

She had given him everything. Her body. Her affection. Hope for his people. There was nothing he would not give her in return.

She fixed those great green-and-gray eyes on him and said, "I want to go home."

* * *

Conn's face wiped clean of expression, becoming dark and flat as a chalkboard.

Lucy felt a chill that had nothing to do with the cold draft prying through the stones.

"Not to stay," she added hastily. "Just for a visit."

"I cannot let you go," Conn said.

Which sounded good, except he immediately released her and climbed out of bed. She made a grab for the covers as he stalked to the fireplace.

Lucy eyed the smooth, strong lines of his back with frustration. "I want you to come with me. To meet my family."

He crouched to make up the fire. The soft gray morning light slid lovingly over the curve of his muscled haunches, the flex of his arm. "We have met," he said in a damping voice. "I know your brother better than you do yourself."

"You know Dylan. Caleb is the one who raised me."

Yellow flames shot upward on the hearth. Conn stood

and faced her, magnificently naked, superbly unself-conscious. "So?"

She jerked her gaze from his penis to his face. Awareness of her reaction glinted in his eyes. It was another weapon in this quiet battle they waged, his experience, knowledge, and sensuality pitted against her will.

She raised her chin. "So, where I was brought up, when you love someone, you bring them home to your family."

Her heart banged against her ribs.

"Sweetheart." Something softened in Conn's posture and in his eyes. He looked almost . . . shaken.

Abandoning his post by the fire, he sat beside her on the bed, his weight depressing the thick, soft feather mattress. He took her hands, this selkie male who never touched except as a prelude to sex. His gaze, his hands, enveloped her. "You must see I cannot leave Sanctuary now. Even to please you."

She did see.

"Because of Gau," she said.

Yet an unreasonable disappointment hollowed her chest. Like any girl in love, she wanted the people she loved together around her.

I want Conn to say he loves me back. She swallowed hard against the realization.

He was nodding, agreeing with her for once. Maybe because she was agreeing with him.

Funny, how that thought didn't make her feel any better.

"I cannot leave my people leaderless," he said.

As his own father had done.

She admired Conn's devotion to his duty and his people. But the empty feeling in her chest did not go away.

"I could go myself," she suggested.

"No."

She knew that look. Every woman with a brother knew that look. "Just to let them know I'm all right," she said.

"They have not even noticed you are gone. Stay," he urged, his gaze warm, his hands steady on hers. "You will be safe here."

She wanted to believe him. But his assurances hadn't kept her safe yesterday, and her presence had put both Madadh and Iestyn in danger.

"What if the demons come back?"

"They will not. They cannot. We seal the springs today."

Lucy frowned. Not over the loss of hot water, but because she couldn't imagine the power it must take to close a rift in the earth's crust. "You can do that?"

"We must," he said grimly, releasing her hands. "Gau's trespass cannot go unanswered."

She watched him cross to the hip bath on the hearth. He rang a rag over his face, his armpits, his genitals, his gaze abstracted, his movements brisk and automatic.

Like Caleb's, before he deployed.

In Conn's mind, he was gone from her already. She recognized the signs.

Her heart sank. She was sick of being left out, tired of being left behind.

Already she couldn't leave the island or go beyond the castle walls. Was she going to sit by quietly, passively until her world narrowed to this tower? This room? This bed?

"I could help," she offered.

Conn dropped the washrag into the bath water. "It is a warden's job."

Her brother was a warden.

Lucy remembered the day after Regina's attack, when Dylan had been desperate to protect her. Lucy had stumbled upon her brother kneeling in the alley behind the restaurant, his hands splayed on the bricks and his face taut with concentration. She recalled the slow seep of power like water gathering underground, collecting in the cool, quiet chambers of her heart, pouring forth in response to his need.

She met Conn's gaze again. "I could help," she repeated, and this time she was sure.

Conn's eyes narrowed. "It could be dangerous. If Gau senses your presence—"

"Yesterday I blasted a bunch of his wolves," Lucy said as dryly as she could. "I think I already have his attention."

Conn's brows rose in surprise.

Lucy sat very still, her pulse beating in her throat.

Please, she thought. She knew he would not go home with her. He could not leave his responsibilities here. Not now. Perhaps not ever. But they had to find equal footing somewhere.

He could not enter into her old life. Would he accept her into his?

He stood naked before her, tall, dark, and formidable as always. A corner of his mouth curved in his slow, rare smile. "Then we will face him," he said, "together."

Her heart trembled. "You're sure?"

"Sure," he said and raised her by their joined hands and kissed her.

* * *

Caleb Hunter curled his fingers over his wife's smooth, flat belly. She didn't feel any different. Here or . . . He stroked upward toward her lush, full breasts. "You're sure."

Maggie chuckled and stretched like a cat, almost purring under his touch. "Yes."

"So soon."

"Yes."

Joy, concern, fear crowded his chest. He inhaled carefully. "Don't you need to take a test or something?"

"Darling Caleb." Her hand cupped his cheek. "I know how much you policemen like proof. But I know this in my heart. We are having a baby."

"When?"

"I would say a few months after Dylan and Regina's child."

So soon. The demons had targeted Regina as soon as she became pregnant.

"Is it . . ." He paused, worry weighting his tongue. Tightening his throat.

Maggie's eyes glinted in the dark. "Human?"

He didn't give a damn if their baby was born with flippers and a tail, as long as his wife was happy. And safe.

"Healthy."

Maggie smiled. "The baby is fine. I am fine. Never better."

"Good." He pulled her into his arms, holding her slim, naked body close. "I'm shaking," he confessed.

"I noticed." She kissed him. "Do not worry, my love. You will be an excellent father."

Oh, God. All the blood left his head. Good thing he was already lying down. "You'll be a wonderful mother."

"I hope so." She laughed breathlessly, sounding young and uncertain. "I do not have much of an example to follow."

Caleb thought of his mother, who had abandoned him, and his father, who had drowned his grief and resentment in the bottle.

"Neither do I," he said dryly.

But Maggie's joy left no room for doubts.

"Oh, your family!" she exclaimed. "We must tell them."

Fear stabbed him. "Not yet."

"Yes," she insisted. "Now. I'm so happy. I want them to be excited, too."

"Maggie . . ."

"Everything will be fine," she told him. "Everything is wonderful. What could possibly go wrong?"

16

❧

THE TENSION IN THE CAVERNS WAS AS THICK AS the steam or the smell of sulfur. Blue mage light ran over the dank walls and rippled on the surface of the water.

Conn had summoned the lights for Lucy's sake, to keep her from stumbling in the dark. Her eyes were not attuned like selkie eyes to see below the surface.

She did not belong here, whatever he had told her in the tower.

Conn fought to keep his face carefully blank and his thoughts even more carefully focused. Lucy had earned the right to stand with his wardens. And the full and unfortunate truth was he might yet need her and her power.

The children of the sea did not command this portal to Hell, formed and framed by rival elements, by earth and fire. Conn and his wardens could not close a gap between continental plates. But they could seal it, plugging the rift with their magic like crofters caulking mud between the stones of a house.

If Conn could bind their strengths together. He glanced

around the circle. The selkie were solitary by nature. They did not work easily or well together. Even here, even now, their energies pulled against his control, darting in every direction like fish caught in a net.

Deliberately, Conn relaxed his clenched fists, letting his thoughts float below the cloudy surface of the pool, sending his spirit drifting down through the warm, bubbling currents, spiraling into the murky depths, dragging the wardens after him like an anchor chain in the dark.

Sweat poured from his face. Rushing filled his ears, his head, as his spirit self sank down through the silken water, down through the mineral silt.

His eyes stung. His lungs burned. His spirit continued its descent, his body anchored at the side of the pool. The wardens' presence tugged behind him like so many buoys on a line. Lucy floated above him, sunlight on the water.

He must go deeper still to seal the portal.

Down through the scalding water where the blue-green algae bloomed. *Down*, until the heat killed all life and nothing grew, breathed, moved but rock and the water trickling through the rock.

Conn's temples throbbed. He had been too long in his tower, in the clear light, in the cold air. The pressure of the deeps crushed his chest. His doubts churned like sediment, clouding his mind.

And still he pushed, filtering down, down through tiny passages in the stone, seeking the bright molten thread, the rent in the world, the balance between earth and fire.

He could not breathe.

The roaring in his ears was not water, but fire. Smoke and darkness blinded him. Vibrations shook him, like the sound of an approaching army on the road or the shudder of a burning house before it collapsed in flames.

He had been noticed.

Someone was coming.

Gau.

Did he feel, just for a moment, Lucy tremble above him?

"*My lord Conn.*" The voice was in Conn's head, Gau's voice, unformed by lips or tongue but still recognizable. Breathless, if words without air could be so described. The demon lord must have hurried to intercept him. "*This is a surprise.*"

Conn's anger flared, a gout of rage that ate the soft tissues of his mouth and scorched his throat. *Not a surprise, you sodding son of a bitch. You violated Sanctuary.*

But rage was Gau's weapon, Conn recognized. To distract him, to deflect him from his purpose.

If Conn engaged the demon at this level, he could not win. He might not survive.

He stopped his eyes and ears. He made himself like water, clear and calm, sinking down through layers of stone, disintegrating as he went.

He felt Enya like a flash of quicksilver and Griff, steady and persistent as rain. Morgan cut his own path through the rock, a spear of ice. Lucy . . . *Where was Lucy?*

Fear flickered, bright, consuming.

Another trap, Conn realized, and focused his thoughts toward the portal.

There. A red, seething gap in the wounded crust of earth, boiling with energy. The gateway to Hell.

Gau was with him, in him, still. The demon's words burned in his mind like holes through paper, scorching, empty.

You cannot do this.

Do not provoke our enmity.

Do not . . . Do not . . .

Your father knew better.

Will you risk the peace for this? For her.

Lucy.

The thought formed, his or Gau's, their minds so close Conn could no longer separate them. The demon leaped on her name, fed on it, on her image, fueling his energy and Conn's fears.

She is not worth this.

The daughter of Atargatis, Conn spoke or thought.

But mortal. A human. She will not live. Nothing lasts that is not of the First Creation.

Their thoughts clashed, thrust, parried, their arguments sharp and flexible as steel. Conn had withstood the demon's assault on his emotions, but Gau's mental challenge lured him to fight. His intellect had always been his strength and his weakness. His arguments quickly outpaced his wardens. Soon he was alone, locked in furious mental combat with the demon lord.

You broke the peace.

You disturbed the balance.

An act of aggression . . .

Self-defense . . .

The portal blazed. Heat scorched his hair, his flesh, his his hope. His nostrils clogged with the stench of burning.

Give her to us, the fire sang, *and we will have peace again.*

Conn opened his mouth to defy the flames, and the fire rushed in, eating his tongue, searing his throat and lungs. *Give her to us, or we will destroy Sanctuary.*

He staggered. Mind and heart were dead and dry as bone. He must . . . What? There was something he wanted. Something he must do.

Close the gap. A whisper like water.

Lucy. Her name sizzled, a drop in his mouth. He gasped, pressed between hundreds of feet of rock above him and the fiery pit below.

Close the gap.

He shook as he laid down lines of magic, emptying

himself to form a tissue seal across the door to Hell, spilling himself into the spell.

Too little, Gau whispered. *Too late.*

A vision scorched Conn's brain and shriveled his soul. His wardens lost, trapped like sea creatures abandoned by the tide, each in his private pool, his separate Hell. Dying. Drying up.

The flames howled.

Desperately, Conn drew magic like moisture from his flesh and bone, poured it out like blood.

He drained himself out like a cup of water into the burning sand.

And felt his strength, his spirit, evaporate away.

*   *   *

Lucy's nose itched.

She fought not to scratch. She didn't want to make a move that might disturb Conn or distract the wardens from whatever they were doing, standing around, staring into the pool.

The surface of the water trembled like a dreamer's eyelids. The air was hot and close. Lucy measured the time in heartbeats, fighting to stay awake. What was going on?

In the beginning, she'd at least had a sense of the others' presence. They glowed in the dim cave like gemstones in a mine: Conn, brilliant and hard as diamond, and Griff with his great warm ruby heart. The one Conn called Morgan, dark as onyx; and the woman beside him, round and shining as an opal.

But as the minutes—hours?—passed, Lucy's awareness of them faded. Maybe if they were holding hands, the way children did in line, for comfort and to keep from getting lost . . . But the selkie did not touch.

"*I touch you,*" Conn had objected. "*I have been inside you.*"

The memory made her smile.

The blue lights had dimmed. An effect of the steam? Or was everybody else nodding off, too?

The heat was stunning. Numbing. Lucy's head drooped. A bead of sweat rolled down her nose and plopped onto her shirt.

With a surreptitious sideways glance, she wiped her nose on her wrist.

No one noticed. *Good.*

No one moved. *At all.*

In fact . . .

Lucy frowned, a funny quiver in the pit of her stomach. In fact, they barely appeared to be breathing.

"Conn?" Her voice shivered like the surface of the water.

No answer. The quiver spread. Grew.

"Conn!" Her cry bounced off the cavern walls and ran into the corners. Just like in her nightmares. "Griff? *Conn.*"

* * *

Pain consumed him.

Pain and burning. He stretched across the mouth of Hell like a prisoner on a rack, like melted wax on the seal of a bottle. His bones ran with fire. Flame coursed through his veins, pumped his heart.

Lucy, my heart . . .

He had not thought to love her. The selkie did not love. Or die. He would live forever in agony as long as his body above survived.

As long as his will held out.

He lay and burned.

* * *

Lucy seized Conn's arm, as stiff, as cold, as unresponsive as his face. Terror closed her throat.

"Help me!" she shouted.

But everyone who could help was already here, blind and voiceless as mannequins in a department store window.

She grabbed Griff on her other side. Energy sparked and snapped through her body. Her pulse jumped. Her nerves sizzled. Like jamming a fork in a toaster. As if her touch had completed a connection.

Griff groaned and took a shuddering breath.

Fear and urgency overrode her relief. She tightened her grip on his arm. "Conn?"

Griff blinked bleary eyes at her. "Too deep," he murmured. "I could not—"

She had no time for explanations. No patience. Love sharpened her brain. Fear pressed like a knife at her throat. She shook him. "*Help* me," she said fiercely.

"Lass . . ."

"Like this." She would not release her hold on Conn, so still, so cold beside her. With her free hand, she reached past Griff, fumbling for the woman on his other side. "Hold her. Her arm. We need to . . ."

What?

"Make a circle," she decided. "All of us."

Griff shot her a confused look but obeyed.

The woman beside him gasped and stirred.

Lucy danced from foot to foot in an agony of impatience as the wardens woke and grumbled, as Griff prodded them into a circle, linking hands like reluctant fifth graders forced to square dance.

The silver-haired man, Morgan, took the arm of the man beside him. He looked at Lucy, his mouth compressed. "Why?"

She bit her lip. She had no answer. She only knew, with a teacher's instincts, what to do in an emergency. *Hold hands. Stay in line. Stay together. So no one is lost.*

The pressure swelled in her chest. Her breath escaped on a sob.

Oh, Conn.

* * *

He wept without tears. Screamed without sound, without throat or mouth. Throat and mouth were burned away; being and memory, gone. Only his will remained, a spider thread stretched across the door of Hell.

Oh, Conn.

A name raked from the ashes.

His name, in a voice . . . *Her* voice. His beloved's. She was saying his name and crying.

Her tears were sweet balm and precious rain to him. He roused, trying to summon strength to answer, to thank her for her tears, but there was not enough of him left to respond.

He closed his lidless eyes and burned.

But her voice would not let him go.

Her words dripped into his arid soul, trickling along his veins, seeping into the marrow of his bones. Her golden tears opened channels for other streams to follow, springs of strength, rivulets of power. Griff's. Morgan's. Enya's. The streams joined and mingled. The gush became a spring, the spring a torrent that thundered through Conn like a flood. He was battered, blinded, deafened, grateful.

The golden flood rushed along the passage and scorched through his soul, drowning out the roar of the fire, inundating the threshold of Hell. He was taken up, taken over, by a great wave of power that flung him up and cast him on the shore.

When he opened his eyes, he was in the caves under the castle, and Lucy was holding him as if she would never let go.

She smiled at him with tears in her eyes. "Welcome back."

* * *

"Walk with me?" Conn invited in his cool, uninflected voice.

At the word "walk," Madadh lurched from the hearth, panting at the prospect of escape.

Lucy knew exactly how the dog felt. "Outside the castle walls?"

Conn nodded.

She eyed the sword at his hip. "Is that safe?"

"The portal is closed," he reminded her. "Thanks to you."

She shook her head. "I didn't have a clue what I was doing."

"You united us. You enhanced our power."

"Did I? I just . . . I had to do *something*, you know?"

"Yes."

He didn't need to say more. More than anyone else, this son of Llyr understood that you did what you could with what you had in the face of overwhelming odds.

He looked . . . not his age, exactly. But he looked tired tonight. Human. The strain of the day had etched deeper lines at the corners of his mouth and drawn the skin taut across his cheekbones. Concern tightened her throat.

"I'll get my cloak," she said.

He smiled at her, the rare, brilliant smile that transformed his austere face. But the shadows lingered in his eyes.

Warrior's eyes, she thought with another quick squeeze of concern. She could drag him back from the brink of Hell, but she could not ease the memories of what he'd suffered there any more than she'd been able to help Caleb when her brother returned from Iraq.

As she pulled her cloak from the wardrobe, a memory

flashed across her brain: Conn, carved of marble and moon-light, gazing out to sea, so weary, so proud, so alone.

Well, he wasn't alone anymore.

Dragging the sealskin off their bed, she turned to face him. Her heart hammered in her chest. "Ready," she said.

He froze.

She stumbled to explain. "I thought . . . After the day you had . . . Here." She thrust the pelt at him.

He made no move to take it. "You are releasing me."

Did she imagine the question mark at the end?

"I guess." He was a child of the sea. The sea could heal him. She had not attached any larger significance to her gesture than that. But . . . "I mean, yes. I don't want you to feel like my prisoner."

He raised his eyebrows. "You humans have a saying: If you save a life, it belongs to you. You saved more than my life today."

"You saved mine yesterday."

"After bringing you here against your will," he pointed out. "I merely restored the balance between us."

She swallowed. She was no good at putting feelings into words. Her family didn't. And selkies supposedly had no feelings to speak of. But a combination of hurt and fairness drove her to blurt out, "The hell with the balance. I'm not fucking keeping score, okay? I'm here because I want to be here. I choose to be here. Now. With you."

His silver eyes gleamed. "And you think to offer me the same choice."

"I . . ." She drew a sharp, bitter breath. "Yes."

He crossed the room in two strides. He took her hands. The sealskin fell between them. He raised her hands to his lips, one after the other, kissing the backs and then the palms. His lips were warm. So were his eyes.

"Then I choose you," he said. "Only you. Now and for-ever."

* * *

Later, much later, they climbed down the narrow rutted path to the beach. The sea had the texture of beaten silver; the sky was molten gold.

Lucy felt weak-kneed, warm, and satisfied. Every time Conn made love to her, she felt closer to him. More free to be herself.

Yet after only two weeks, how well did they really know each other? He had never said he loved her. She had never seen him Change.

She eyed the black sealskin slung over his shoulder and fought a little shiver. "You go ahead," she said. "I'll watch."

He tugged his loose shirt over his head. He had a beautiful body. "Come with me."

She jolted, the impositions and restrictions of a lifetime clenching her stomach. "Oh, I . . ."

Couldn't.

Can't.

Won't.

"You have been in the water before," he reminded her.

Her heart tripped in panic. "Not when it was this cold."

He stooped to unbuckle the knife from around his knee; divested himself of his pants. His long, arched feet were already bare. His toes . . . For the first time, she noticed his toes were webbed.

She jerked her gaze back to his face.

"You braved Hell for me," he said softly, holding her gaze. "Will you not come with me into the ocean?"

Put that way, how could she refuse?

She gritted her teeth and stood while he unfastened the buttons of her cloak, untied the skirt at her waist, and slid her blouse over her head. The clothes she wore on Sanctuary offered more coverage and fewer challenges to a man than her jeans back home. All the while he undressed her, his hands were busy, touching, brushing, stroking, cupping. By the time he had her naked, she was shivering with cold and fear and desire.

Her nipples peaked. She crossed her arms over her breasts, pressing her thighs together.

"You know, on World's End, when the ice breaks, we have this thing called the Polar Bear Plunge," she babbled nervously as he herded her toward the line of foam, his muscled arm around her waist. "But nobody actually goes into the water naked."

Conn smiled at her, his eyes very bright. "Trust me," he murmured. "Trust yourself."

"Easy for you to . . . *Shit*, that's cold." She hopped from foot to foot.

Conn steadied her against his broad, naked side as the water ran over her knees. "It will be all right. Hold on to me now."

She clutched him, grateful for his warmth. His support. "What about your, um." With her free hand, she gestured toward the shore, where his sealskin lay in a lump.

"Not this first time. Not your first time. You will need me with you." His face was serious, intent, like the first time they'd made love.

With another internal quiver, Lucy realized he didn't expect this to be easy. What had Iestyn said? *"The first time, you must generate your own skin from the inside. It hurts. Like your guts being torn out."*

Crap.

She sucked in her breath and waded into the icy water. Cold speared her feet, gripped her legs, swirled toward the juncture of her thighs. She clenched; inched into the ripple of the surf.

"Brave girl," Conn said.

She nodded weakly and slid another foot forward.

Pain shot through her belly, white-hot, nauseating. Her body locked. Spasmed. She felt like a poker was being driven into her stomach. She couldn't see. Couldn't breathe. Couldn't yell.

Conn's arm was an iron band around her waist. He held her upright in the freezing water as the agony battered her in waves. Like the worst kind of cramps, like what she vaguely imagined childbirth might be, like death . . .

Sweat broke out on her face. Panting, she leaned her head against his shoulder and prayed for the pain to end.

Surely it must end.

Conn swore and hauled her out of the surf. She stumbled. He held her tight, his body her shelter. She clung to him, trembling. He pressed his lips to her hair.

"I'm . . . okay," she managed. "Just let me get my"— *nerve*—"breath, and we can try again."

Maybe. If she didn't throw up or pass out first.

He frowned. "Something holds you back."

"Yeah," she joked through chattering teeth. "Incredible pain."

He shook his head impatiently. "Something else."

"You mean it's not supposed to feel like that?"

"Not without Changing."

She winced. At least he wasn't still suggesting she was suppressed or repressed or whatever.

"I did try," she said defensively.

"Yes."

That single syllable—"yes"—sounded good and solid. The sick feeling in her stomach eased slightly.

But Conn was still frowning, staring out to sea.

She bit her lip. "Maybe I'm not selkie, after all," she suggested.

He did not answer.

"Are you disappointed?" she asked.

He glanced down in apparent surprise. "No," he said simply. "You have accepted me as I am. I can do no less."

His near echo of her words made her breath hitch: *All my life I have waited to be wanted for who I am . . .*

"Come." He swept her cloak from the sand and wrapped it around her. "We must get you warm."

Her gaze dropped to the sealskin lying just beyond the reach of the waves. "What about you?"

His face set in familiar, formidable lines. He stooped for her skirt and blouse. "I will not put my pleasure before my duty to you."

That, she thought, was his strength. And her problem. She appreciated his care of her. But who took care of him?

"You can't always put off what you want, what you need, because you feel responsible for everything and everybody else."

Speaking the words, she even believed them. Who knew?

Conn's mouth compressed with annoyance. That was okay, Lucy told herself. Annoyance was an emotion. She could deal with his emotions.

"I *am* responsible," he said, very coolly and precisely.

"Which is one of the reasons I love you," she told him honestly. "But sometimes—now, for instance—those responsibilities can wait. I can wait."

"You should not have to."

She dug her heels in the sand. "Neither should you."

She could see the turmoil swirling in his eyes, gray as storm clouds.

"What are you afraid of?" she asked gently.

"The selkie flow as the sea flows. The water is our blood, our home, our life, our delight. Yet if we are to survive, someone must remain on shore to reason and to rule."

"Someone has to be the grown-up," she murmured.

"I beg your pardon?"

She shook her head. She admired Conn's decision to step up, to step into his father's role. Hadn't she and Caleb, in their different ways, tried to do the same? But doing so had cost them a part of their childhood.

It had cost Conn a piece of himself.

"You think if you Change, you'll forget who you are? That you'll stay out at sea like your father?"

Conn's face was bleak as February. "That I will want to. Yes."

"I don't believe it." She stooped, as he had done, and raised his sealskin from the sand. "You'll come back."

"You cannot know that." His voice was strangled.

"'Trust me,' you said, remember?" she quoted back at him softly. "'Trust yourself.' And the crazy thing is, I did. I do."

Contrary to all her expectations and experience, she trusted him not to leave her.

She held the heavy pelt out to him. "I know because I know you. We're connected. Forever, just like you said."

*　　*　　*

The wet leather of Lucy's boots chafed her ankles as she climbed the track to the tower. Madadh loped ahead.

Conn had insisted she return with the dog to the castle. As she reached the ridge, however, she turned for one final sight of the beach.

Her lover stood at the water's edge, a statue of male beauty cast in gleaming bronze. The setting sun burnished the hard curve of his shoulders, the long muscles of his legs, and set the gold medallion at his neck aflame. A burst of foam ran over his feet.

Lucy's breath caught. She hugged his shirt to her chest.

With a matador's grace, he swung the sealskin into the air, aided by a gust of wind that lifted the heavy pelt and blew Lucy's hair into her eyes. She pushed hastily at the blowing strands.

Conn was gone.

An enormous black bull seal reared on the beach in his place.

She bit her lip to keep from crying out in shock, loss, wonder, protest.

It was so big. He—*Conn*—was so big, at least twice the size he had been as a man.

It—*he*—hunched over the rocks, ungainly, awkward, and powerful. The water rushed to meet him.

The first wave rippled along his sides. The next broke over his head. The surf exploded in a burst of force and movement, and then he was beyond the breakers, one with the water, suddenly graceful, suddenly free.

His beauty closed her throat. Yearning filled her chest.

She had seen seals before.

In Maine.

At a distance.

She had glimpsed the sleek, dark heads appearing in the shining sea, rarely enough to *seem* like magic. Their eyes were wide, wise, and round, human enough to spark legends or stir the longings of lonely sailors.

Or so Lucy had thought.

She had never imagined anything or anyone like Conn.

He crested and dived with liquid power and fluid joy, moving away from her, heading toward the open ocean. *We flow as the sea flows.*

Her face was wet. She tasted salt. Spray or tears?

He would come back, she told herself fiercely. They were connected. Forever.

She stayed on the path a long time, her heart swollen with longing, watching the sea.

17

CONN'S SIDE OF THE BED WAS EMPTY, HIS PILLOW cold and undented, when Lucy woke.

She flipped onto her stomach, wrestling the covers and her concern. What did she expect? He wasn't some harried executive out for an after-work jog. He wasn't her father, stumbling home when the bars closed.

Conn was selkie. He was . . .

A scrape. A thump. A rustle from the wardrobe.

Her heart leaped with love and relief. *He was here.*

She lifted herself on one elbow, shoving her hair back from her face. Conn stood before the wardrobe. She glimpsed a slice of his naked back before his shirt dropped over his head. His sealskin lay like a rug before the hearth, the rich, dark fur gleaming in the last embers of the fire. Her breath caught.

Conn turned. "I woke you. Good."

"You're home." Her voice was husky with sleep and welcome.

"Yes." He strode briskly to the bed, his austere face relaxed and open, his eyes dancing silver. "I brought you a present."

She blinked. She barely recognized him in this mood, warm and playful. His early morning energy made her want to burrow right back under the covers.

And drag him with her.

"I can't wait," she said. "Give it to me."

Conn grinned like . . . okay, not like a little boy. No little boy had that wicked, knowing curve to his mouth. But he looked amazingly pleased with himself and with her. He flipped back the covers. "In the courtyard."

"Hey!" Laughing and shivering, she made a grab for the blankets. "I'm naked here."

"I noticed." The glint in his eyes became even more pronounced. She shivered again in pleasure. "Very nice. Come on."

Lucy gawked. She had received presents before. Cal had seen to that. On Christmas Eve, after the bar closed, their family would gather in front of the TV and unwrap their gifts to each other: a ball, a board game, a pair of gloves. But she had never had the experience of waking early Christmas morning and scrambling downstairs.

Heart fluttering with unfamiliar excitement, she dragged on her clothes and followed Conn down the tower's spiraling stairs.

"It's not a pony, is it?" she joked.

He stopped at the bottom of the steps so that she almost ran into his broad shoulders.

He turned. "You want a pony."

She stood on the step above him, their faces almost on a level. She smiled into his eyes. "Not since I was about eight."

"I am relieved to hear it," he said dryly.

Love for him tightened her chest. Her throat.

"Conn."

He waited, eyebrows raised.

He was selkie. How could she make him understand what it meant to her to have her desires considered, her needs met? By him. More than by any other man, any other human, she had ever known.

"I . . . Thank you," she said softly. "You've already given me everything I ever wanted."

His eyes deepened with emotion. His mouth curved, tender and amused. "You might have said so earlier," he complained, his voice wry. "I could have been back hours ago."

She laughed and jumped off the last step into his arms.

* * *

"A rosebush," Lucy said.

Her voice was flat. Stunned.

Conn shifted his gaze from her downturned head to the wet burlap sack on the courtyard stones. Four thorny canes protruded from the mouth of the bag. The damned bush had been the very devil to transport.

Despite his own disappointment with her reaction, he could not blame her for her lack of enthusiasm.

"Not much of one, I am afraid." It was almost winter, after all. "I brought it from Scotland. For your garden."

"You . . . dug it up?"

He remembered—too late—that she had problems with him taking things. He clasped his hands behind his back. "Yes."

"How did you get it here?"

Dragging it with him through the sea. "There was some little magic involved," he admitted.

Lucy regarded the pathetic bundle of sticks with their sharp, wicked thorns. Anything looking less like a rose-bush would be hard to imagine.

"There are seeds, too," he offered, feeling like a fool.

Never surrender to impulse.

He should have brought her pearls or gold, precious treasures to show her she was precious to him. But Griff had advised him to pay attention to her character and habits, to find something she wanted but could not ask for.

He ought to strangle Griff.

She raised her head. Her eyes were huge and translucent with tears. Her expression struck him like a quick blow to his gut.

"You brought me a garden," she whispered.

He shrugged uncomfortably. *Never admit emotion. Never reveal weakness.* Yet with her, his defenses crumbled like the mortar of the tower. "Only the beginnings of one. To remind you of home."

"Oh, Conn." To his horror, the tears welled and began to roll.

She scrambled from the ground and launched herself at his chest.

He had just enough presence of mind to catch her. Soft hair, soft breasts, soft, foolish, female sounds beyond his understanding like the gurgle of the fountain. He deciphered enough, however, to comprehend that she was pleased, that he had pleased her, and the slippery knot in his gut eased.

He stroked her back, pressed a kiss to her hair. An unfamiliar tenderness swelled his chest until he could scarcely breathe. All this fuss for sticks and seeds. She had not cried like this—noisy, abandoned tears—when he kidnapped her or when she faced the demon wolves or when she dragged him back from the gate of Hell.

"You . . . So thoughtful . . . Love it," she wept.

He was baffled. "Then why are you crying?"

She shook her head, mumbling something into his chest.

He put a finger under her chin and lifted her head. "Tell me."

"I know I can't . . . And I don't want to," More tears spilled. "Not to stay."

His heart froze in his chest.

"You do not wish to stay here." It was possible, he discovered, to form words, to speak calmly and precisely, even as his whole world turned to ice.

She raised those soft, drowned eyes to his. "Of course I want to stay," she said. "I miss them, that's all."

His heart began beating again. "Miss . . ."

"My family."

Ah. He released her.

Her teeth dented her lower lip. "It's all right. I totally get you can't leave Sanctuary for a two-week jaunt across the ocean. I'm sure they're all fine. It's just . . ." Her voice trailed away.

Conn clasped his hands behind his back. What had she said to him last night? "*You can't always put off what you want because you feel responsible for everything and everybody else.*" Yet she was willing to sacrifice her desire for his sake.

"Would it ease your mind to see them?" he asked.

She blinked. "You said that wasn't possible."

"Not possible to visit," he conceded. "That does not mean you cannot observe them."

"Can you do that?" Lucy asked.

"I saw you," he reminded her simply.

Taking her hands, he led her to sit on the edge of the fountain, bubbling with magic, sparkling with memories.

"Picture your family," he instructed quietly. "Imagine them all together. Can you see them? Caleb and Margred; Dylan and Regina; your father, Bart . . ."

Their names merged with the murmur of the fountain.

"All your family. All together. Now."

A wind swept over the surface of the water, shimmering with ghosts and reflections.

Lucy shivered.

*   *   *

A wind swept over the threshold of Antonia's restaurant, carrying the scent of wood smoke and fallen leaves.

Maggie shivered.

Caleb put an arm around her as the door jangled shut behind them. "You okay?"

She looked up at him with big dark eyes. "Did you feel that?"

"Yeah. Damn cold out tonight."

The snap in the air had brought the locals out to dinner. Caleb exchanged nods with the former mayor, Peter Quincy, greetings with lobsterman Manny Trujillo. Glassware clinked. Plates clattered. The smell of Antonia's red sauce and Regina's mussels in white wine and garlic hung over the dining room.

Nick Barone, Regina's eight-year-old son, hopped into the aisle between the tables. "Hey, Chief. Can I show Danny your handcuffs?"

"Sure, Houdini." As Caleb unhooked the cuffs from his belt, Regina pushed through the swinging door, her thin face flushed beneath a red bandana.

She gave him a grin and Maggie a kiss. "Special tonight is bluefish with capers, soup's minestrone. Booths are full, but I can get you a table. Unless you want to share with your dad and Lucy?"

Caleb narrowed his eyes. Bart Hunter went out in search of alcohol, not food or company. Most nights he favored the bar at the inn. "Dad's here?"

Regina nodded. "In the corner."

Caleb glanced over the dining room. Dylan had strolled out of the kitchen and picked up two plates from the pass-through. Caleb smothered a grin at the sight of his elegant older brother, the selkie son, the warden of the sea, bussing tables. He carried the plates to a corner booth, where Caleb could see a flannel sleeve and his sister's blond hair.

"They've been in almost every night this week," Regina continued.

A muscle ticked in Caleb's jaw. Not too long ago, he'd hauled his father out for breaking bottles behind this very counter. "He give you any problems?" he asked evenly.

"None." Her gaze met his. "He's changed, Cal."

Caleb grunted, watching the family tableau. "He going back to the AA meetings at church?"

"I wouldn't know."

Caleb rubbed the back of his neck. "Well, I'll talk to him."

"Dylan says he's been taking real good care of Lucy," Regina offered.

"That would be a first." Caleb shifted until he could see his sister sitting opposite their father in the high-backed booth. Something about the color of her skin, the expression in her eyes, nagged at him. "She looks a little off."

Regina shrugged. "She's been sick."

"We will sit with them," Maggie said.

Caleb frowned in concern. "I don't want you catching anything."

"Oh, please," Regina said. "Lucy's fine now. Nick said her class spent most of yesterday outside."

Maggie touched Caleb's arm. "I want to sit with them. They should hear our news, too."

"What news?" Regina's gaze darted between them.

Maggie's dark eyes shone. Her lips curved.

"Oh my God." Regina's mouth dropped open. "You're . . ."

Maggie nodded, her smile widening. "Having a baby."

* * *

The joy on her face, the pride in her voice, stung Lucy's eyes.

"Oh, that's wonderful. Isn't that wonderful? They're having a baby." She grinned at Conn through her tears. "I'm going to be a two-time aunt!"

"A child is a blessing," he agreed. "We have had too few."

She shook her head impatiently. "I'm not talking about the selkie birthrate. I'm happy for them. Aren't you happy for them?"

He raised his eyebrows. "I am happy for us all."

She opened her mouth. Shut it. Maybe his lack of reaction was a selkie thing. Or a prince thing. Or a guy thing.

He met her gaze and smiled very faintly, with amusement and affection. *Teasing* her.

Her heart somersaulted in her chest.

"My lord Conn." Griff paced across the courtyard from the keep. He sketched a bow to Lucy before turning to Conn, his eyes dark and serious in his broad face. "Ronat has discovered a new vent to the northwest."

Conn's features froze. "He is here?"

"In the hall, lord."

Conn released Lucy's hands and stood. "I must see to this. Will you—"

"I'm fine here," she assured him. "I'll . . . plant my rose-bush or something while you're gone."

His smile rewarded her for her understanding. "Get Iestyn to help you with the digging," he tossed over his shoulder as they strode away.

She watched them through the arch, their shadows stretching across the cobblestones of the outer bailey. The fountain gurgled and flowed. The pool reflected only the sky and the castle towers.

Lucy sighed and tried to recall her family's faces, to hold on to their memory in her heart and in her mind, to imagine their joy and their conversation. Did they miss her?

But no, they had the corn maiden. Sitting there with Lucy's family. With Lucy's face. A little worm of jealousy uncoiled and gnawed at her heart.

Taking a deep breath, she focused on the silver surface of the water. Think about babies. Think about nieces and nephews, a little girl with Dylan's black eyes, a little boy with Caleb's slow smile. She could almost see them, sturdy chubby legs and small grubby hands and skin smooth as an egg or the inside of a shell. Her heart was full and tender for them, these children who would always know their parents loved them.

The water shimmered deep, deeper . . .

"*How pretty.*" The voice—*that voice*—drove into her brain like an iron spike and ripped her throat. She opened her mouth, but no scream came out. "*How unfortunate they will not live to be born.*"

Her stomach twisted. Her mind shrank. This couldn't be happening. Gau shouldn't be here. They had warded the springs.

"*Oh, I am not here.*" Gau's chuckle drew blood like the rusty edge of a saw. "*I am already on my way to World's End to visit your family. Since you couldn't take the time.*"

She quivered, fear and guilt making her shrivel like a jellyfish left in the sun.

"*Do you know what I'll do to them when I get there? Your pathetic excuse of a father. Your big brave brothers and their bitches.*"

The pool roiled and darkened.

"*Perhaps I'll let you watch . . .*"

Her stomach churned like the waters of the fountain. She saw things, dark, horrible, vile things, wavering just below the surface, Dylan fighting and Regina screaming and Caleb covered in blood. Maggie, pale and torn, weeping as though her heart would break.

"*No!*" Lucy shouted, or tried to shout, but she had no voice.

Just like in her nightmares.

"*Too bad about the babies,*" Gau said, and laughed while the water ran stained with blood.

The scream built in her chest and in her head until her throat was raw, until her ears rang, until the pressure behind her eyeballs exploded.

And she never made a sound.

When the last echoes died away across the courtyard, she stood on trembling legs. Staggering to the corner by the fountain, she threw up on the cobblestones.

*   *   *

After the freedom and relief of the sea, the stone keep closed around Conn like a prison.

They all felt it, he saw, looking around at his wardens. They were used to the vast reaches of their own territories. Being on land, in human form and together, strained them as much as any demon threat. Morgan wore a perpetual sneer. Enya's voice was as brittle as her smile. Even Griff's normally impassive face creased in worried lines.

The weight of responsibility pressed on Conn's neck and pounded in his temples. It fell to him to unite them, to direct them, to protect them all, however uncomfortably they bore with each other or his control.

"We closed the door," he said grimly. "Hell has opened a window."

"Unless the vent was already there," Enya said. "We do not know everything that goes on in the deeps."

"The eruption could be merely a warning," Morgan said.

"Not a warning," Conn said. "A threat. We must deal with it."

Gau's words seared his memory. *"Give her to us, or we will destroy Sanctuary."*

He would never give Lucy up.

He listened to the wardens squabble like seabirds on the cliffs.

He had hoped that they would have weeks or months before the demons moved against them. Time to be together. Time for Lucy to understand her gift.

She was operating solely on instinct and raw power. In healing Madadh and in closing the portal, she had channeled that power through Conn. She needed to learn control.

Morgan said something that made Enya flush and snap at him.

Yet perhaps Lucy's ignorance was also her strength, Conn reflected. Deprived of training, she had no preconceptions of what she could or could not do. Her power, like her loyalty, was not dictated by logic or duty.

Lucy's magic sprang from love. From passion.

That love had saved his hound. Her love had rescued Conn from the gate of Hell.

Griff rumbled, intervening in the wardens' argument. Conn listened to them debate, aware as always of the tensions that flowed below the surface, threatening to pull them apart.

He needed Lucy's magic to save his people. But how could she save them unless she accepted she was one of them?

She loved him, Conn reminded himself. She had said so. For now, that must be enough.

He must rein the council to the crisis at hand. Conn looked at Ronat. "How active is this vent?"

"I cannot say, lord. I sensed the plume, but I could not

approach the chimney. It was too deep for me—more than a mile below the surface."

"Could the finfolk go there?" Conn asked Morgan.

"I could," Morgan said.

"Then—"

The door swung open. A shaft of sunlight spilled across the floor. Lucy followed it in.

For a moment Conn simply enjoyed the sight of her, long and lean and graceful, bathed in light.

Then he saw her face, and his heart clenched like a fist.

"What is it, lass?" Griff said. "What's the matter?"

She stumbled from the beam of light, moving stiffly, blindly, like an old woman. "Gau."

Conn surged from his seat to catch her.

"What?" A voice behind him.

"Where?"

Lucy raised her drowned green eyes to Conn. "In the fountain."

He supported her forward, his heart beating again.

"A vision," he said with relief.

Gau must have taken advantage of the opening in the fountain to bypass the wards. At least the demon had not harmed her physically.

Lucy clutched his arms. "I have to go home."

Conn stiffened. She was distraught. She did not mean it. She could not leave him. "No."

*　　*　　*

Lucy trembled.

He didn't understand.

"Gau threatened my family. I have to go home."

A muscle bunched in Conn's jaw. "You cannot leave Sanctuary."

Despair tore her. "You don't understand. I saw—"

"Visions can lie," Conn said patiently. Implacably. "Gau lies."

"Gau is on his way to World's End!" The words burst from her.

"Then he will be there before you," a voice drawled.

Lucy turned her head to identify the speaker. Morgan, with the white-blond hair and eerie yellow eyes.

"Whatever you imagine you can do," Morgan said, "you are already too late."

Too late. Horror shook her. The internal scream started again in her head.

Conn pierced the warden with a look before turning back to Lucy. "Dylan is there," he said soothingly. "And Margred. They will protect your family."

Lucy's visions rose like smoke, searing, dark. They choked her. "That's not enough. They need a warden."

"Dylan is a warden."

"Dylan's only one person."

"I will send the *whaleyn* to him with a warning."

She stared at him in disbelief. "My family is in danger. My brothers. A boy you've known since he was thirteen. And you're going to send a *warning*?"

Conn's mouth compressed. "Your family accepted their danger when they refused to come to Sanctuary."

"Conn." Her voice caught. "You must help them."

His face hardened. "My duty is here."

"What about my duty?"

"You are the *targair inghean*."

"Oh, let her go," Enya snapped. "Let her take on Gau on someone else's turf. That would solve our problems with Hell."

"One way or the other," Morgan said.

Conn shot them a glare that shut them up.

Lucy turned to them, her frantic gaze scanning the circle of interested, noncommittal, selkie faces.

"You could help. Help my family. Please." Her heart pounded. "Won't any of you help me?"

Griff shuffled his feet and looked away.

"They are human. Mortal." Her eyes begged for understanding. For sympathy. "They will die."

Conn took her hands in a strong clasp. "Lucy, Sanctuary itself is threatened. Without it, our people will die."

"You're immortal."

"Not in human form. Not outside of Sanctuary."

"So what?" Was that her voice, sharp and cold as the wind? "So you only live eighty, ninety years?"

His face set. "It is not for the children of the sea to grow old and die."

"My family won't have the chance to grow old. They'll just die. Gau will kill them. Unless you send help."

"No one can be spared from the defenses here."

"Then I must go."

"You can be spared least of all. We need you here. I need you here." Conn lowered his voice. How he must hate this display of emotion in front of his wardens. "I cannot do this without you."

His eyes—warm silver—bored to the bottom of her soul. Her hands trembled in his.

But her voice was perfectly steady as she said, "I'm sorry. I love you. But my family needs me more."

Slipping her hands from his grasp, she walked out of the hall.

No one moved or spoke or tried to stop her. She walked swiftly, so no one could catch her. She did not look back. She couldn't afford to.

Across the courtyard and into the tower, down the stairs, and through Conn's private door. Madadh whined and trotted after her.

On the path that led to the beach, she turned. "Go!" she shouted. "Go on. Go back to him!"

The hound pressed closer, thrusting its bearded muzzle into her hand. Her eyes stung. Her chest was on fire.

She stumbled down the track.

She had never wanted to be like the mother who had abandoned her. But she could be herself. She must not think of the ones she was leaving behind, but the ones she was leaving to save.

Lucy swallowed hard. Maybe her mother had done the same.

On the beach, she stripped off her borrowed clothes and folded them in a pile.

"*Something holds you back,*" Conn had said.

Yes. Pain.

Fear.

Love.

Naked, she stood at the water's edge.

Or nearly naked. The aquamarine glinted against her belly. Conn's words teased at her memory: "*The selkie do not alter or adorn their skin.*" Was she selkie? She remembered the tearing pain at her midsection the last time she had braved the water. Maybe . . .

With shaking hands, she fumbled with the piercing and laid it on top of the pile of discarded clothes. The tiny jewel shimmered against the rough linen like a tear. A promise. A farewell.

Her heart hammered against her ribs as she turned to face the water. Conn had cautioned her against going alone into the sea. What had Iestyn said? Without a guide, a selkie Changing for the first time could be lost forever beneath the waves.

But she was connected to the land in ways no selkie had ever been, anchored by duty and bound by love.

Taking a deep breath, she walked naked into the sea.

The water foamed around her ankles. Cold and apprehension shook her. She didn't want to do this. She had no choice. Admitting it was a kind of relief. No choice. No control.

She slogged forward.

Pressure built under her skin, beneath her ribs, deep in her gut, swelling in slow rolling breakers along her sinews, bones, and nerves.

She recognized the precursors of pain, the onset of the Change. She'd always resisted it before. Now she welcomed the pain, waded into it, with tears streaming down her face and outstretched arms.

She needed the pain to take her where she had to go.

Her vision blurred. Her hearing sharpened. Smells, a rich stew of kelp and brine, swept over her. The current dragged at her knees. She staggered, and the water bore her up, wrapped her in a lover's embrace. Pain ripped her belly. Confusion rent her mind as the world dissolved and swirled around her. Her limbs shortened and fused. Her body thickened. Panic closed her throat. She couldn't . . . She must. She struggled forward, wallowing in the surf, ungainly and powerful. Her skin quivered, her fur rippled under the caress of the water.

We flow as the sea flows . . .

The water broke over her head. Her heart leaped and surged.

Yes.

The waves whispered and sang. With a sigh of release, she surrendered her body, surrendered her will, surrendered control to the sea.

18

THE DOOR THUDDED SHUT BEHIND LUCY. SI-
lence fell over the hall.

None of Conn's wardens would meet his eyes.

"Will you go after her, lord?" Griff offered at last.

Conn's headache simmered behind his eyes. He was
aware of having upset her. Hurt her. Disappointed her. But
what else could he have done or said? His duty was to his
people, as Lucy's must be.

She was not thinking rationally. She did not grasp the
larger picture. She did not know Gau as he did.

"Go where?" he asked. "We are on an island."

And Lucy could not swim. He would let her cool off before he sought her out, before he found her and explained . . .
What? That her family must be sacrificed to her destiny?

Griff frowned. "Even so . . ."

"Oh, let the girl have her exit," Morgan said. "She has
earned that much."

"She has earned much more," Conn said harshly. "In-
cluding the right to be left alone."

*   *   *

Alone.

In the clear cold dark, sound rushed upon her. Thought faded and fell away. Her nostrils were tightly sealed, her eyes wide open, her body as sleek and barreled as the swells she rode. The pulse of the surge was her pulse. The briny beating heart of the sea throbbed in her chest.

She moved with the currents and by instinct, bubbles spangling the water like stars. Dazzled by the constellations of her breath, immersed in wonder and sensation, she spiraled among swaying forests of kelp, over ridges of sea flowers. Every quiver and vibration, the darting fish, the swaying weed, the ponderous song of the whales, was caught by her whiskers. The texture of the water rippled through her fur.

She surfaced, and the world burst on her, explosions of light and air against a liquid horizon, harsh and overwhelming.

Breathing, she dived again.

Her sorrow was a weight in her chest, her fear and purpose a pressure at the base of her skull.

But beneath the waves, everything was buoyant and clear. With a flick of her flippers, she wheeled and soared, breaking the flat planes of her previous existence like a bird. She had slipped the shackles of land, the burden of responsibility. In the ocean, she was graceful, weightless, and alone.

She was free.

*   *   *

Lucy was not in their room.

Conn stood in the doorway, aware of an unaccustomed hollow in his chest.

Selkie were solitary. He had always preferred his own thoughts, his own company, his own space.

Yet after centuries in the splendid isolation of his tower, he had somehow gotten used to seeing Lucy's face over dinner at the end of the day, had grown attached to her quiet conversation and her unexpected passion and the glow of her eyes by fire and candle light.

The hearth was empty. Lucy was gone.

Conn frowned. When had he begun to count on her presence, to want her company?

When had he started listening like Madadh for the sound of her voice or her footsteps?

Madadh, he thought. The vise around his chest eased. Lucy must have taken the dog for its evening walk on the beach.

Reassured, he crossed to the window and swung open the glass. The light faded from sea and sky, leaving behind a gray and purple luster like the inside of an oyster shell and Sanctuary like the rounded pearl at the heart of the world.

He scanned the scalloped line of foam rushing and retreating along the shore.

He saw the dinghy, pulled up against the rocks, and an unacknowledged tension left his shoulders.

He saw the dog, a long, lean shadow.

And there, dark in the dying light, he saw the red of Lucy's cloak, crumpled on the sand.

Conn's heart pounded. His eyes strained to see as his mind struggled to process. Lucy sleeping, Lucy hurt, Lucy . . .

Gone.

His heart howled in silent protest.

Snatching up his sealskin, he plunged down the steps of the tower, his own careless words drumming in his ears.

"Will you go after her, lord?"

"Go where? We are on an island."

And Lucy could not swim.

Could not . . .

Should not . . .

Buggering hell. He slammed through the postern door.

She must not go alone into the sea. Not the first time. Without guidance, she could become dazzled, disoriented, lost beneath the waves.

Lost.

As his father was lost.

Conn stumbled and burst onto the beach, more bull than human, blind with fear, uncoordinated with worry. Madadh guarded a slim pile at the water's edge. Lucy's cloak. Lucy's clothes.

Lucy was gone.

His heart turned to ice in his chest. She had left him.

He wanted to scream her name and plunge into the sea after her.

He fought the impulse. He had no way of knowing where in all the vast ocean she was. Or what she was. If she was Changed or lost or drowned.

His hands fisted at his sides.

He stood listening, casting his heart and all his senses out to sea to find her. But all that came back to him was the low roll of the breakers and the high seabirds' cries.

Madadh rose, ears drooping, skinny tail pressed between his legs, as if his dim, doggy brain accepted responsibility for Lucy's leaving.

"Not you," Conn said hoarsely. "Me."

He reached for her cloak, as if the touch of the fabric which had touched her skin could provide a hint of comfort, a clue to her presence or her fate. Something fell from the cloak's folds, flashing as it tumbled to the sand.

Conn picked it up, his hand trembling.

The aquamarine drop glinted in his palm, pale as a diamond in the twilight.

His heart clenched. His hand closed.

Dropping to his knees on the hard sand, he bowed his head.

Lucy.

* * *

Lucy. A finger touch on her soul.

She was Lucy.

Her name was a chain around her neck, tightening her throat. She dived to escape, but the sound followed her into the depths like the ringing of a buoy's bell.

She scythed through the water, pursued by her name, by the memory of his voice.

She had left him, the one who called her. The one she loved. She wept tears into the sea from large, moist, round eyes that saw in the dark.

But she did not turn back. The siren song of the sea rushed in her ears, drummed in her head, as she plunged in the wake of the sun, driven by a need deeper than hunger, more compelling than exhaustion, goaded on by visions of blood and tears that stained the water.

Wave upon wave.

Day after day.

She slept in snatches, bobbing in the waves, breathing brine. Woke and swam. Slept and swam again. Until her strength was nearly depleted, until her mind was almost gone, until she existed only as a purpose and a shadow gliding in the shadows of the water.

Following the sun.

Going home.

She carried the one she loved with her, a fish hook caught in her heart, and every mile she swam from him ripped her chest and made her bleed.

* * *

The wardens gathered around the ancient map imbued with magic on Conn's desk. The tall windows barred the tower room with rose light and with shadow.

As if, Conn thought, the castle already burned. He clasped his hands behind his back, refusing to entertain the fantasy or the fear.

"There are no signs of life anywhere near the fissure," Morgan said. He had just returned from the vent. "No squid, no shrimp, not even worms."

"Killed by the heat," Griff suggested.

Morgan shook his white-blond head. "Life thrives in the heat around the vents."

Ronat frowned. "So if there is no life . . ."

"Then the vent opened only recently. After Gau's visit," Conn said grimly.

The issue was not the cause, but their response.

On the map, the demons' activity was revealed as a throbbing red threat off the west coast of Sanctuary.

Never admit emotion. Never reveal weakness.

"How large is the seep?" he asked calmly.

Morgan shrugged. "The magma has not built up. But the cracks are deep. I could see the sulfur plume before I was down a hundred feet."

Brychan whistled, obviously dismayed. "We cannot seal such a gap."

"No." Morgan turned his unblinking golden stare on Conn. "I should say . . . not without help."

Not without Lucy to boost and bind their powers together.

They all looked at Conn, as if expecting him to produce the *targair inghean* from thin air and save them all.

Conn quelled the impulse to shout at them. She was gone. She had left him. He could not save them.

"Even if we seal this fissure, there will be more," Conn said.

"There are always vents," Morgan said. "Thousands of them across the ocean floor."

"But not this close to home," Conn said. "This goes beyond a diplomatic skirmish at our borders. Hell strikes at our heart. The demons cannot break the wards on Sanctuary itself. So they open a fissure mere miles beyond our shore to use our own element against us. When the vent erupts—and it will erupt—the surge will flood us. We must control the surge. And evacuate Sanctuary."

"Evacuate?" Enya's voice was shrill. "No. Without Sanctuary, we are no more than mortals. We must go beneath the wave or age and die."

There had been centuries when Conn might have welcomed death as a variation in his endless existence. Might have given up his responsibilities to join the king in the land beneath the waves. But to grow old cowed and conquered, knowing his death was defeat for his people . . . To die, knowing he would not see Lucy again . . .

No, Conn did not want to die. Not now.

He drew a breath. Loosed it. "Which is why the wardens will stay," he said. "To hold the island if we can. And to fall with it if we must."

Griff looked at him steadily. "And if we fail?"

Then his life and his love would both be forfeit.

"Then we will trust to be reborn on the tide," Conn said. He regarded the few scattered blue sparks on the map, a taste like ashes in his mouth. "The youngest will survive. Along with however many of our people still exist in the sea or under the wave."

"Survive, how?" Byrchan asked.

"There is a boat in the harbor," Conn said. "Iestyn can sail."

"Why a boat?" asked Enya. "Why can't they simply Change?"

"With the right winds, a boat will get them clear. And there are things I would save from Sanctuary that they could take with them."

Morgan lifted an eyebrow. "We flow as the sea flows. We have no need of possessions. What the surge seizes, we can retrieve again from the deep. What would you take from Caer Subai?"

Conn looked around the tower room where he had lived and ruled since before the *sidhe* fled to the west and Britain was overrun by the Romans and the Vikings and the monks. His room was furnished with treasures, his desk from a Spanish galleon, the fish-shaped lamp from the temple of Enki.

What would he save from the salvage of centuries?

"My dog," he said.

An embarrassed silence fell.

"How very . . . human of you," Enya said.

"The Creator gave us human form, too," Conn said. "Perhaps it is only our pride that makes us deny our human affections."

"Much good those affections have done us," Morgan said.

Another silence.

Ronat cleared his throat. "There is no sign of the *tar-gair inghean*?"

"No," Conn said shortly.

Griff grunted. "Well, if you cannot find her, neither can the demons."

"Unless she swims into a trap." Morgan tapped the other side of the map, where a smattering of red dots clustered, demons off the coast of Maine. World's End.

The possibility that Lucy might have fled to greater

danger twisted Conn's gut. But Hell's focus was on Sanctuary. The activity on the map proved it.

"The demons were already active on World's End," he said evenly. He put his finger on a glowing spark north of the island. "One of them, Tan, is imprisoned here, beneath the water."

Which accounted for that submerged stain.

At least he hoped Tan was the cause.

*   *   *

She came ashore in early twilight under a sky that smelled of snow. She raised her whiskered face to the breeze that blew from inland, scented with wood smoke and spruce. Recognition pierced her exhaustion. She knew this outcrop of rock and sand. This was the point on World's End, a mile and a half from home.

The gray sea reached long fingers over the frozen beach. The air was cold and still.

She struggled on the broken shore, levering her weight on the rocks. For one awkward moment, as she flailed in the surf, panic swelled and threatened to swallow her. Would she . . . How would she become human again?

Her flippers scrabbled. Her belly scraped the shale. She tightened her stomach to shove herself forward and sprawled naked, half in and half out of the water, her wet hair in her face and the sea foaming around her ankles.

Lucy gasped. Shivered with shock and cold. Her fingers curled into the gritty sand.

Fingers. She had fingers. And ankles. Toes.

She staggered to her feet to see. Ten toes. Webbed.

Like Conn's.

She swayed, unsteady as a newborn foal or a hospital patient after surgery. Naked. Naked and cold, tired and hungry. Her sealskin washed in the retreating waves like seaweed caught in the tide.

She raised her head, and the shore jumped out at her, etched in black and white, sharp and bright. Frost coated the rocks. Ice encrusted the frozen bladders of weed. The clouds, the same turbulent gray as the sea, were pregnant with snow.

Pregnant.

The word leaped in her mind like a flame, warming her, reigniting her sense of urgency.

Maggie was pregnant.

Lucy had to find . . . She had to warn her family.

She stooped for her pelt.

The fur rippled in the water. She hauled the heavy, wet pelt from the surf, streaming water. With trembling hands, she stroked the fur, a brindled silver gray, smaller and lighter than Conn's in both weight and color. In her arms, it felt no more than damp.

Selkie magic? she wondered.

Why not?

She wrapped the pelt around her like a beach towel, over her breasts, under her arms. Her skin prickled with goose bumps. She was cold, but not intolerably so. She should be freezing . . .

Her heartbeat quickened. And then she realized. She was different. Changed. Her journey through the sea had changed her. She wondered if, when night fell, she would be able to see in the dark.

Her stomach growled.

She stumbled over the rocks on long, awkward legs and tender feet, picking her way up the beach to the trees standing sentinel along the road. She needed shoes. Shoes and clothes and food.

She could not remember the last time she had eaten. Days ago.

As she stepped from under the trees, a light snow began to fall. The soft, wet flakes dissolved against the black asphalt, softening the outlines of the trees, blurring the boundaries between earth and sky. She trudged along the shoulder of the road. Going home.

She didn't want to be seen. Noticed. What would she say to a driver, a neighbor, the parent of a student, if they stopped and wanted to know why the teacher of the island's first grade class was walking along the snowy road half-naked and wrapped in a fur?

"Think of it as wearing a fur coat," Conn had said.

She smiled. *Yes.*

But the memory of Conn hurt her chest. Like poking a bruise. Like picking a scab. Bowing her head, she concentrated on putting one cold, bare foot in front of the other. The gravel stung her soles. Her stomach cramped. She was dizzy with hunger, trembling with fatigue.

Almost home.

She would not need to worry about encountering her father. At this time of day, he was always at the inn.

She spotted their rusting mailbox, lurching a little to one side ever since Bart Hunter swiped it in the truck one night. Staggering in exhaustion and relief, Lucy turned up the driveway and climbed the steps to the porch. The key was hidden under a lobster buoy by the door. But when she reached for the knob, it turned easily in her hand.

Sick panic lurched to her throat.

Gau's voice played in her head. *"Do you know what I'll do to them when I get there? Your pathetic excuse of a father. Your big brave brothers and their bitches."*

She whimpered and opened the door.

Old smells, old memories rushed at her, must and mildew and old carpet. The house was cold and quiet.

"Dad?" She croaked and cleared her throat. "Dad?"

Silence.

Heart thumping, she closed the door behind her. She

should go upstairs. She needed warm clothes and a hot shower.

She shivered. She needed to call Caleb.

She went through the dark house to use the kitchen phone. A loaf of bread sat on the counter.

Oh, God, she was so *hungry*.

She seized the bread, ripping open the plastic sleeve, and jammed a slice into her mouth. It tasted so *good*. Her stomach demanded more. Still chewing, she grabbed a jar of peanut butter from the cabinet and slathered a second slice.

She would call Caleb in a minute. In just a minute. She ate standing up, like a horse, tearing into the food like an animal, almost choking in her eagerness to replenish her body. Water. She needed water. Her hand shook as she reached for the kitchen tap.

She heard the creak of the front door, felt a rush of cold air, and froze with her hand under the faucet.

She blushed like a dieter caught on a midnight raid of the refrigerator, like a drunk with his hand in the liquor cabinet. Like her father.

She swallowed hard. "Dad?"

Thumps. Footsteps, coming down the hall.

Lucy turned, pulling her sealskin more closely around her, her heart thudding in her chest. She was home. She didn't need to hide what she was or be ashamed. Her mother was selkie. So was her brother. Her father knew.

"In here! In the kitchen," she called.

More footsteps. Bart Hunter appeared in the kitchen doorway, lean, weathered, and gray as driftwood, all the life battered and bleached from him years ago.

His eyes rounded. His mouth dropped open in shock.

Lucy's smile wobbled. So did her knees. "It's okay, Dad. I'm really here."

"What the fuck are you talking about?" he said.

Lucy worked moisture into her dry mouth. Swallowed. "I'm home."

Behind her father was a girl. A blond girl, with a face . . . With *her* face.

Lucy's heart lurched. *Oh, no.*

The girl took one look at Lucy and froze. A sigh escaped her before she fell, crumpled on the floor of the hall.

Lucy pressed her hands to her mouth.

Bart turned in time to see the corn maiden slither to the floor. He dropped to his knees at her side.

He looked up at his daughter, his face twisted in grief, his eyes hard with accusation. "What the hell did you do to her?"

"I . . ."

"What have you done to Lucy?"

Stricken, Lucy watched as he pulled the unconscious girl into his arms, cradling her head against his chest.

"Dad," she whispered. "I am Lucy."

But he did not hear.

19

"LET ME GET THIS STRAIGHT," CALEB SAID EVENLY. "You're not just selkie; you're the one the demons have been sniffing around for. The daughter in the prophecy."

Lucy clasped her hands together tightly in her lap. They had all come over as soon as she called, all of her family. First Caleb, in his marked police Jeep, to carry the unconscious-but-still-breathing corn maiden to Lucy's bed and convince their father not to call the doctor. Then Dylan, driving Regina and Margred carefully through the falling snow in the white restaurant van.

Bart remained with Lucy—the *other* Lucy—upstairs.

The rest of them sat in the drab brown living room, Caleb on the arm of Maggie's chair, facing the door, and Dylan and Regina together on the couch. Caleb's hand rested on Maggie's shoulder. Dylan had an arm around Regina's waist.

Matched sets, Lucy thought dully, like the candlesticks on the mantle or the fireplace tools on the hearth. She perched on the edge of her seat, her feet flat on the floor.

The whole setup looked remarkably like the family conference she had interrupted three weeks ago.

Only this time she was a part of it all.

This time she was the center of attention.

She had never felt more alone.

"Yes," she said. "But that's not why I'm here. I came because Gau threatened you."

Dylan leaned forward, his face tense and concerned. "I know the demon lord Gau. Know of him," he corrected. "He's a powerful enemy."

"And he's here," Caleb said. "On World's End."

"Yes," Lucy said.

"No," Dylan said just as certainly. "I've crawled over every inch of this island. I would know if the wards were broken or tampered with."

Gau's voice seared Lucy's brain. *I am already on my way to World's End to visit your family. Since you couldn't take the time.*

"Then he's on his way," Lucy said.

"Maybe . . . a visitor?" Regina suggested. "If this Gau person possessed somebody—"

"I would still know," Dylan said. "Newcomer or not."

"Nobody comes to the island in November anyway," Caleb said. "It's too damn cold for tourists. Even the homeless camp's cleared out."

Lucy's fingernails dug into her palms. She was exhausted and grieving and wracked with fear and guilt, and they weren't taking her seriously enough. They weren't taking their own danger seriously enough.

"Does it really matter how he gets here? The important thing is you're in danger. All of you. I saw . . ." Impossible to describe the horrors she had seen with Maggie and Regina sitting there. "He threatened you. Hurt you. In a vision."

Caleb nodded. "Okay. So you came home—"

"Swam home," Lucy said.

He shot her an older brother look, running his hand over his short hair. "Swam home to warn us."

"To protect you," Lucy said.

Dylan raised his eyebrows. The expression made him look fleetingly like Conn. She pressed her hand against the pain in her chest.

"Protect us, how?" Dylan said.

Lucy swallowed. "I, um . . . On Sanctuary, I was kind of a link, an enhancement. Like a . . . a channel for the other wardens' power."

Margred's eyes widened. "You were in the hall," she said. "The first time I stopped the rain."

Dylan stood. Paced. Turned. "When I warded the restaurant . . . That was you?"

Lucy nodded, her throat tight.

"Well." Caleb smiled at her wryly. Admiringly. "The daughter of Atargatis, huh?"

Tears pricked her eyes. To have him see her . . . To have him accept her . . .

"Conn knew this?" Dylan asked.

Pain speared her heart. *"You can be spared least of all,"* Conn had said. *"We need you here. I need you here. I cannot do this without you."*

She cleared her throat. "He . . . Yes."

"Then I am surprised he let you go," Margred said.

Lucy stared at her, stricken.

"Oh, my God." Regina's dark eyes widened with feminine instinct. "He didn't. He doesn't know she's here."

"He knows," Lucy forced herself to say. "We talked before I left."

"You mean, you fought," Regina guessed shrewdly.

"The important thing is, she's here," Caleb said. "She's home. Where she belongs."

Something turned over in Lucy's chest, like a small animal startled into flight. "Not to stay," she said. "I'm only here until you're not in danger anymore."

"And when," Dylan said, "will you know that?"

Lucy opened her mouth. Shut it.

Her brothers exchanged a long look.

"In the military, you have a defined objective," Caleb said. "Identify the threat, take it out. But you can't neutralize a threat you can't see. We don't know where this demon, Gau, is coming from. How he'll strike. Which means we'll be running patrol a long time. You can't leave."

Panic beat strong wings in her chest. She caught her breath in despair. *Never* leave? Never return to Sanctuary? Never see Conn again?

But she had always known in her heart that she could not go back, she accepted numbly. She had made her choice. Taken her stand. She was home now.

She had only herself to blame that it didn't feel like home anymore.

* * *

The earth groaned. The tower trembled. Conn shifted his weight on the castle wall, riding the swell like a man on the deck of a ship.

His world was already shaken when Lucy left.

The demons' work would only finish the job.

He gazed out over the horizon, a void where his heart used to be.

Griff climbed the wall to stand beside him. "They are gone?"

Conn nodded without speaking. The ship that bore Iestyn, Madadh, and the others had gradually disappeared from view, fleeing south before the wind he had summoned to carry them away. He had dispatched the ship at dawn, as soon as the first rumble made itself felt through the castle stones. There had been no time for long instructions, no delay for farewells, no interval for Kera's pleas to stay and aid in Sanctuary's defense. She was a talented weather worker. Better to preserve her gifts if the island fell.

At Conn's insistence, she had boarded the boat, seething with resentment and distress. Iestyn had been pale, Roth subdued. Conn had known the children from the time he had taken them from their human families, from the time they had played with the hound's many-times-great-grandsire on the rushes of the hall. They carried Sanctuary with them, a few small, precious objects for remembrance. They carried Conn's prospects for the future and a closely guarded portion of his heart. They carried his dog, tied shivering and barking to the rail.

It was unlikely that Conn would see them or that they would see Sanctuary again.

He watched until their sails slipped out of sight, lost in the hazy blue curve of the sea, sailing south toward the Azores. And then he turned and looked to the west, where Lucy had gone, taking his soul and his hopes with her. He watched the ocean where Gau and his cohorts labored under the earth, applying pressure to turn the sea itself against Sanctuary.

Griff stirred as another rumble vibrated through the stones at their feet. "My prince, you are not safe up here. Come down."

Conn shook his head without taking his eyes off the ocean. "Not yet."

The castle would not yield to the quake.

It would fall, if it fell, to the sea.

* * *

"What are you going to do about Lucy?" Regina asked.

Lucy looked up in mild annoyance. "I'm still here."

Forever, she thought, and shivered with loss and grief.

"No, I meant . . ." Regina's thin face flushed. "The one upstairs."

Caleb rubbed the back of his neck. "Damned if I know."

"Don't look at me," Dylan said. "I never made a *claidheag*. I don't have the power. But I think she's supposed to wither away when she isn't needed anymore."

"Perhaps she is still needed," Margred suggested.

Dylan raised an eyebrow. "Needed?"

"By your father," Margred said gently.

"Oh, Christ," Caleb said. "This will blow his mind."

"Or knock him off the wagon," Dylan said.

Lucy bit her lip. She remembered their father's face as he kneeled on the floor of the hall—"*What the hell did you do to her?*"—as he cradled the corn maiden in his arms. Her heart wept for him. For Conn. For herself.

What the hell had she done?

Caleb rubbed the back of his neck. "Maybe not. He's been going to his AA meetings. And last time I checked, Lucy—the other one—was still breathing."

"Yeah, but magic can't keep her alive indefinitely," Dylan said.

Margred looked at them both in dark-eyed reproof. "There is another magic that might."

"What magic?" Dylan asked.

Regina poked him in the ribs.

Lucy hugged her arms to herself. "Love," she said quietly. "Love could save her."

In the silence, a candlestick fell and shattered on the hearth.

The windows rattled.

Regina pressed a hand to her stomach. "What was that?"

Somewhere down the road, a car alarm blared, muffled by distance and by snow.

"Felt like a bomb," Caleb said.

Lucy's stomach dipped in dread.

"Or an earthquake," Margred offered.

"An earthquake." Regina snorted. "In Maine."

"Wouldn't be the first time," Dylan said.

Caleb nodded. "Nineteen twenty-six."

All the little hairs rose on the back of Lucy's neck and along her arms. "What are you talking about?"

"Last recorded tsunami on Mount Desert Island was caused by an earthquake in nineteen twenty-six," Caleb said promptly.

Regina laughed. "Boys and their fact books."

But no one else smiled. Looking at Dylan and Margred, Lucy saw a shadow of the same instinct in their eyes.

Something in Caleb's words, something in Dylan's expression, tickled her memory. Griff, his face grave, hurrying to find Conn in the courtyard, saying . . . What had he said? *Ronat has discovered a new vent to the northwest.*

"An earthquake," Lucy repeated slowly. "Not a vent? Or a volcano?"

Caleb narrowed his eyes, responding to some clue in her question or her voice. "What difference does it make?"

"Maybe none," Lucy said.

That's what she was afraid of. Maybe there was no difference at all.

The car horn continued to blare an intermittent warning.

In her mind, she saw the glowing line of fire in the caves beneath Sanctuary.

Her lips felt numb. Stiff. "What happens if there's an earthquake?" she asked. "Here on World's End."

Caleb frowned. "Not a lot. Some structural damage. We're mostly one- or two-story single-family dwellings. We might get some fires from downed lines or chimneys."

"Fire?" Margred repeated.

"The island is warded," Dylan said.

"Now, a bigger danger is an earthquake at sea," Caleb said. "Depending on the magnitude and the distance and the tide, you could be looking at some serious flooding then."

Lucy trembled. She had always dreamed of the sea. The sea and drowning. In her dreams, the oceans came for her, a hungry wall of water that swept everything, destroyed everything, killed everyone she loved.

She raised her head and looked at her family.

"Then I know where Gau is coming from," she said steadily. "I know how he'll strike. The demons caused that earthquake. And unless we stop them, they will flood World's End."

*　*　*

Lucy watched Caleb anxiously as he ended his radio call. Not because she didn't expect it to confirm everything she said. But because she did.

"That was the county sheriff." Her brother's voice was grim. The last time she'd heard him speak in quite that tone, Maggie was missing. "The U.S. Geological Survey is reporting a six point two magnitude earthquake south of the Bay of Fundy. Damaged cable lines from here to Halifax. They've ordered mandatory evacuations along Penobscot Bay."

"What about World's End?" Regina asked.

Caleb's mouth tightened. "No evacuations."

"In a fast boat—"

"Not in the dark. Not through the surge. The first wave will hit us in less than an hour."

Dylan put his arm around Regina. "What about helicopters?"

"Not in this snow. We couldn't get more than a few people off that way anyway."

"I only care about a few."

"Wait," Lucy said.

"Can't," Caleb answered briefly. "I need to sound the hurricane warning, get everyone up to high ground."

"The community center," Regina said.

Caleb nodded. "Tell your mother. She's mayor. Get her started making calls. We'll need volunteers to get the word out, move folks along."

"We'll need food," Regina said. "I'll load the catering van."

"You're pregnant. You're not loading anything," Dylan said.

She patted his cheek. "Fine. You lift, I'll drive."

Lucy pushed to her feet. She could feel the pressure building outside her, inside her, the wall of water bearing down, the power boiling up. "I need Dylan to stay with me. Dylan and Maggie."

Dylan's black eyes blazed. "Then you can help load the van. I'm not leaving Regina."

"Maggie's going to the community center," Caleb said. "Where she'll be safe."

Lucy's legs shook under her. All her life, she had shrunk from confrontation. All her life she had given in to avoid raised voices and hard looks. Until Sanctuary. Until Conn.

"You are stronger than either of us imagined," he had said.

Strong enough to leave him.

Strong enough to do what needed to be done.

Lucy raised her chin and stared down her brothers. "You can't save them," she said. "I can."

"You should listen to her," Bart Hunter said.

Lucy's heart thumped. They all turned.

The old man stood in the hallway at the bottom of the stairs, in almost the exact spot where Lucy had stood however many weeks ago.

"You should trust her," he said. "That was my problem. I never trusted your mother. I didn't listen."

Lucy's throat ached. "Thank you," she whispered.

Something flickered in his eyes that might have been sorrow or pride or regret. "You were always a good girl," he said and shuffled away.

"Dad," Caleb called urgently.

Bart stopped.

"You need to get the . . . girl ready to move to the community center," Caleb said. "My Jeep. Five minutes, okay? Bring plenty of blankets."

Bart nodded and continued up the stairs.

Lucy blinked back tears and found Margred watching her. Her sister-in-law's lips curved in a faint, approving smile. "Tell us what to do," Margred said.

*   *   *

Small waves slapped the rocks below the towers of Caer Subai, rushed in, and drained away. Conn watched them ebb and flow, ebb and . . .

Ebb again.

He sucked in his breath through his teeth, fear cold in the hollow where his heart had been. It had begun.

"Call the wardens," he ordered quietly.

As Griff ran to obey, Conn watched the water crawl away from the shore, exposing the fragile communities that live at the water's edge, crabs and mussels and shining weed, barnacles and starfish abandoned by the grumbling tide.

And still the water drained away, drawing down, pulled by the waves still building out at sea, the powerful waves of displaced water created by the demons' activity offshore. Soon those waves would reach the shallower waters around the island; and then the roaring flood would crest and fall on Sanctuary.

Unless Conn could hold his wardens together and hold back the sea.

"*I cannot do this without you,*" he had told Lucy.

He eyed the retreating water bleakly. He had no choice.

But he would have liked to see her one last time.

To tell her he loved her. To say good-bye.

*   *   *

The wiper blades scraped ineffectually at the windshield as Dylan drove their father's truck through the dark and snow to the headland above the point. Lucy squeezed shoulder to shoulder between Dylan and Margred on the bench seat. A cold wind whistled through the faulty seals. The ancient heater blasted at their knees.

"You do realize," Dylan said as the truck caromed over another icy bump, "that if we had any sense at all, we'd be driving the other way?"

Margred showed her teeth in what might have passed for a smile. "Bitch, bitch, bitch. At least you still have your pelt."

Dylan threw back his head and laughed.

After a shocked moment, Lucy joined in.

They were going unprepared into battle together. Her long lost brother. Her newly acquired sister. Her unborn niece or nephew. She thought fleetingly of Caleb, risking his own safety to bring in the sick, the elderly, and the reluctant from all over the island, and Regina at the community center, cooking enough food for the entire town. Or an army.

Whatever Lucy lost, whatever she had given up, she could take comfort in this moment. She could cling to this hope. Different as they were, they were family. And maybe, one day, she could have more.

If they defeated Gau.

If they survived this.

If Conn could forgive her.

Dylan drove the truck under the black shelter of the trees. Yanked on the brake. The wind howled. White caps and skippers' daughters ran in rows over the black water below. High tide, Lucy thought, her stomach clenching. That would worsen the effects of the surge.

Dylan cocked a brow at Lucy, letting the engine run. Steam curled off the hood into the night. "Cal said the epicenter was south of the Bay of Fundy. So the water will be coming from this direction. You want to try here?"

She consulted her bones, her heart, her gut. "Yes."

Dylan cut the engine. They climbed from the truck. The snow had stopped, but an icy wind whipped tiny crystals into the air, swirling like a matador's cape, silver on black.

Margred's face appeared as pale and perfect as the snow. "Now what?"

Lucy took a deep breath and held out her hands. "Now we stop this."

* * *

Conn stood on the castle wall in the path of the approaching flood, watching the wave roar out of the west, dark as an eclipse, loud as an attacking army, carrying destruction on its crest like foam. Spears of debris and pennants of spume flew before it.

His wardens stood with him, naked and unarmed, pelts at hand. Griff, sturdy as a tower, and Morgan, mysterious as the deeps, and Enya, blazing like the sea at sunset. Their faces were white with fear and stark with awe and alight with a terrible pride. For the sea was coming to the children of the sea, horrible and beautiful as death, and its voice was the voice of the deep.

And Conn knew that Gau had made a mistake.

For the sea was theirs.

They were united, for that one moment, in appreciation for the Creator's awful power and the water that gave them being. Conn poured himself out along the channels Lucy had etched in his soul, drawing the wardens' power to him, funneling their magic through him, until his gift thundered in him like the roaring of the surge and he held the flood poised on the cusp of Sanctuary.

He held it.

They held it.

Barely.

Conn trembled. He only needed one push, one soul, one gift more to tip the balance. To turn the tide.

He needed Lucy.

And at that moment, when the fate of Sanctuary hung sparkling like drops at the curl of a wave, he heard her voice, his heart's own voice, calling out to him in his own words.

"*Conn. Help me. I cannot do this without you.*"

Conn staggered, and the wall of water slipped.

"Hold!" Morgan shouted, and the water halted, roaring like the waterfall at the edge of the ancients' world.

Sweat broke out on Conn's face.

Griff's worried face swam before him. "Lord, what is it?"

Lucy. He saw her, blazing in his inner vision as she had blazed in the waters of the tide pool. She stood surrounded by snow and night, holding the hands of . . . Margred, Conn recognized. And Dylan. They balanced on a headland as he balanced on his tower, and above them threatened a flood.

They were holding the waters back.

She was holding the waters back.

Barely.

He felt the struggle Lucy exerted, heard the desperation in her voice. "*We need you. I need you.*"

His soul answered hers, spinning a golden thread of love and need, a wavering bridge across the sea.

He shook with effort and the enormity of his choice. He could not do both. He could not save both her and Sanctuary.

Either he drew on her power to hold the wave back here, or he sent his spirit self to help her turn the flood there.

Love or duty?

Life or Lucy?

The past or the future?

Her magic sprang from love, he remembered thinking. Could his do less?

He licked his lips, bitter with brine and defeat. "You must Change," he ordered his wardens. "Save yourselves."

"But my lord," Griff objected.

"He goes to her," Morgan snarled. "Fool!"

Enya's mouth dropped open in shock.

"Change, damn you!" Conn cried before his heart was plucked from his chest.

For a moment, he hovered, his spirit winging like a bird above the tower. As he wheeled, he saw his body drop abandoned on the wall, and Morgan grab the chain about his neck.

And then his spirit was drawn away, sucked across the sea.

The wave reared taller than the towers and fell like a hammer on Caer Subai.

20

LUCY HELD TIGHT TO MARGRED'S AND DYLAN'S hands as if they were drowning.

Or she was.

The flood roared down on them like a train in a tunnel. The earth shook. The wind rushed in her ears.

She felt Dylan's spirit draining and Margred's spirit ebb, and the wall she had built to protect them, the dike to dam the demon flood, began to crumble and crack under the strain. Her knees trembled. Her soul cried out.

Never to return to Sanctuary.

Never to see Conn again.

"We need you. I need you." An echo of his words.

I love you. A cry wrenched from her soul.

And as if her love were a bridge, a channel, he was suddenly there, with her, in her, his strength propping up her faltering strength, his power thundering through her veins.

She felt the demons' surprise, heard their howls of pain and protest as she turned the ocean back on them, as the sea wall she had constructed burst to become one with this new surge of power, boulders tossed in the flood, missiles hurtled against an enemy.

Conn's spirit flowed into her spirit. Her magic rose like the sea, shining, vengeful, smooth and towering as the wave.

"*Gau!*" she shouted. "*I bury you!*"

The wave crashed down, turning the flood back out to sea, where it was swallowed by the deeps.

But even as her magic crested and crashed down, even as she clung to her family's hands, she saw another wall, another wave, across the sea.

Like a bird high in the sky, she saw the castle wall on Sanctuary, topped with tiny figures, human and seal, and a wave rearing over them like the hammer of Hell.

She saw Conn, unconscious, helpless, lying on the wall; and she watched in horror as the hammer fell.

*   *   *

The next morning Lucy crept toward the stairs, aching and stiff in every muscle and sinew, sore and sick at heart. In the hallway outside her old room, she paused, caught by the sound of her father's voice, reading aloud to the figure on the bed.

" 'Goodnight to the cow jumping over the moon . . .' "

Lucy's breath hitched.

Bart looked up and saw her. His spare, worn face flushed. "That new doctor told me it might help to read to her. He saw us—saw her—saw Cora at the community center last night." He cleared his throat. "I'm calling her Cora. Too confusing to have two Lucys in the house."

Tears sprang to Lucy's eyes. She blinked, leaning against the door jamb. "That's . . . great, Dad. Pretty name," she offered, because what else was there to say?

"I found this with your teaching stuff." Bart held up the

orange-and-green-striped cover of *Goodnight Moon*. "You don't mind, do you?"

"No," she said truthfully. "I don't mind at all."

Bart frowned at the figure lying on the bed, so still, so pale, her chest rising and falling softly with her breath. "She doesn't look anything like you," he said. "I don't know why anybody . . . I don't know why I thought she looked like you."

Lucy's laugh sounded more like a sob. Walking into the room, she bent and kissed the top of his head. "I don't know either, Dad."

Her father reached up and patted her hand awkwardly where it rested on his shoulder. "Caleb and the rest of them's downstairs," he said. "You should go down. Get some breakfast."

"Yes." She swallowed hard. "I will."

They were gathered in the living room: Caleb in his uniform, and Margred tired and beautiful, Regina with eight-year-old Nick on the couch, and Dylan with his back to the room, staring out the window at the snow.

Caleb and Regina were speaking in hushed voices, like schoolchildren in the library or visitors to a house where somebody has died.

Lucy's heart squeezed with terrible grief. Somebody *had* died. Conn. She had not been able to feel him, touch him, sense his presence, since they had turned the flood the night before. The golden cord that stretched between them had snapped completely, leaving her cut off. Adrift.

". . . dissipated in the Atlantic," Caleb said. He looked up and saw her. His face sharpened with concern. "Lucy."

Dylan turned.

Her gaze sought his, an impossible hope raging like a fire in her chest. "Any word?" she begged. "Anything."

Dylan shook his head, his eyes black with regret. And she remembered that he, too, had loved Conn, had known the selkie prince since he was a sulky thirteen-year-old boy.

Regina nudged Nick, who jumped off the couch. "We don't have school today," he announced. "Because of the snow and, like, the evacuation and stuff. So Danny and me are going sledding." He cocked his head. "Are you sick again?"

Lucy opened her mouth, but to her horror no words came out.

"She's just tired," Regina said, ruffling her son's hair. "Come on. Let's make Miss Lucy some tea."

He trotted after her down the hall, and Lucy walked across the room and into her brother Dylan's arms.

United in grief, they embraced for the first time. His body was hard and lean and spare, like their father's.

"I'm sorry." Dylan's voice was hoarse.

She shook her head wordlessly. He patted her back awkwardly, briefly, before releasing her to follow his wife and son into the kitchen.

Lucy stood bereft in the middle of the living room. Margred watched her, her dark eyes deep and sympathetic.

"You did good," Caleb said quietly.

"I feel so empty," Lucy whispered.

He enveloped her in a hug. He smelled of uniform starch and spruce and snow. Caleb smells. World's End smells.

"It always feels like that after a battle," he said. "Even when you win."

But they hadn't won, she thought numbly, resting her head against his shoulder.

Her family was safe, for now. World's End was safe. Gau was defeated, buried under sea and stone.

But Lucy had lost.

She'd lost Conn.

* * *

The week wore on, measured by the deepening ruts in the snow and the thickening ice layer around Lucy's heart.

Island life resumed, marked by the rotating flyers in the window of Wiley's Grocery and the changing daily specials at Antonia's restaurant. Ferry and cable service were restored.

Lucy's classroom filled with squirming bodies and the smell of wet coats and boots. Regina and Margred went shopping on the mainland for maternity clothes. Caleb rescued cars from ditches and checked on the elderly in the cold. Dylan walked the frozen beaches, casting for signs of Sanctuary.

Cora opened her eyes and smiled at their father.

Everything went back to normal.

Lucy's life went back to normal.

A life without Conn in it.

She couldn't eat. She couldn't sleep. Her days were haunted by thoughts of Conn, her dreams by the falling towers of Caer Subai.

Grief, Regina told her, dropping by the house with a pot of Antonia's minestrone.

Shock, Caleb said, when he came by after school.

Stress, Dylan concluded, his mouth compressed in sympathy.

Their well-meaning concern battered at the ice encasing her poor, bruised heart and scraped her nerves raw.

She fled to her garden for solitude and solace.

But the ground was hard and barren, as frozen as her heart. Frost lay on the pumpkins and the broken stalks of corn.

She turned from the untidy rows, desolation blooming in her chest.

Someone was watching from the edge of the field. Her heart thumped. A man, taller than Dylan, broader than

Caleb, watching her with an intensity that charged the air like a storm.

Something stirred in Lucy like the trickle of ice, like the melting of her heart. Her throat tightened. The blood drummed in her ears like the sea.

He strode across the field, his boots crunching the frozen furrows, a lean gray shadow trotting at his heels. Madadh.

Madadh and Conn.

The ice shattered, and Lucy burst into tears.

She stumbled forward, meeting him halfway. He caught her close, his breath warm, his arms strong. He was real and warm and solid and alive.

She clung to him, sobbing. "I thought you were dead."

Conn kissed her hair, her cheek, her mouth. She tasted her tears on his lips like the salt of the sea. "Almost," he said. "Morgan saved me. He dragged me out of the sea by the chain around my neck, and he and Griff kept watch over my body until I could return to it."

"I love Griff," she said in a choked voice.

"You love me," Conn said, a hint of arrogance in his tone.

She didn't mind. She loved his arrogance. He was the lord of the sea. The master of her heart.

She smiled. "Yes. Always."

Emotion swirled in his gray eyes. "Do you forgive me?"

She blinked. "What for?"

"For not coming with you when you asked."

"You came to me when it mattered the most." A splinter of pain pierced her happiness, a tiny icicle of doubt. "Can you forgive me?"

He raised his dark eyebrows. "For what?"

It had to be said. Had to be faced. "I left you."

"Yes." A single word like a stone between them.

She swallowed hard. "I destroyed Sanctuary."

"The demons destroyed Sanctuary."

"But I could have stopped them."

"You made the better choice. The only choice for either of us. Sanctuary is the past. You are my present and the future of our people."

She wanted so desperately to believe him. "But the prophecy . . ."

"Is fulfilled." His voice was strong with hope and purpose. "The balance of power is changed. The children of fire have suffered a defeat they cannot quickly forget or recover from. And my people, our people, have remembered the magic of the sea."

"But the castle . . . everyone on Sanctuary . . ."

"Caer Subai can be rebuilt."

She eyed him doubtfully. "Just like that."

He looked down his long, elegant nose at her. "I did not say the effort would be easy. It will take cooperation. And time."

She nodded. She could help with the rebuilding, she thought. She was the *targair inghean*. But under her resolve, worry stirred. "How much time?"

Conn raised his eyebrows. "You are impatient?"

"No. Yes. Conn . . ." Her gaze searched his face. "Where will you live? You cannot stay in human form forever. Without Sanctuary, you will age. You could die. All of the children of the sea will age and die."

He shrugged. "Some may choose to live beneath the wave. Until Sanctuary is restored."

"But—"

"Lucy. Each of us must use the gifts that we have, in the time that we have, in the place that we are. You taught me that. No more is required of us. And no less."

She touched his face. "I don't want to lose you."

He turned his lips into her palm. "You told me you trusted me to come back to you. And so I have."

Her heart swelled. "And the others?" she asked anxiously. "Griff? Iestyn?"

"Griff is well." Conn slanted a look at her. "He sends his love."

Conn still had not said he loved her. But that small worry was swallowed by a bigger one.

"And Iestyn?" Lucy persisted.

Conn hesitated. "I sent them away," he said, grief roughening his voice. "Iestyn, Roth, and Kera. I sent them on a boat with Madadh, before the wave struck. We found pieces of the craft drifting in the sea."

Lucy's heart contracted. She glanced down at the dog, its tongue lolling at their feet. "But Madadh survived."

Conn's mouth curved. "Yes."

"So there's a chance that Iestyn and the others survived, too."

Conn met her eyes gravely. "That is," he said, "my second greatest wish."

Her gaze locked with his. Her breath caught in her chest.

"What . . ." Her mouth was dry. "What is your first wish?" she whispered.

Conn took her hands again, her cold, frozen hands, and folded them in his. He raised their clasped hands to his lips and kissed her fingers. "That you will come back with me to Sanctuary to rebuild," he said. "To raise the castle and make the roses grow. To walk with me and rule with me. To bear our children. To be my love."

He dropped on his knees in the snow. Her hands trembled in his. "I did not know I could love," Conn said in his deep voice. He looked up, and his eyes were the color of the sea at dawn, reflecting her joy as the dancing waves reflect the sun. "But I love you. Be with me now and forever. Fill my life with magic and my heart with love."

Lucy's heart welled with emotion. Her eyes brimmed

with happy tears. Tugging him to his feet, she threw herself into his arms. "*Yes.*"

"You will never leave me?"

"Never," she promised.

"I love you."

At last, they kissed, rediscovering each other with lips and hands and hearts, and for that moment the air around them was as warm as spring and the garden bloomed like summer.

Because love is the greatest magic of all.

TURN THE PAGE FOR A SPECIAL PREVIEW
OF THE FIRST BOOK IN THE FITZ
CLARE CHRONICLES

*Kissing
Midnight*

BY EMMA HOLLY

COMING JUNE 2009 FROM
BERKLEY SENSATION!

Paddington
Station, 1933

~∞~

GRAHAM FITZ CLARE WAS A SECRET AGENT.

He had to repeat that to himself sometimes, because the situation seemed too ludicrous otherwise. He was ordinary, he thought, no one more so, but he fit a profile apparently. Eton. Oxford. No nascent Bolshevik tendencies. MI5 had recruited him two years ago, soon after he'd accepted a job as personal assistant to an American manufacturer. Arnold Anderson traveled the world on business, and Graham—who had a knack for languages—served as his translator and dogsbody.

He supposed it was the built-in cover that shined him up for spywork, though he couldn't see as he'd done anything important yet. He hadn't pilfered any secret papers; hadn't seduced an enemy agent—which wasn't to suggest he thought he could! For the most part, he'd simply reported back on factories he and his employer had visited, along with writing up impressions of their associated owners and officials.

Tonight, in fact, was the most spylike experience he'd had to date.

His instructions had been tucked into the copy of *The Times* he'd bought at the newsagent down the street from his home.

"Paddington Station," the note had said in curt, telegraphic style. "At 11:45 tonight. Come by Underground and carry this paper under your left arm."

Graham stood at the station now, carrying the paper and feeling vaguely foolish. The platform was empty and far darker than during the day. The cast-iron arches of the roof curved gloomily above his head, the musty smell of soot stinging his nose. A single train, unlit and silent except for the occasional sigh of escaping steam, sat on the track to the right of him. One bored porter had eyed him when he arrived, shaken his head, and then retired to presumably cozier environs.

Possibly the porter had been bribed to disappear. All Graham knew for sure was that he'd been waiting here fifteen minutes while his feet froze to the concrete floor, without the slightest sign of whoever he was supposed to meet. Doubly vexed to hear a church clock striking midnight, he tried not to shiver in the icy November damp. His overcoat was new, at least—a present from the professor on Graham's twenty-fifth birthday.

That memory made him smile despite his discomfort. His guardian was notoriously shy about giving gifts. They were always generous, always exactly what the person wanted—as if Edmund had plucked the wish from their minds. He always acted as if he'd presumed by wanting to give whatever it was to them. The habit, and so many others, endeared him to his adopted brood more than any parent by blood could have. The professor seemed to think it a privilege to have been allowed to care for them.

All of them, even flighty little Sally, knew the privilege was theirs.

Though Graham was old enough to occasionally be embarrassed by the fact, there really was no mystery as to why Edmund's charges remained at home. Graham's lips pressed together at the thought of causing Edmund concern. If tonight's business kept him waiting long enough to have to lie to the professor about where he'd been, he was not going to be amused.

Metal creaked, drawing his eyes to the darkened train. Evidently, it wasn't empty. One of the doors had opened, and a dainty Oriental woman was stepping down the stairs of the central car. Her skintight emerald dress looked straight out of wardrobe for a Charlie Chan picture. Actually, she looked straight out of one, too, so exotically gorgeous that Graham's tongue was practically sticking to the roof of his mouth.

He forced himself to swallow as her eyes raked him up and down.

"Hm," she said, flicking a length of night black hair behind one slender shoulder. "You're tall at least, and you look healthy."

Graham flushed at her dismissive tone, and again— even harder—when she turned her back on him to reascend the stairs. Holy hell, her rear view was smashing, her waist nipped in, her bum round and firm. Graham knew he wasn't the sort of man women swooned over, not like his younger brother, Ben, or even the professor, whose much-younger female students occasionally followed him home. No, Graham had a plain English face, not ugly but forgettable. Normally, this didn't bother him—or not much. It just seemed a bit humiliating to find the woman who'd insulted him so very attractive herself.

That green dress was tight enough to show the cleft

between the halves of her arse. His groin grew heavy, his shaft beginning to swell. The sight of her lack of underclothes was so inspiring he forgot he was supposed to move.

"Don't just stand there," she said impatiently over her shoulder. "Follow me."

Shoving *The Times* into his pocket, he followed her, dumbstruck, into a private compartment. She yanked down the shades before flicking on two dim sconces.

"Sit," she said, pointing to the black leather seat opposite her own. Her hand was slim and pale, her nails lacquered red as blood.

Graham sat with difficulty. He was erect and aching and too polite to shift the cause of the trouble to a different position. Hoping his condition wasn't obvious to her, he wrapped his hands around his knees and waited.

The woman stared at him unblinking—taking his stock, he guessed. She resembled a painted statue, or maybe a mannequin in a store window. In spite of his attraction to her, Graham's irritation rose. This woman had kept him hanging long enough.

"What's this about?" he asked.

She leaned back and crossed a pair of incredibly shapely legs, a move that seemed too practiced to be casual. Her dress was shorter than the current fashion, ending just below her knee. Graham wasn't certain, but from the hissing sound her calves made, she might be wearing real silk stockings.

"We're giving you a new assignment," she said.

"A new assignment."

"If we decide you're up for it."

"Look," Graham said, "you people came to me. It's hardly cricket to suggest that *you're* doing *me* favors."

The woman smiled, her teeth a gleaming flash of white behind ruby lips. Graham noticed her incisors were unusually sharp. "I think you'll find this assignment more intriguing than your previous one. It does, however, require a higher level of vetting." She leaned forward, her slender forearm resting gracefully on one thigh. The way her small breasts shifted behind her dress told him her top half had no more undergarments than her bottom. Graham's collar began to feel as tight as his pants. The space between their seats wasn't nearly great enough.

"Tell me, Graham," she said, her index finger almost brushing his, "what do you know about X Section?"

"Never heard of it," he said, because as far as he knew, MI5 sections only went up to F.

"What if I told you it hunts things?"

"*Things?*"

"Unnatural things. Dangerous things. Beasts who shouldn't exist in the human realm."

Her face was suddenly very close to his. Her eyes were as dark as coffee, mysterious golden lights seeming to flicker behind the irises. Graham felt dizzy staring into them, his heart thumping far too fast. He didn't recall seeing her move, but she was kneeling on the floor of the compartment in the space that gaped between his knees. Her pale strong hands were sliding up his thighs. His cock lurched like it could hasten their possible meeting.

"We need information," she whispered, her breath as cool and sweet as mint pastilles. "So we can destroy these monsters. And we need you to get it for us."

"You're crazy." He had to gasp it; his breath was coming so fast.

"No, I'm not, Graham. I'm the sanest person you've ever met."

Her fingers had reached the bend between his legs and torso, her thumbs sliding inward over the giant arch of his erection. She scratched him gently with the edge of her bloodred nails.

"Christ," Graham choked out. The feathery touch

blazed through him like a welder's torch. His nerves were on fire, his penis weeping with desire. He shifted on the seat in helpless reaction. Her mouth was following her thumbs, her exhalations whispering over his grossly stretched trousers.

"I'm going to give you clearance," she said. "I'm going to make sure we can trust you."

He cried out when she undid his zip fastener, and again when her small, cool fingers dug into his smalls to lift out his engorged cock. Blimey, he was big, his skin stretched like it would split. She stroked the whole shuddering length of him, causing his spine to arch uncontrollably.

"Watch me," she ordered as his head lolled back. "Watch me suck you into my mouth."

Graham was no monk. He watched her and felt her and thought his soul was going to spill out of his body where her lips drew strong and tight on him.

He didn't want to admit this was the first time a woman had performed this particular act on him. He could see why men liked it. The sensations were incredible, streaking in hot, sharp tingles from the tip of his throbbing penis to the arching soles of his feet. She was smearing her ruby lipstick up and down his shaft, humming at the swell of him, taking him into her throat, it felt like. Her tongue was rubbing him every place he craved.

The fact that she was barking mad completely slipped his mind.

"Oh, God," he breathed, lightly touching her hair where she'd tucked it neatly behind her ears. The strands were silk under his fingertips, so smooth they seemed unreal. "Oh, Christ. Don't stop."

She didn't stop. She sucked and sucked until his seed exploded from his balls in a fiery rush. He cried out hoarsely, sorry and elated at the same time. And then she did something he couldn't quite believe.

She bit him.

Her teeth sank into him halfway down his shaft, those sharp incisors even sharper than he'd thought. The pain was as piercing as the pleasure had been a second earlier. He grabbed her ears, wondering if he dared to pull her off. Her clever tongue fluttered against him, wet, strong . . . and then she drew his blood from him.

He moaned, his world abruptly turned inside out. Ecstasy washed through him in drowning waves. She was drinking from him in a whole new way, swallowing, licking, moaning herself like a starving puppy suckling at a teat. All his senses went golden and soft. *So good. So sweet.* Like floating on a current of pure well being.

He didn't know how long it lasted, but he was sorry when her head came up.

"You're mine now," she said.

He blinked sleepily into her glowing eyes. Was it queer that they were lit up? Right at that moment, he couldn't decide.

"I'm yours," he said, though he wasn't certain he meant it.

"You're not going to remember me biting you."

"No," he agreed. "That would be awkward."

"When I give you instructions, you'll follow them."

"I expect I will," he said.

She narrowed her eyes at him, her winglike little brows furrowing.

"I will," he repeated, because she seemed to require it.

She rose, licking one last smear of blood from her upper lip. As soon as it disappeared, he forgot that it had been there.

"Zip yourself," she said.

He obeyed and got to his feet as well. It seemed wrong to be towering over his handler, though he couldn't really claim to mind. She handed him a slip of paper with a meeting place in Hampstead Heath. As had been the case with the note tucked into his paper, the directions were neatly typed—no bobbles or mistakes. He had the idle thought that Estelle would have approved.

"Tomorrow night," the woman said. "Eleven sharp. You'll know when you've seen what we need you to."

"Will you be there?"

He thought this was a natural question. Any male with blood in his veins would want to repeat the pleasures of this night, if only to return the favor she'd shown him. But perhaps he wasn't supposed to ask. She wrinkled her brow again.

"*I* won't be," she said, "but chances are our enemy will."

USA Today Bestselling Author

Virginia Kantra

delivers a haunting novel of suspense and passion,
in which the sins of the past are never forgiven—and
murder is never forgotten...

HOME BEFORE MIDNIGHT

Years ago, Bailey Wells left behind her small-town
North Carolina roots for the high life in New York
City, working as a personal assistant to bestselling
true crime author Paul Ellis. Now, Ellis and his wife
are moving to rustic Stokesville, North Carolina, and
Bailey follows them—right back home.

When Ellis's wife is murdered in their new house,
Bailey attracts the attention of tough police detective
Steve Burke, who cannot share his growing feelings
for her as long as she is a murder suspect. But Bailey
soon discovers that the violence is far from over. And
that to bury a secret from the past, someone is willing
to kill again.